THE HEARTS WE MEND

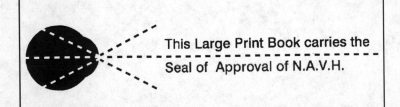

This Large Print Book carries the
Seal of Approval of N.A.V.H.

A BANISTER FALLS NOVEL

The Hearts We Mend

Kathryn Springer

THORNDIKE PRESS
A part of Gale, Cengage Learning

GALE
CENGAGE Learning·

Farmington Hills, Mich • San Francisco • New York • Waterville, Maine
Meriden, Conn • Mason, Ohio • Chicago

LIBRARY OF CONGRESS CATALOGING-IN-PUBLICATION DATA

Names: Springer, Kathryn, author.
Title: The hearts we mend : a Banister Falls novel / by Kathryn Springer.
Description: Large print edition. | Waterville, Maine : Thorndike Press, 2016. | © 2015 | Series: Thorndike Press large print clean reads
Identifiers: LCCN 2016003257 | ISBN 9781410488367 (hardcover) | ISBN 1410488365 (hardcover)
Subjects: LCSH: Widows—Fiction. | Single mothers—Fiction. | Large type books. | GSAFD: Love stories. | Christian fiction.
Classification: LCC PS3619.P76 H43 2016b | DDC 813/.6—dc23
LC record available at http://lccn.loc.gov/2016003257

Published in 2016 by arrangement with The Zondervan Corporation LLC, a subsidiary of HarperCollins Christian Publishing, Inc.

Printed in Mexico
1 2 3 4 5 6 7 20 19 18 17 16

To God — Master builder, restorer,
and multiplier of loaves and fishes
To you be the glory — always

CHAPTER 1

"You're up next, Evie! Then you can check karaoke off your list."

Evie Bennett had a lot of lists. Karaoke wasn't on any of them. Neither were bachelorette parties, and yet here she was, watching Raine and Ginevieve Lightly strut around the living room of their trailer, belting out the lyrics to Taylor Swift's "Shake It Off."

Gin had shown up at her door that morning while Evie was bundling Jordan almonds and mints into little bags made of cream-colored tulle. The firefighters at Second Street Station had decided to host an informal get-together for Cody, so Gin thought it would be nice if she and Evie did something special for the bride-to-be too.

Evie had hesitated, wondering how she could possibly squeeze one more thing into a day already packed with last-minute wedding details.

"What did you have in mind?" she'd asked cautiously.

"Oh, the usual." Gin shrugged. "Texas Hold'em. Jell-O shots."

Five months ago Evie might have believed her.

Raine bounded over to the karaoke machine, her loose-fitting sundress no longer able to disguise the rounded curve of her belly. "Eighties or golden oldies?" She shot a mischievous grin over her shoulder. "Wait, isn't that the same thing?"

It was one of *those* moments. When Evie understood why Cody, her sensitive, serious son, had proposed to this girl.

She just wished they were . . . older.

An argument that hadn't taken Evie very far, considering that she and Max had gotten married before the ink was barely dry on their high school diplomas. And welcomed Cody Maxwell Bennett into the world eleven months later.

The opening notes of The Turtles "Happy Together" began to play, and the plastic microphone swept up Evie's sigh and funneled it through the speakers.

Max was the one who'd loved this kind of stuff.

A familiar ache spread through Evie as she started to sing the words unfolding across the screen. She'd become adept at multitasking over the past thirteen years. Missing Max while handling all the little tasks that required her attention throughout the day.

Gin grabbed the remote control from the TV, holding it like a microphone in one hand while she flipped a glossy curtain of mahogany hair over her shoulder with the other and joined Evie on the chorus.

"Come on! Shake those hips!"

Gin demonstrated, and two thoughts collided in Evie's head. She envied the woman's ability to surrender to the beat of the music — and thought that it would be easier to shake her hips if she actually *had* some.

Still, she made a half-hearted attempt, and Gin laughed. "Come on, Raine. Let's show the girl how it's done."

Raine plucked a soup ladle from the bouquet of kitchen utensils on the counter and looped her arm around Evie's waist. Sandwiched between them like a Rockette, Evie tried to mimic their synchronized moves. Knee up. Kick out. She could only imagine what the women on her ministry team would say if they saw her . . .

"This looks way more fun than basketball."

Evie whirled around and almost dropped

the microphone. Dan Moretti and Cody stood in the doorway, the grins on their faces proof they'd been there long enough to witness the performance.

"Hey, this is a girls only party!" Raine complained.

Cody held up a red-and-white cardboard box from Cicero's. "We brought pizza."

"What kind?"

"Deluxe no mushrooms."

"Yes!" Raine abandoned the chorus line and danced across the room to Cody's side. "The golden ticket."

"I told you it would work." Dan sauntered in, his eyes fixed on Gin. They weren't as openly affectionate as the teenagers, but Evie saw the look that passed between them. The hint of color that stole into Ginevieve's cheeks when Dan reached for her hand.

Their relationship was brand new, but Evie had no doubt that Dan and Ginevieve would be the next couple walking down the aisle.

She was happy for Dan. Really. She was. But over the past few months, their friendship — the one forged in the Morettis' sandbox when she and Dan were three years old — had been undergoing a subtle change too. Ginevieve was the one Dan spent time with now.

The one Dan looked at the way Max used to look at her.

Evie set the microphone down on the table. "It looks like everyone's ready for a break, so I should probably go. I still have a few last-minute things to do."

Her announcement raised an instant chorus of protest.

"But we just got here." Cody kept one arm around Raine's waist while he raised the lid on the takeout box. "It's kind of hard to be a party crasher if there isn't a party."

"We could have a karaoke contest." Raine hip-checked Cody and snitched a slice of pizza before he could. "Guys against the girls."

Two guys. Two girls. And Evie.

She silently switched around the items on her to-do list. "I have to stop by the church and check out the centerpieces we're going to use on Saturday. I might have to make up a few more for the buffet table."

"Do you need some help?" Gin asked. "Raine and I can go with you."

"No, stay here. Eat pizza. It shouldn't take me very long." Evie grabbed her cardigan off the back of the chair. "Your grandparents will be here tomorrow afternoon, Cody. I invited them to the rehearsal dinner."

"Are they staying with you?"

Not us. *You.* The footings under Evie's heart shifted again. Cody hadn't physically moved into the house that Dan's parents had offered to rent to him and Raine, but in Cody's mind he'd already left.

"Grandma said it will be easier if they stay at the bed-and-breakfast."

Based on past experience, Evie knew what Betty really meant was that it would be easier on *them.*

She glanced at Dan and saw the smile in his hazel eyes change to concern. More than anyone, he knew her relationship with her former in-laws had been strained since Max died. Well, maybe *strained* wasn't quite the word. *Nonexistent* would be a better choice.

Evie understood that everyone grieved differently, but it seemed like the Bennetts had simply decided not to do it at all.

After Max died, Neil and Betty sold his childhood home and moved across the country. Unlike Evie's parents, missionaries to Uganda who could only fly back to the United States once every four or five years, Betty and Neil had the time and money to return to Wisconsin for regular visits. But coming back to Banister Falls meant accepting the fact that Max was really gone. Annual Christmas cards and a phone call on

Cody's birthday became a substitute for being part of their grandson's life, which was why Evie was a little shocked when Betty called to let her know they planned to attend the wedding.

"I took the day off tomorrow." Dan followed her to the door. "Do you need help with anything? I can set up tables and chairs in the fellowship room. String up those little white lights you bought."

Dan didn't ask out of habit; helping people was embedded in the Moretti family's DNA. But out of habit, Evie almost said yes. She'd depended on Dan over the years — maybe more than she should have — but the friendship she and Ginevieve had was new too. Fragile. Evie didn't want to put any additional strain on it.

"I left Harvey some notes before I took vacation time, and I'm sure he's got everything covered. You don't want to start a turf war." She looped the strap of her purse over one shoulder and looked at Gin. "Thank you for inviting me over. It was . . . fun."

"Then we'll have to do it again sometime." Laughter kindled in Gin's light-green eyes, proof that Evie hadn't fooled her a bit.

"Bye, Mom." Cody loped over and pulled her into a hug. "I'll see you later."

Evie patted his back, oh so careful not to

cling. "Don't forget to pick up your suit tomorrow at two o'clock."

"I'll remind him," Raine sang out.

Evie knew that — but it didn't prevent her vision from becoming as blurry as her place in Cody's life.

Everything was changing so rapidly she could hardly keep up, let alone get in front of it. After the honeymoon, Cody would be living with Raine in a house on the other side of town. Creating a home of their own. A *life* of their own.

There were times Evie didn't even recognize her son anymore. It seemed like only a minute ago he'd been chasing Diva, their golden retriever, around the house in his footie pajamas, and now he was going to be a husband. A father.

A firefighter. Like *his* father.

Evie hadn't seen that coming any more than she'd seen Cody falling in love with Raine. Or maybe she hadn't wanted to see it. Maybe the only thing she'd wanted to see was the future that she'd imagined for her son.

A future a little safer, a little more secure, than the one Max had chosen . . .

A dog lunged from the shadows of the trailer next door as Evie walked to her Jeep. Heart pounding, she quickened her steps and slid into the driver's seat as its owner snarled a reprimand through the screen door. Plastic garbage bags waiting for pickup lined both sides of the road that cut through the trailer park, overriding the sweet scent of the late June breeze, and Evie rolled up her window.

At least Cody and Raine wouldn't be living on Fifth Avenue after they got married. And if Dan got his way, Evie suspected Ginevieve wouldn't be living there much longer either.

She drove down Main Street, following a familiar set of landmarks to Hope Community.

The parking lot, a patchwork of asphalt squares that had grown in direct proportion to the building over the years, was empty. Most of the scheduled activities — the kids' club program, youth group, and adult Bible studies — took place on Wednesday evenings. Unless there was a meeting or special event, the building remained vacant for the remainder of the week.

Evie parked behind the building and unlocked the door that opened into the fellowship room. At the end of the hallway, a seam of light glowed underneath the door of the custodian's room.

Harvey Kinnard lived in an apartment

complex just down the street, and it wasn't unusual for him to work late if there was something specific that needed his attention — or if he wanted to watch a Brewers game on the big-screen television in the youth wing.

Evie cut through the kitchen to the walk-in storage closet.

The air-conditioning unit began to hum as she flipped on the overhead light and scanned the rows of plastic bins that lined the shelves, each one color-coded to represent a different event the women's ministry team had hosted over the years.

When she picked out the antique brass lanterns and ivory tulle for their last conference, she never dreamed she'd be recycling them as centerpieces for Cody's wedding reception.

Cody's *wedding* reception.

God . . .

Evie's prayer, like so many others lately, trailed into silence after the opening beat. She tried to give it some momentum — reciting verses she'd memorized, singing bits of a praise chorus — but they couldn't seem to get past the knot of . . . of *something* that had lodged in her heart over the past few months.

She couldn't label it. And because she

16

couldn't label it, she had no idea what to do with it.

Candles. Floral arrangements. Those were so much easier.

Evie heard the soft tread of footsteps as she reached for one of the bins. "It's just me, Harvey. I'm checking the decorations for the reception."

Silence.

Evie glanced over her shoulder and the air emptied from her lungs. A man stood in the doorway. A shadow of stubble, several shades darker than the tawny hair brushing the frayed collar of his denim shirt, accentuated his lean, chiseled features. Slashes of black paint stood out like graffiti against faded, loose-fitting jeans.

Silver-gray eyes locked on Evie, holding her in place. "I remember you."

Evie remembered him too.

He'd been standing in the shadows that other night too. Holding a baseball bat.

CHAPTER 2

There were times Jack Vale wished he still believed in coincidence.

This was definitely one of them.

How many people lived in Banister Falls? Six . . . eight thousand? How many churches were scattered throughout the city limits? At least half a dozen?

But here *she* was. Looking at him with those incredible blue eyes — yeah, Jack remembered those too — like *he* was the one who was trespassing.

Now they were even.

Because the first time they'd met, Jack had assumed the people sneaking around Travis's backyard were two of the neighborhood's friendly drug dealers, taking their party right to his brother's door.

So, yes, he'd confronted them . . . but Jack hadn't realized they were women until they'd turned around and the porch light illuminated their faces. And *they* probably hadn't realized that the baseball bat resting in the crook of his arm was more of a prop, meant to emphasize Jack's opinion of their presence, than an actual threat.

"What are you doing here?" She glanced at the purse on the floor between them. A cell phone sprouted from a pocket in the side.

He could practically *see* her dialing 911.

"Look . . . I'm sorry if I startled you." Jack raised his hands, slowly. Smiled. *See, no bat. No weapon of any kind.* "I heard a noise and thought I should check it out."

Usually a smile put people at ease. Not Blue Eyes.

"Check it . . . How did you get inside?" Her expression didn't change, but Jack heard the undercurrent of tension in her voice. "The church is closed."

"I work here. I'm the custodian."

"The custodian." She took a step closer to her purse.

Not quite the reaction he'd expected.

It suddenly occurred to Jack that he might look a little . . . rough. Pauline, the church secretary, had told him there was nothing going on at Hope Community on Thursday nights, so he hadn't bothered to change clothes after he'd worked on his brother's car. Hadn't bothered to shave off a two-days' growth of beard either.

"Just for a few weeks." It might be a good time to start dropping names. "Harvey was called out of town for a family emergency, so Pastor Keith hired me right before he left for a conference."

"He hired *you*?"

In all fairness, Jack had been kind of surprised too.

"You can call the secretary. Pauline put me on the payroll." Jack started to extend his hand but changed his mind when he saw the grease from Travis's carburetor still trapped underneath his fingernails. "Jack Vale."

"Evie . . ." She hesitated a moment, but at least it looked like she was finally starting to believe him. "Bennett."

"Bennett." The name sounded familiar. Familiar because Jack remembered seeing it on the door of one of the offices he'd vacuumed earlier in the week. "You work here too?"

One coincidence, God. Just one. That's all I'm asking for.

"I'm the director of women's ministries."

Jack wasn't sure what a director of women's ministries *did,* but he knew what it meant. Evie Bennett wasn't just a member of the congregation. She had the power to get him fired.

Jack's gaze swept over her, taking in the crisp white shirt and the khaki pants that tapered down to trim ankles.

Evie looked as put-together as her office, with its pastel furniture and watercolor prints featuring peaceful landscapes with coordinating verses of scripture, artistically arranged on the pale-green wall behind her desk.

Jack supposed there were some women who would find the room a comfortable, inviting place to pour out their hearts. But not someone like Cheryl, who'd be afraid that what was in *her* heart would permanently stain the fabric on one of Evie Bennett's dainty, little chairs.

He'd tried to tell his sister-in-law about forgiveness and grace, but Cheryl viewed God as some kind of heavenly parole officer glaring down at her from heaven, ready with a lightning bolt if she made another mistake. At least that was a starting point. Travis refused to acknowledge God's existence at all.

"I've been on vacation all week," Evie said, yanking Jack from the shadowy detour that his thoughts had started to take him down. "Will Harvey be back by this weekend?"

"By the weekend . . . no." At least Jack hoped not. He needed this job. Not only for the income it provided, but as an excuse to stay in Banister Falls a little longer. "Pastor Keith told me it would be about a month."

"A month."

For the first time, Jack saw a ripple in the calm blue waters of Evie Bennett's eyes. "Is something wrong?"

"*You're* the one in charge of getting everything ready for the wedding on Saturday?"

Well, that explained the ripple. As the director of women's ministries, Evie was probably in charge of special events at the church.

"The secretary did mention something about a wedding." Jack couldn't resist teasing her a little. But once again, it seemed to have the opposite effect.

"Didn't you see the notes I left in Harvey's office?"

By "office" Jack figured Evie was referring to the oversize utility closet adjacent to the furnace room. And her "notes," the grid of Post-its perfectly aligned above the shelf of cleaning supplies.

"I saw them." Fluorescent pink was pretty hard to miss. "I took care of everything marked Tuesday and Wednesday, and I was just finishing up the list" — the very detailed list — "for today. I've got everything under control."

Evie didn't look exactly reassured as she reached down and scooped up her purse. "I . . . if you'll excuse me, I have to carry some things out to my car."

"I can do it." Jack went to reach for one of the plastic bins, but she beat him to it.

"That's all right. I . . . I really don't need any help."

The rigid set of Evie's shoulders, the way she averted her eyes, translated the words more accurately.

I really don't want your *help.*

Okaaaay . . . message received.

Jack backed into the hallway, giving her some space. "I'll have everything else ready by Saturday afternoon."

If he still had a job by then.

CHAPTER 3

Evie heard a thump when she let herself into the house.

The soft but unmistakable sound of four paws connecting with the floor. A moment later, Diva peeked around the corner.

Evie clucked her tongue in mock disapproval. "You know you aren't supposed to be on the sofa."

The golden retriever padded up to her, head down, plumed tail wagging in repentance.

"I'm surprised you can even jump up there anymore." Evie bent down and rubbed the dog's snow-white muzzle. "What do you say we make a batch of popcorn and watch a movie until Cody comes home? Girls night part two. Minus the karaoke."

Diva's tail thumped the floor three times. Canine Morse code for yes.

Evie smiled. Funny how the one permanent fixture in her life was a dog she hadn't wanted in the first place.

It had been Max's idea, buying Cody a puppy for his fifth birthday. There were seven in the litter, golden balls of fluff with liquid-brown eyes and rough bubblegum-pink tongues. While six of the puppies wrestled with Max and one another, one of them had ambled up to Evie while she was filling out the paperwork. But instead of viewing Evie's favorite pair of shoes as a potential chew toy, the puppy had sprawled on top of them and fallen sound asleep.

"That one looks like a rhinestone-collar kind of girl." Max eyed the puppy in amusement while his top two contenders battled for attention in his arms. "Hey, little diva."

Nothing. Not even a twitch.

Max had laughed, but Evie pointed out that it was her signature on the dotted line.

"She's calm and I'm already outnumbered," she'd told him. "If we're going to get a puppy, at least we can get one who seems to appreciate a stylish pair of shoes."

Diva — the nickname stuck — had slept in Evie's arms all the way home.

Just as Max predicted, Cody and Diva had become inseparable over the years. But after the funeral, the dog sneaked into Evie's room, the only one in the house that Evie had declared off-limits even on the nights

Max bunked at the fire station.

The mournful cry at the foot of the bed gave voice to the one Evie had been forced to stifle all day. She'd patted the foot of the bed.

"One night," she'd whispered.

Diva had slept there ever since.

Evie tried to ignore the packed cartons lining the walls as she walked down the hallway to the living room.

What was she going to do with all the empty space?

After Cody proposed to Raine, Evie thought about downsizing. But Max had spent every penny of an inheritance his grandmother had left to him to build her a house in Rosewood Court, the first subdivision in Banister Falls.

I'll fight fires and you keep the ones at home burning, he'd told her.

Every time Evie let Diva out the back door, she saw the wreath of handprints stamped in the concrete patio. Three sets, three different sizes. Cody's as small as the wings of one of the sparrows that nested in the awning over Evie's kitchen window every summer.

It wasn't just the memories though. In Rosewood Court, the neighbors looked out for each other. Most of them had built their homes in the subdivision at the same time as Evie and Max. It was quiet. Peaceful.

The kind of neighborhood where people felt safe leaving their doors unlocked . . .

"I remember you."

An image of Jack Vale's face suddenly flashed in Evie's mind.

Even without closing her eyes, she could see him standing at the bottom of the rickety porch steps, a baseball bat resting casually in the crook of his arm.

It was the first time Evie had been caught while taking part in what her women's ministry team called a blessing burglary. That night the target had been Nicki Chapman, a single mom who waited tables at My Place, the diner on Radley Street where Gin worked.

Evie and Gin were sneaking up under cover of darkness with a few bags of groceries when Jack showed up — and misunderstood their intention.

And now here he was again.

There had to be at least a dozen men in the congregation who would have agreed to serve as a temporary custodian. Why had Keith hired Jack Vale?

But at least "temporary" meant that Harvey would return in a few weeks and everything would go back to the way it was supposed to be.

Evie moved a box of Cody's books off the sofa and smoothed out the wrinkles in the fabric.

Something had to.

CHAPTER 4

Jack couldn't believe the transformation that had taken place when he unlocked the door of the church on Saturday morning.

A slender glass vase holding an arrangement of peach-colored roses and glossy ferns marked the center of every linen-covered table in the fellowship room. Gold satin covered the fifty chairs Jack had set up the day before. He could practically *see* Evie Bennett wrapping each one like a Christmas present and then topping it off with a tidy little bow.

And speaking of tidy . . .

His first stop was the custodian's room, where, just as he suspected, a new row of Post-it notes had appeared on the wall in the last twenty-four hours.

At least the first one — changing a burned-out lightbulb above the stage — would be an easy fix. Especially when its replacement had been positioned directly under the note calling it to Jack's attention.

He resisted the urge to take a quick detour into the kitchen for a cup of coffee as he made his way down the hall to the sanctuary.

Roses scented the air, and antique lanterns hung from the two decorative posts stationed at the end of the aisle. Like the fellowship hall, the overall effect was elegant. Beautiful.

Like the woman who'd been in charge of decorating it.

Jack shook that thought away before it had a chance to take root. His gut told him that if he wanted to keep this job, he'd better stay as far away from Evie Bennett as possible.

"Morning!"

"Hello." Jack tracked the cheerful greeting to a sandy-haired teenage boy sitting on the stage. "Can I help you with something?"

"Nope." The boy cast an appealing, lopsided smile in Jack's direction. "Just hanging out with God for a few minutes."

The way he said it, without a hint of self-consciousness, had Jack returning the smile. "Sorry for interrupting then. I'll get out of your way."

"No problem. I have to finish getting dressed before the ceremony anyway. You

30

don't happen to know how to tie a Windsor knot, do you?"

"Sorry. Not a clue." A Windsor knot? Jack didn't even own a tie. For the first time he noticed the kid's white dress shirt and charcoal gray pants. "You're in the wedding party?"

"I'm the groom."

"The groom," Jack repeated. Just to make sure he'd heard him correctly.

"Go ahead and say it."

A low laugh told Jack that the kid — because, honestly, the new information didn't change the fact that he still looked like one — hadn't taken offense.

"Everyone else has."

Jack made it a habit never to say things the collective "everyone" said.

"Congratulations."

"Thanks." The kid hopped off the stage, stuffing the tails of the shirt into the waistband of his pants as he loped over to Jack. "You're the guy who took Harvey Kinnard's place, aren't you? I've been praying for Harvey and his family."

Jack liked him even more. "Jack Vale."

"Cody. It's nice to meet —"

"Cody?"

Jack turned at the sound of a familiar voice.

31

He'd expected to see Evie again. But not this soon.

And not wearing a dress made from some sparkly fabric that matched her eyes and skimmed over curves Jack hadn't noticed on Thursday night. Much. Evie's ash-blonde hair, swept into a sleek coil at the base of her neck, drew attention to the perfect symmetry of her face.

She reminded Jack of a sculpture he'd seen in a gallery once. A marble statue of a woman kneeling in a garden, her face lifted toward the sun. Jack had lingered for a moment, admiring the sheer beauty of the workmanship, while a thin satin rope reminded him to keep his distance.

And so did the thin gold wedding band on Evie's finger. The one she was twisting with the careful precision a person would use to unlock the combination on a safe. The one Jack hadn't noticed until now.

Cody grinned. "Hey, Mom."

Mom.

Jack was still trying to come to grips with that when Evie stepped through the doors of the sanctuary.

"The photographer will be here in about twenty minutes." She took a sweeping inventory of her son's attire, from the unbuttoned shirt to his stockinged feet.

"I'm almost ready." Cody reached for the gray suit jacket draped over one of the chairs to back up the statement. "Have you met Jack yet?"

"Yes." A hint of color tinted Evie's cheeks, making Jack wonder which of the two meetings she was remembering. The one when he'd cornered her on his brother's porch or the one in the storage closet at the church.

"Jack and I were just discussing the Windsor knot," Cody said cheerfully.

Evie aimed a pointed look at her son's open collar. "I believe it starts with a tie."

"And I happen to have one of those." Cody searched the pockets of his jacket. "Somewhere."

Apparently Evie wasn't immune to the kid's charm either because a smile tempered her exasperated sigh. "Well, once you find it, you have to stay put until you hear the music start. No wandering the halls trying to catch a glimpse of Raine."

Cody's feet practically left the floor when Evie said the name. "Have you seen her? How is she doing? Is she okay?"

"Raine is fine. The last time I saw her, she and Gin were on their way to the Morettis' house. Liz offered to do their hair." Evie nudged Cody toward the double doors. "Now go. Watch for John. He has your boutonniere."

"I hope he brought something to eat too." Cody patted his stomach. "I'm starving."

"Would you like a cheese sandwich?" Jack offered his lunch from the day before. The one he hadn't had a chance to eat because his schedule had been dictated by a cheerful row of pink Post-it notes. "Help yourself. Bottom drawer of the fridge . . ."

Cody didn't wait for him to finish the sentence. The doors swung shut behind him.

Leaving him alone with Evie Bennett. Again.

Okay, Lord. What's going on?

Because suddenly, getting a job at Hope Community Church didn't feel like a blessing.

It felt more like a test.

Jack Vale managed to look intimidating even when he was surrounded by sunlight instead of shadows. Maybe it was because Evie was used to Harvey, who showed up for work every day wearing tan Dockers and a dark-green polo with a lighthouse, the Hope Community logo, embroidered on the pocket.

Jack, in faded, loose-fitting jeans, a black T-shirt that stretched across his broad shoulders, and a pair of scuffed Frye boots, looked more like the leader of a biker gang.

"I didn't realize your son was the one getting married today." Jack speared his hands into his front pockets. "He seems like a nice kid."

Evie's spine straightened. "Emphasis on *kid,* I suppose?"

"No emphasis at all. But I'm guessing his age is a touchy subject?"

Evie was so taken aback by the blunt honesty of the question that she couldn't help but respond in kind.

"It shouldn't be. At least not for me. Max . . . my husband . . . and I were Cody's age when we got married. We just seemed . . . I don't know. *Different.*"

"Funny how that works." Jack's eyes crinkled at the corners, making him appear more approachable.

Evie pivoted toward the entrance to the sanctuary. "I should check on Cody —"

"There you are!"

Ginevieve blocked Evie's path on the other side of the double doors. She wore the dress Evie had helped her pick out at Felicity's Bridal Shop on Main Street, a dark-gold satin that complemented her mahogany hair and green eyes. "Lisa and Liz smuggled Raine into the church through the back . . ." Her gaze locked on Jack, who'd followed Evie into the hallway. "What are *you* doing here?"

Judging from the way Jack's eyes narrowed, he'd recognized Gin too. "You're the partner in crime."

Gin didn't look the least bit offended by the label.

"Ginevieve Lightly. But today I'm the mother of the bride." Gin suddenly smiled — *smiled* — at Jack as if they were long lost friends. "And you're the baseball-bat guy."

"Baseball bat?"

Evie tried not to wince when Dan joined them.

"Remember the night we planned the blessing burglary for Nicki?" Gin was still smiling. "I told you about the guy who thought Evie and I were providing the party instead of dinner, remember?"

"I don't remember you mentioning a baseball bat."

Dan wasn't the kind of person who judged someone by the length of his hair or the type of clothing he wore, but the frown that settled between his brows meant he'd switched into protective mode. Evie had always considered it one of her friend's more endearing qualities. Now she was struck with the sudden, inexplicable urge to stomp on his foot.

"That's because it wasn't important." Gin's way of reminding Dan to mind his manners was a playful but equally effective shoulder bump. "Just a lack of communication."

Dan's gaze shifted back to Jack. "You communicate with a baseball bat?"

"I was *holding* a bat." Jack's lips quirked. "So it was more like a nonverbal *mis*communication."

The frown between Dan's eyebrows eased. A little. "Our pastor is busy at the moment, but is there something I can help you with?"

"Actually, I'm here to help *you*. Your pastor hired me to fill in for your custodian." Jack stretched out his hand. "Jack Vale. And I'm guessing you must be the father of the groom."

CHAPTER 5

The expression on Dan Moretti's face — no, on *all* their faces — told Jack he'd guessed wrong.

"Dan Moretti." Jack could feel the tension in the guy's grip as he shook his hand. "I'm . . . a friend of the family."

The redhead — Ginevieve — broke the awkward silence that suddenly weighted the air around them. "I think I'll steal Evie for a few minutes so she can see how beautiful Raine looks in her wedding gown."

"Hey, Evie!" A slim brunette in her late twenties jogged past, a dry-cleaning bag draped over one arm. "Marie just got here, and she was wondering if there are any extra power strips lying around. She needs them for the buffet tables."

Jack looked at Evie, who refused to look at him at all. Further proof he'd messed up somehow.

"Evie?" Jack waited until she made eye

contact with him. "I'll take care of it."

"Thank you." It was Ginevieve who responded — because Evie was already walking away.

"I think I'll tag along with Jack." Dan
bared his teeth in what anyone other than
Jack might have mistakenly interpreted as a
smile. "He's probably still trying to figure
out who's who and what's what around
here."

Oh . . . Jack thought he had it pretty much
figured out.

Ginevieve caught up to Evie, and Moretti
fell into step beside him.

Five. Four. Three . . .

"You aren't from Banister Falls." It wasn't
phrased in the form of a question.

"Milwaukee." Jack could have narrowed it
down to a specific area of the city, but he
had a feeling that Dan Moretti wasn't nearly
as interested in where Jack was from as he
was in why Jack was *here.*

"Did you work at a church there too?"

"Construction."

"A little overqualified for this job, aren't
you?"

"Not if you need one." Jack didn't give
Moretti an opportunity to chew on that.
"Look, I enjoy small talk as much as the
next guy" — that pulled a reluctant smile

out of his escort — "but I have work to do."

Dan paused as they reached the end of the hallway, and Jack braced himself for another round of questions.

"Evie's husband died when Cody was six years old."

Jack felt like he'd been sucker punched. *"Died?"*

Dan nodded. "Max . . . Cody's dad . . . he was my best friend. And I'm Cody's best man."

Evie was a widow. A widow who still wore a wedding ring — Jack silently did the math — even though she must have lost her husband over a decade ago.

"I'm sorry." The words you said when you didn't know what else to say.

"So am I." A shadow skimmed across the surface of Dan's eyes. "Max was like a brother. I would have done anything for him."

A brother.

The two words sliced deep. More than anyone, Jack understood the bond between brothers.

A flash of blue in the fellowship room caught his eye. Evie, working her way from table to table. Smoothing a hand over the linen tablecloths. Adjusting a centerpiece.

She reminded Jack of a ballerina. All

40

graceful movements and measured steps. He had a hunch that Evie Bennett measured everything.

Thoughts. Words. Gestures.

Post-it notes.

Jack didn't realize he was smiling until Dan shifted his weight, blocking her from view.

"I've known Evie since we were kids. She was devastated when Max died, but there are a lot of people in this town who care about her. Look out for her."

Dan turned and walked away without another word, but it didn't matter.

Jack understood that too.

Evie didn't cry when Dan escorted Raine down the aisle and then took his place next to Cody at the front of the church. Or when Cody slipped a gold band on Raine's finger — right next to the diamond ring Max had given Evie the night he'd proposed.

But she could feel the tears backing up in her throat as Cody and Raine began to recite their vows.

To have and to hold, from this day forward.

For better or for worse.

For richer or for poorer. In sickness and in health.

To love, honor, and cherish.

Until we are separated by death.

Evie had stood in this church, stood in the exact spot where Raine was standing now, the promise of a bright future shining in her eyes the day she'd made that promise to Max. Never dreaming they wouldn't have a whole lifetime of days together.

Evie felt that familiar bittersweet surge of emotion as she watched Cody take Raine's hand.

"You may kiss your bride." Pastor Keith was smiling at the couple, and Evie looked down at the corsage of rosebuds on her wrist as Cody drew Raine into the circle of his arms.

A cheer erupted from the firefighters. Most of the crew at Second Street Station had known Cody since the day he was born. They were the ones who'd grieved right alongside her at Max's funeral. Replaced the shingles on her roof after a hailstorm. Made Cody an honorary member of their basketball team.

Following the crew's lead, Amanda and Emily, Dan's nieces, began to shriek and clap their hands. No one even tried to shush them.

The Moretti family took up the two front rows. The church hadn't been divided down the middle, with one side reserved for the bride and the other for the groom. Other than Sara, Gin's half sister who'd flown in from Maine for the weekend to serve as Raine's maid of honor, Gin didn't have any family. It didn't surprise Evie at all that Angela and John Moretti had simply absorbed Gin into theirs.

Evie slid a glance at Max's parents, who'd slipped in at the very last minute. Betty had called after they'd checked in at the bed-and-breakfast on Friday and bowed out of the rehearsal dinner, claiming they were too tired from traveling. But the sour expressions Evie saw on the couple's faces made her wonder if they were remembering another wedding. Neil and Betty had tried to convince her and Max to wait too.

But *waiting* wasn't a word in their son's vocabulary, and with Evie's parents leaving for the mission field a week after she graduated from high school, Max had presented a list of reasons — Evie's idea — why it made sense for them to get married right away.

Just as Cody had done, the night he'd told Evie that he was going to propose to Raine.

With the baby due in September, he and Raine had opted for a short engagement. Evie, who'd assumed she would be getting ready to send her son off to college, had found herself planning a wedding instead.

Invite the people you know will be happy for us, Mom. Really happy, not just pretending.

Evie's gaze shifted to the table on the stage as Cody and Raine started down the aisle hand in hand. Instead of the flowers that matched Raine's wedding bouquet, she saw a satin banner winding through a spray of red roses.

Beloved husband and father.

Evie wanted to be happy for Cody and Raine, but she knew the truth.

If your dreams came true, your deepest fears could too.

CHAPTER 6

"It was a beautiful wedding, Evie."

Chrissy Anderson, Pastor Keith's wife, linked arms with Evie as she made her way to the kitchen to box up the leftover wedding cake.

"Thank you for coming. I know it meant a lot to Cody and Raine."

"Well, they mean a lot to me and to Keith." Tears glistened in her friend's eyes. "I talked to Cody before they left. He said they're going to Whisper Lake for their honeymoon."

"Kimberly and Wade Russell, Dan's aunt and uncle, are letting them stay in one of their cabins for the week as a wedding gift."

"That was so sweet of them! I'm sure you'll appreciate some time to yourself. I know I couldn't plan a wedding in less than a month."

Planning the wedding had been the easy part. It was the "time to herself" Evie didn't

45

know what to do with.

"Evie?" Jennifer Moretti, Dan's sister-in-law, appeared in the doorway, the elegant line of her chiffon dress slightly distorted by the enormous pink-and-purple plaid diaper bag looped over one shoulder. "Stephen and I are going to take Bree home and put her down for a nap before things get ugly. Is there anything else you'd like me to do before we leave?"

"Yes . . . round up all the Morettis and take them with you." Gin and Dan, his parents, and most of his siblings had tracked Evie down and asked the same question after the reception ended. "They've done more than enough."

"I will."

"And take another piece of cake."

"I was hoping you'd say that." Jennifer plucked one from the counter and dashed out of the room.

"I should go too." Chrissy enveloped Evie in a quick hug. "Keith promised the boys we'd take them to a baseball game this evening. Are you sure you don't —"

"Bye, Chrissy."

"Fine." Laughing, Chrissy let Evie bump her toward the door. "I'll see you tomorrow morning."

The voices in the hallway faded, and

silence replaced the laughter and the hum of conversation. Outside in the parking lot, car doors slammed as the last of the guests drove away.

Evie rinsed out an empty vase and put it in the rack to dry. It was a task she could have put off until the next morning, but right now the thought of going home to an empty house left her feeling hollow. Restless.

"Could I talk to you a moment, Evie?"

One look at her mother-in-law's face, and everything Evie had eaten at the reception welded together in a solid lump in her stomach. "Of course."

"That girl — Raine — is pregnant, Evie." Betty folded her arms, flattening the corsage pinned to the lapel of her linen jacket. "Don't bother to deny it."

Evie released a slow breath. "I wasn't going to."

"I thought the short engagement was because they didn't want to . . . you know . . . *wait.*" Betty glared at her. "You didn't bother to mention it was because they hadn't."

"I didn't think it would matter."

"Of course it matters! When we talked on the phone at Christmas, you said Cody was going to be valedictorian. That he was doing well."

"Cody *is* doing well, Betty." *Steady, Evie.* "He was awarded the Mansfield Merit scholarship."

"A scholarship he's not planning to use," her mother-in-law retorted.

"Cody doesn't want to go to college."

"We know what Cody wants." Betty's voice trembled under the weight of emotions Evie guessed had been building up since she and Neil had arrived in Banister Falls. "Did you even *try* to talk him out of it?"

"It wouldn't have done any good. Cody is an adult. Whether or not I agree with his decisions, I'm going to support him."

"Like you supported Max?"

Bile rose in Evie's throat as the words found their mark.

You raised Max, she wanted to shout at her mother-in-law. *Didn't you know him at all?*

A challenge, a look of doubt, a dare — they only made Max more determined to succeed.

He'd announced he was going to be a firefighter after a sixth-grade field trip to Second Street Station, but his parents had dismissed it as one of those little-boy dreams. A dream Max would eventually

48

outgrow, like winning a gold medal at the Olympics for downhill skiing or playing quarterback for the Green Bay Packers.

It didn't seem to matter that Max had never shown the slightest bit of interest in running the hardware store on Main Street. Betty and Neil made it clear they expected their only son to join his father in the family business.

When nothing Max's parents said could get him to change his mind, Betty had invited Evie over a few days before the wedding and made it clear that *she* should. But who would have thought Betty still resented her for refusing?

"You know Max would have been miserable," Evie said quietly.

"At least he would be *alive.*" Betty's mouth snapped shut.

Evie glanced over her shoulder. Jack stood in the doorway, a steaming cup of coffee in his hand.

"I thought you'd left." Why hadn't *he* left? Evie searched Jack's face, but there was nothing in his expression that hinted he'd overheard their conversation.

"One of your notes . . . I'm supposed to pick up an envelope after the reception?"

Evie had totally forgotten. She always gave Harvey a little thank-you when he worked

49

extra hours for a special event. She'd purchased the gift certificate from Marie's Bistro, Harvey's favorite coffee shop, in advance, but put it in a new envelope with Jack's name on it.

"That's right." She turned back to Betty, who was staring at Jack the way she would a bug that had landed on her piece of wedding cake. "This will only take a few minutes."

"Neil is waiting for me in the car. It's been a long day, and we have to be at the airport at five tomorrow morning."

It took every ounce of Evie's strength to scrape up a smile, but she didn't want to leave things like this between them.

"Cody and Raine will be gone, but you're welcome to come over to the house this evening. There are plenty of leftovers from the reception."

Betty hesitated for a moment, and then her hands rolled into fists at her sides. "No, thank you. Please tell Cody that his grandpa and I will be in touch." Betty gave Jack a wide berth as she swept out of the kitchen.

Jack's eyes narrowed. "Are you all right?"

"I'm fine." Evie kept her smile in place. "The envelope is in my office. I'll be right back."

Instead of waiting for her to return, Jack

followed her into the hall. He didn't say anything, but Evie was acutely aware of his presence. The loose-limbed, confident stride. The subtle blend of freshly laundered cotton and some masculine soap that sifted into Evie's lungs every time she took a breath.

She fumbled with the light switch and walked over to her desk, her knees still a little wobbly after the confrontation with Betty. Opening the drawer, Evie withdrew the long white envelope.

"Here you —" *Go.* Evie almost bumped into Jack as she turned around.

"I'll trade you."

"Trade?" The word slipped into the space between them.

"I think you need this more than I do." Jack took the envelope and pressed the coffee mug into her hands. But instead of leaving, he took another step closer. Cupped her chin in his hand.

Evie felt the imprint of each blunt fingertip, still warm from the ceramic mug, as he tilted her face toward his.

"W-what are you doing?"

"Looking for proof that you're fine." Jack's wry smile made Evie's heart stutter midbeat, but then it stopped altogether when his thumb grazed the curve of her jaw. "I know from experience that turning the other cheek can be painful."

CHAPTER 7

Jack made a point always to knock first before he walked into his brother's house. Not this time. This time he wrenched the front door open and followed the muffled sobs to the kitchen, where Cheryl was kneeling on the rug in front of the sink.

"Did you cut yourself?" Glass crunched underneath Jack's feet as he crouched down and took hold of his sister-in-law's hands. Gently pried her fingers apart to check for blood.

"No." Cheryl shook her head, her broken whisper a sign that all the damage was on the inside. "The plate that Travis bought me for my birthday . . . it broke."

Jack didn't waste time wondering if it had been intentional or an accident. The end result was the same. "Where's Trav?"

"He's not here. He called me about an hour ago and said he picked up some overtime."

Overtime. Is that what he's calling it now?

Even as the thought began to form in Jack's mind, he stomped it out. No one said this was going to be easy.

"Come on." Jack helped Cheryl to her feet and relocated her to a chair at the table before he grabbed the broom.

Her lips twisted in a parody of a smile. "Practicing for your new job?"

His new job. Right. For a guy who'd claimed he needed the job at Hope Community, Jack seemed to be on a personal mission to get himself fired.

What were you thinking, Vale?

He hadn't been. That was the trouble.

Jack hadn't heard exactly what the woman who'd cornered Evie in the kitchen had said to her, but he'd heard the bitterness in her tone.

How many times had Jack stood in silence while Travis berated him for something he had or hadn't done? All Jack had wanted to do was let Evie know he understood. Knew how difficult it was to look past a person's anger and see their pain.

Sure, there were times Jack wanted to get in Travis's face. Grab him by the front of the shirt and shake some sense into him. But whenever his younger brother was at his most frustrating, his most unlovable,

54

Jack saw his own reflection in Travis's eyes.

What he would be — *who* he would be — if God hadn't gotten his attention.

Well, he'd sure gotten Evie Bennett's attention.

"Where's Lily?" Jack deliberately focused his thoughts on the here and now. He hoped his niece hadn't witnessed her mother's meltdown. In spite of all the upheaval in the ten-year-old's life over the past six months, Lily hadn't lost a bit of her sweetness or sparkle.

"With Nicki." Cheryl listlessly kicked a stray shard of glass toward the dustpan. "She took all the kids to the park this afternoon."

"You didn't want to go with them?"

"Travis said he'd take me out for dinner tonight. Someplace nice, like we used to go."

Jack struggled to keep his expression neutral. His brother didn't exactly have the best track record when it came to keeping promises. And as far as Jack knew, Trav didn't have the money to take Cheryl to a nice restaurant either.

Or maybe he did.

Now *Jack* wanted to break something.

"If you're at loose ends, you can hang out at my place for a while," he said casually.

"So you can make sure I don't run down

to Eddie's for a six-pack?" Cheryl glowered at him. "I don't need a babysitter, Jack. I'm sober."

She had been, up until six months ago. And the last time Jack had heard those words come out of his sister-in-law's mouth, she'd been arrested for shoplifting and having open intoxicants in her vehicle a few hours later.

"Then let me drop you off at the park." Jack emptied the dustpan into the wastebasket under the sink. "I'm sure Nicki wouldn't mind some company."

"I guess." Cheryl's shoulders twitched in a shrug. "I'll be right back. I'm going to do something with my hair."

Jack took advantage of the time alone to look for signs that his brother's life wasn't sinking into the same state of disrepair as the house he was renting.

The pillow and rumpled blanket on the couch weren't a good sign. It was Trav's standard MO, to pull away from the people who cared about him when he needed them the most.

God . . . whatever it takes to get his attention. Don't give up on him. Show Trav You're the kind of father a guy can trust.

Because their earthly one sure hadn't been.

"I'm ready." Cheryl drifted into the living room, her hair scraped back into a ponytail, a shirt thrown over her tank top to hide a stain. But other than that, Jack didn't see a whole lot of difference in her appearance. Except maybe for the weary slump in her shoulders that seemed more pronounced every time he stopped by.

His sister-in-law blamed her constant fatigue on working swing shifts at the Leiderman plant outside of town, but Jack had a hunch it had more to do with the swings in Travis's moods.

The floorboards on the porch shifted under Jack's feet when he stepped outside. "Did the landlord call you about tearing down the shed yet?"

"He said he'd get around to it."

Right. That's what Phil had said two months ago.

Jack had already boarded up the door and windows after he'd stopped over one afternoon and found Lily sweeping out the top layer of grime, trying to convert the dilapidated shed into a playhouse. The structure, fashioned from scraps of plywood and strips of ragged metal, was not only an eyesore, it was practically caving in on itself.

Not that the rental house itself was a whole lot better. Jack had fixed a few things around the place, but Travis had turned down his offer to replace the broken tiles in the kitchen floor, claiming he didn't want to invest in something he didn't own.

Jack had wanted to say, *How about investing in your marriage? Your family?*

He'd toyed with the idea of talking to Coop, his employer back in Milwaukee, about putting in an offer on the place. In addition to the finishing work Jack did for Coop's construction company, they'd recently partnered together to flip houses. Coop bought them, and Jack fixed them up in his spare time. One of the buyers told Jack he had a gift for looking past the flaws and seeing what a house could be.

Maybe that was true, but it didn't mean there wasn't a whole lot of blood and sweat — and yeah, maybe a few tears — along the way.

But Jack figured the end result was worth it.

"I'll give Phil a call and let him know I'm going to rip that thing down tomorrow." He opened the passenger-side door of his pickup, and Cheryl slid inside. "Trav can help."

"If he's around."

Jack closed the door a little harder than necessary. He understood Cheryl's frustration. She and Travis had moved to Banister Falls to start over, but it was difficult when his brother preferred to live in the past.

"I don't know why you came here, Jack." She turned toward the window as he hopped into the cab. "You have your own life."

"I like Banister Falls."

It was the truth — even if the move hadn't been a completely altruistic gesture on his part. The bottom line? He was selfish.

He *did* have a life — and he wanted his little brother in it.

Jack pulled into the parking lot next to the playground equipment. On this beautiful summer afternoon the park was packed with families, but he spotted Cheryl's sister, Nicki, right away, pushing her fifteen-month-old Grace in the baby swing. Lily was with Nicki's two older children, Luke and Ava, playing tag on the monkey bars.

The change Jack had seen in Nicki over the past few months was nothing short of miraculous. She had left Victor, her abusive boyfriend, taken a job as a waitress, and moved into a duplex subsidized by donations from the local domestic violence shelter. Jack hoped the gold cross she had started wearing was more than simply a piece of jewelry to her too.

He tapped the horn to get her attention.

A grin broke out on Lily's face when she recognized him. His niece swung down from the bars and skipped toward the truck, waving both arms.

"Lily looks happy to see you," he said.

Cheryl perked up a little, absorbing the warmth of her daughter's sunny smile. "If you talk to Trav, will you tell him that I'm with Nicki and the kids?"

"Sure." Even as Jack made the promise, he thought about how many Travis had broken.

Cheryl slid out of the truck and came around to his window. "Thanks, Jack."

"Anytime."

"I-I'm trying, you know."

Jack's throat tightened. "I know."

They all were.

"Can you stay, Uncle Jack?" Lily jumped onto the running board of the truck, her infectious grin conjuring up images of Travis at that age.

"Not this time, Peanut." Jack tweaked her nose. "But I'll drop by tomorrow afternoon."

"Okay." Lily hopped down and tugged on her mother's hand. "Come on, Mom! I can hang upside down for fifteen seconds. You can time me."

Jack watched them walk toward the playground hand in hand.

You're missing this, Trav.

Why couldn't his brother see that by holding onto his anger, he wasn't getting back at their dad — he was turning into him?

Jack left the window down as he drove away, letting the scented breeze roll in. Banister Falls, tucked into a fold between rolling farmland and hardwood forest, felt as remote as another planet from the urban area where Jack and Travis had grown up.

His cell phone rattled the console between the seats as Jack pulled alongside the curb in front of his apartment building.

Unknown number.

His stomach lurched.

It never quite went away. The feeling that he was only one phone call away from the next disaster.

"Hello?"

"Jack? This is Pastor Anderson."

Jack closed his eyes, bracing himself for what was coming next. The last time they'd spoken, the pastor had told Jack to call him Keith.

"What can I do for you, Pastor?"

"Can you stop by my office when you come into work on Monday morning?"

"Sure. Not a problem."

Jack had a problem.

But at least now he didn't have to wonder what Evie thought about his stepping across that invisible line.

CHAPTER 8

"We're going to have just enough paint to finish." Gin stepped back to admire her handiwork. "I hope Raine and Cody like the color we picked out."

"Me too." Evie swiped her paintbrush against the plastic tray to catch a drip before it hit the carpeting. "It would have been easier if we'd had more information. Like whether the baby is a him or a her."

"I hear you, but they want it to be a surprise."

"Did you know Raine was a girl?"

"Not until the doctor put her in my arms," Gin admitted. "What about you?"

"We knew." Evie didn't like surprises. The day she'd found out she was going to have a boy she had stopped by the hardware store and picked out a color for the nursery. A pale, barely there blue called Morning Sky, the perfect backdrop for the clouds she then sponge-painted on the ceiling above

Cody's crib.

Gin rolled another stripe of paint down the wall. "Angela said this shade of green reminds her of new beginnings."

Evie smiled. That sounded like something Dan's mother would say.

Angela was the one who'd organized a work party after Sunday dinner, the Moretti clan's weekly get-together. Everyone except Bree, Trent and Jennifer's one-year-old daughter, had been drafted to fix up the house next door so they could surprise Cody and Raine when they returned from their honeymoon at the end of the week.

Lisa and Liz were put in charge of removing outdated wallpaper from the rooms, Jennifer and Carissa assigned to the kitchen. Dan's sisters-in-law had even raided their own cupboards, filling the cabinets with surplus pots and pans and stocking the freezer with enough meals to last a month.

The men armed themselves with rakes and fanned out across the yard while Angela and her two older granddaughters, Emily and Amanda, planted bright-yellow marigolds along the sidewalk leading up to the front door. Which left Gin and Evie in charge of painting the nursery.

"Looking good, you two!" Liz poked her head through the doorway. The undisputed fashionista in the Moretti family, Dan's sister had dressed for the work day in a cute pair of khaki shorts and a striped T-shirt that coordinated with the colorful bandana that covered her sable-brown hair.

"Thanks." Evie took advantage of the momentary interruption to knead away a kink in her lower back. "Are you finished with the downstairs already?"

"Uh-huh. Lisa and I are about to start taking down the wallpaper border in the bathroom at the end of the hall." Liz waggled her fingers. "Good-bye, red canoes. Time to take your cute, little pinecones and bear cubs and sail back to the eighties."

Gin grinned as Liz ducked out of sight. "I feel like I've been transported into one of those home-makeover shows."

Not Evie. Evie felt as if she'd been transported back in time.

She hadn't been inside Max's childhood home since . . . for years. The house had gone through several different owners after Betty and Neil sold it and left town, but there were things even new carpeting and a fresh coat of paint couldn't hide. Like the dent Max and Dan had put in the wall when they'd tried to shoot a potato out of a Nerf gun. The notches in the trim board that surrounded Max's closet, measuring his height at every birthday.

Evie wondered if that was the reason Betty and Neil had moved. Because the memories crowding the air made it difficult to breathe.

"I still can't believe Raine is going to live here."

"Next door to Dan's parents?"

"In a house." Gin traced a finger over the windowsill, her gaze drawn to the people in the backyard.

Dan's brothers were all busy: Will and Stephen were in the process of reseeding bare spots in the lawn while Trent, wielding a hedge clipper, was locked in battle with the overgrown shrub the home's previous owners had planted at the end of the stone wall separating the two yards.

Evie glanced at Gin and realized she wasn't joking. "You've never lived in a house?"

"The double-wide on Fifth Avenue is the closest we got."

Downstairs someone cranked up the volume on the radio. At the end of the hall a series of thumps and bumps, accompanied by shrieks of laughter, told Evie that Liz and Lisa were attempting to choreograph the number.

"They're kind of a noisy bunch, aren't they?" Evie smiled. "Don't worry, you'll get

66

used to them."

"I'm already getting used to them."

"You say that as if it's a bad thing."

"It's a *different* thing."

The flash of vulnerability in Gin's eyes offered a glimpse of her past. What had life been like for her, moving from city to city? Raising Raine on her own?

Evie had been blessed with a strong support system. Dan and his family. The firefighters at Second Street Station. The congregation at Hope Community, who had voted to pay her for taking charge of women's ministries, a position ordinarily filled by a volunteer, because they knew Evie needed the additional income.

"The Morettis love you." Evie had watched them gently draw Ginevieve into the family fold over the past few weeks.

Dan, who'd been tossing branches into the bed of his pickup, suddenly looked up at the window. The slow smile he aimed at Gin brought an instant blush to her cheeks, one that made her look more like a teenager than a grown woman.

"And so does someone else," Evie teased.

"I'm still getting used to that too," Gin confessed. "Dan is just . . . well, Dan is amazing. And scary."

"Scary?"

"It's like he knows what I'm thinking before *I* know what I'm thinking. I don't have to pretend. Or hide. I can just be . . . *me.* Does that make any sense?"

A memory pierced Evie, so sharp and unexpected it hurt to breathe.

The warm brush of Jack Vale's fingers against her skin. The understanding in his silver-gray eyes.

"I know that turning the other cheek can be painful."

Evie turned away from the window, unsettled by emotions that, like Gin, she was afraid to name.

"I'm sorry." Gin bit her lip. "What am I talking about? Of course it makes sense to you. You were married to Max . . . and I know how much you must miss him."

"It's —" *Fine, Evie?* "All right."

But it wasn't.

Because for the first time in a long time, Max wasn't the man Evie had been thinking about.

CHAPTER 9

Keith Anderson's office was the masculine version of Evie's. Plush, dark-green carpeting. Comfortable leather chairs angled in front of a walnut desk that spanned the width of the room. Wildlife prints on the wall. A tiny box plugged into an outlet next to the filing cabinet dispersing an invisible puff of pine-scented fragrance into the air every two minutes.

Jack had yanked the thing out of the wall and opened the window a crack when he'd vacuumed the building on Friday.

The door was open a few inches, but he knocked anyway. Pastor Keith looked up from his computer monitor and smiled.

"Morning, Jack." Keith gestured toward the chair on the opposite side of the desk. "Come on in. Have a seat."

Jack would have preferred to stand up while he was being fired, but he sat down anyway, just to be polite.

69

"I'm sorry we haven't had an opportunity to talk until now, but I've been playing catch-up since the conference, and then there was the wedding."

Yes. The wedding.

But Jack's mind didn't automatically conjure up images of roses and white lace and wedding cake. No, he saw Evie's blue eyes staring up at him. Felt her pulse jump underneath his fingertips.

Because you scared her, you idiot.

"I have to admit I don't usually hire people on the spot, but Harvey had just called from the airport, and we had that problem with the water," Keith went on. "I'd just asked God for a little help, and there you were. I try to pay attention to divine appointments."

So did Jack. A city crew had been repainting the lines at the four-way stop on Main Street, forcing him to take an alternate route from the bank back to Travis's house. Jack had spotted Hope Community's marquee at the end of a quiet, tree-lined street. And felt The Nudge.

His first impulse was to keep right on going.

The church he attended in Milwaukee met in an old theater.

Depending on the time of year, the temperature in the building could either cause third-degree burns or frostbite, but what it lacked in members it more than made up for in enthusiasm. After the service, the worship team took their instruments out on the sidewalk and played another hour or two. The next Sunday, there would be a few more people hunched in the back row of musty chairs, eyes riveted on the floor, hearts finding their rhythm in the opening notes of "Amazing Grace."

Jack had fit right in.

Hope Community, with its steeple and stained glass windows, looked so . . . tidy.

But a nudge was a nudge, so he pulled into the parking lot to check it out. There were only a few cars, so he'd figured he could take a quick look inside without drawing any attention. Except that a harried-looking woman with an armload of towels had almost taken him out when he'd stepped into the foyer.

"Good morning! I'll be with you in a minute," she'd called over her shoulder. "Our custodian isn't here, and we're having a bit of a crisis."

Jack hadn't thought twice about following her down the hall.

There'd been a heavy rain during the night, and water had flowed down one of the walls in the nursery, loosening the wallpaper border decorated with Noah's arks and soaking into the carpet.

Two men were studying the ceiling when Jack came in.

"We sprang a leak," the one in the plaid shirt and cargo pants said cheerfully. "We're just trying to figure out the easiest way to get to these pipes."

Jack took one look at the damage and knew the pipes weren't the issue. "Did you check the roof?"

"Can't be the roof." His companion's gray eyebrows hitched together over his nose. "It's brand new. A group of volunteers just replaced it a few weeks ago."

Exactly why, Jack thought, it could be the roof. "I can take a look at it. I'm familiar with construction."

He could almost hear Coop snort.

"Thank you." The man in the plaid shirt aimed the words at the ceiling and then smiled at Jack. "I'm Pastor Anderson, by the way. And this is Mort Swanson."

"Nice to meet you." The older man still looked a little disgruntled when he gripped Jack's hand.

Just as Jack suspected, the flashing hadn't been installed properly, leaving a gap where the two additions met. He'd explained the problem over a cup of coffee and ended up with a temporary position at the church.

Very temporary, if Jack was right about why he was here.

Keith cleared his throat. "I talked to Evie Bennett yesterday."

Here it comes.

Jack's spine straightened.

"She reminded me the church picnic is coming up in two weeks. I don't know where the time has gone." Keith shook his head and slid a piece of paper across the desk. "Here's the name of the rental company Harvey has used in the past. He oversees the setup that day."

"Picnic?" Jack stared down at the colorful brochure.

"It's an annual event. We always have it the weekend *after* the Fourth of July because the attendance is better. A cookout, carnival games for the kids. I realize this is short notice, but we don't expect you to handle all the details yourself. Dan Moretti's men's group is in charge of grilling the hot dogs and burgers, and the women's ministry team takes care of everything else. Did you get a chance to meet Evie at the wedding?"

Fortunately, Keith didn't wait for Jack to respond. Because his response would have to be *Actually, we met a few months ago in my brother's backyard. She had a bag of groceries . . . I had a baseball bat.*

And she'd lingered in Jack's mind for days afterward.

"Evie's worked at Hope Community for thirteen years. Her office is right next door to mine." Pastor Keith pointed to the wall on Jack's left. "If you have any questions, she knows the answers and she'll be more than willing to help you out."

Jack wasn't so sure about that.

The pastor's gaze shifted to something beyond Jack's shoulder, and he smiled. "Tell Mort I'll be there in a minute, Pauline."

Jack took that as his cue to leave. He rose to his feet, still a little stunned by what had just happened.

He'd walked into Keith Anderson's office expecting to be fired, and instead he'd been put in charge of a picnic. He could almost hear God chuckling.

I believe, Lord. Help my unbelief.

Not the most eloquent prayer Jack had come across in the Bible, but definitely one of the most honest. And one he repeated at least half a dozen times a day.

Fishing the keys from the pocket of his jeans, Jack unlocked the door of the custodian's room and stepped inside. It was a little intimidating, the way Harvey Kinnard kept

74

the space as smudge-free and pine-scented as the rest of the building. The cleaning supplies on the shelf were even alphabetized.

If Pastor Keith had seen Jack's apartment, he might have thought twice about hiring him. But then again, Jack's landlord wouldn't have given him a break on the rent if fixing up the building hadn't been part of the deal.

The toe of Jack's boot bumped into something on the floor. A box filled with plastic trophies that he guessed had something to do with the church picnic.

And so did the line of new Post-it notes that papered the wall.

He recognized Evie's neat handwriting on each one. Tent rental. Booths for carnival games. Bunting. Grills.

Pastor Keith had recommended that Jack talk to Evie if he had any questions.

Well, he did.

And none of them would fit on a Post-it note.

CHAPTER 10

Evie had been the director of women's ministries for so long she knew the exact order in which her team of volunteers would arrive for their bimonthly meeting.

Sonya Olson and Jill Claremont rode together but parted company in the foyer — Sonya to chat with Pauline, who happened to be her first cousin, and Jill to check her lipstick in the restroom mirror. Belinda Mullins inevitably bolted through the door ten seconds before Evie opened the meeting in prayer, the hem of her denim jumper flapping against her ankles, patchwork bag dragging across the floor like a loose tailpipe. While everyone bowed their heads, Belinda would be plumbing the depths of the bag to retrieve a pen that seemed equally determined to elude capture.

But this Monday morning, Evie was the one running late.

76

Cody had called while she and Diva were taking their morning walk.

"Hey, Mom! Miss me?"

"Do I miss you?" Evie pretended to mull that over. "Mmm. No dishes in the sink. No wet towels on the bathroom floor. No shoes in the front hall."

"So, yes?"

Evie closed her eyes for a moment, soaking in Cody's laughter like a warm summer rain. "Yes."

"Raine and I will be back on Saturday afternoon, but we're going to stop over and pick up the rest of my stuff if that's all right with you."

"Of course it's all right." Evie gave Diva's leash a little tug to distract her from the calico cat sunning itself on the neighbor's sidewalk. "What time will you be here? I can have supper ready."

"Raine is . . . she's kind of anxious to settle in and try out the new kitchen, Mom."

"Of course she is." Evie's image of an evening catching up with her son and new daughter-in-law dissolved. She made a mental note to leave a bouquet of fresh flowers on their table as a housewarming gift instead. "We can make it another time."

"Sounds good . . . I should probably go." The sudden lilt in Cody's voice told Evie that Raine was nearby.

"I'll see you on Saturday."

"Love you, Mom."

Evie's eyes began to burn. "Love you too." She glanced at the time before slipping the phone into her pocket. "Come on, Diva, step it up a little or Belinda will get there before I do."

As it turned out, everyone — including Belinda — was already there, passing around a carafe of coffee, when Evie walked into the conference room.

"We want to hear all about the wedding!" Sonya announced.

Belinda, who'd worked with Evie the longest, winked as she slid a cup of coffee in front of an empty chair. "We'll consider it old business."

How could Evie argue with that?

Out of respect for everyone's busy schedules, she kept the meetings to one hour. Which meant they stuck to a three-part agenda. Old business, new business, and God's business. The last one had been Evie's mother's idea — a humorous reminder to make sure that prayer requests brought before the group didn't turn into gossip.

The three women scooted their chairs closer together while Evie touched on the highlights and scrolled through the photos she'd taken with her tablet over the course of the day.

"Cody looks so grown up in a suit and tie," Jill murmured. "I remember when he used to kick off his shoes and socks in Sunday school class and hide them under the beanbag chair because they — and this is a quote — 'made his head hurt.'"

And Evie had encouraged Cody to pursue a degree in business. "I believe the tie came off right after that picture was taken."

Sonya fanned herself with a napkin. "I have to say, Dan sure looks handsome in a three-piece suit."

Evie didn't miss the twinkle in the woman's eyes. She drew in a slow breath and exhaled a smile as she flipped to the next photo. A candid of Dan and Gin holding hands at the reception.

"I'm sure Ginevieve would agree with you."

"Are they . . . are you . . ." Sonya started and stopped, as if she was afraid to fill in the blanks.

"Happy? Yes." Evie did it for her. "Happy for them? Yes."

Absolute silence followed the statement as everyone absorbed the news.

In the past Evie had simply shrugged off

the teasing comments aimed at her and Dan. Friends and, Evie suspected, even some of Dan's family members had kept a close eye on them over the years, waiting for their friendship to develop into something more. And if she was completely honest, Evie knew that Danny had been waiting too.

There'd been times when loneliness had seeped into her bones like a cold spring rain, and her thoughts had drifted in that direction. She could come up with at least a dozen reasons why marrying her childhood friend would be the logical thing to do, but she could never seem to get her heart to agree.

And then she would lie awake at night, in the double bed she'd shared with Max, wondering if she could even trust her heart anymore. Wondering if the only thing it was capable of was pumping blood through her veins.

"Raine's mother is a waitress at that diner on Radley Street, isn't she?" Jill's brows dipped together, an unconscious gesture Evie had discovered to be an accurate gauge of her disapproval.

"My Place." Evie had a feeling it wasn't Gin's choice of a career, or even the diner, that Jill had a problem with. Some of the women who attended Hope Community didn't know what to do with Ginevieve Lightly. To be honest, Evie hadn't known either at first. But the thread that bound them together — their love for their children — had proven stronger than their differences. And now? Well, strange as it might seem, she *liked* Gin.

"A diner?" Belinda clapped her hands together. "I'm a little shorthanded on volunteers in the food tent on Saturday. Maybe I should call Ginevieve and ask if she'd be willing to help out. We could use someone who knows how to handle a hungry crowd."

"That's a good idea." And the perfect segue. *Thank you, Belinda.*

Evie opened her folder and took out the agenda. "We should get started or it'll be lunchtime before we get through the new business. Sonya, will you open in prayer?"

"Of course."

Evie was grateful for an opportunity to close her eyes for a few moments and redirect her focus.

God . . .

Evie stopped and let Sonya's words flow into the space as a familiar pressure began to build.

What was happening to her? That she

couldn't express what was in her heart to the One who knew it the best?

A ragged sigh slipped out and mingled with the chorus of amens. Evie reached for her cup of coffee and hoped no one at the table had noticed.

"Let's skip the first two items and start with the church picnic." She opened her binder, where she'd tucked the notes from the previous year.

The summer picnic was almost as popular as the Chilly Bowl the church held in April. And even though it technically wasn't a women's event, Pastor Keith had asked Evie's team several years ago if they would oversee the details.

"The youth group agreed to be in charge of the carnival games again." Jill's pen tapped against her notebook. "Last year some of the booths were falling apart, but I'm not sure if Harvey got a chance to fix them before he left."

"You could ask the new custodian," Sonya suggested. "I think his name is Jake."

"It's Jack," Evie said. "And I left him a few notes." Five, to be exact.

Had he found them yet? She'd caught a glimpse of Jack walking into Keith's office when she'd arrived at the church, so she'd taken advantage of the moment and slipped into the custodian's room.

The subtle changes had surprised her.

A breeze filtered through the open window, diluting the scent of pine cleaner. The rickety metal table Harvey had confiscated during last year's Bible Olympics looked different too. It no longer listed to one side, and the top had been replaced with a piece of wood that someone had stained a rich golden brown.

Why had Jack bothered to change it, knowing that Harvey was coming back in a few weeks? But then again, why had he taken the job at all . . .

"Evie?"

She snapped back to attention. "I'm sorry. What did you say?"

"We know you've been busy with the wedding, so we've got everything covered for the picnic." Belinda patted Evie's hand. "You can skip right to item seven."

"You guys are amazing. You know that, right?"

Sonya pointed her lemon scone at Evie. "We learned from the best."

"We also had our notes." Belinda thumped her folder. "The picnic doesn't change much from year to year."

"Do people want it to change?" The thought hadn't occurred to Evie until now.

"Of course not." Jill entered the conversation. "That's what makes it a tradition."

"Okay." Evie flipped to the next page in her binder. "I guess that brings us to the garden walk at the end of July. Belinda, you're in charge of publicity. Why don't you start?"

"I e-mailed the local newspaper and two of the radio stations with the date and time. Melanie offered to design the flyers again, but I told her you wanted to wait until you heard from Victoria Kellan."

"Oh no." Sonya reached for another scone. "She isn't planning to back out, is she?"

"Victoria's daughter found out she has to have a C-section, and she wants to be there for the birth. Victoria promised to let me know as soon as they schedule a date."

Jill frowned. "Victoria's rose garden is always the highlight of the tour. The women are going to be disappointed if it isn't included."

"All the gardens on the tour are beautiful, but that's why I think we should wait until the end of next week before we print out the brochures." Evie looked at Sonya. "What about the refreshments?"

"I talked to Marie when I had lunch at the bistro yesterday, and everything is set for the ice cream social afterward."

"Great." Evie checked those items off the list and then checked the time. "I think that covers everything until the next meeting."

"Do you want me to help you clean up, Evie?" Belinda gave her bag a quick shake to settle the contents before she stuffed her notebook inside.

"No, you go ahead. There are only a few coffee cups and plates to rinse out."

"I won't insist — not when I've got a date with my adorable grandson." Belinda's eyes twinkled. "In a few months, you'll know what I mean."

A grandchild.

Evie was still trying to wrap her head around that.

She piled the dishes on a tray and carried them to the kitchen.

Jack's coffee mug was still in the dish drainer where Evie had left it. Bright yellow, with a crooked handle and a daisy etched into the front, it reminded Evie of the art projects Cody had made in elementary school.

It also reminded her of Saturday night.

She'd been trying really hard not to think about Saturday night.

Why Jack had said what he had about turning the other cheek.

Why he'd *touched* her cheek.

Evie picked up the coffee mug and turned it over in her hands, studying the name painted on the bottom in block letters that matched the yellow glaze.

LILY.

Her fingers tightened on the handle as the air in the room seemed to change.

At least Jack hadn't caught her off guard this time. Evie sensed his presence before he even said a word.

She just couldn't decide which one was worse.

Jack thought Evie had looked beautiful on Saturday. But it suddenly occurred to him that it didn't matter what she was wearing. Sparkly blue dress and high heels or a white button-down shirt tucked into a slim-fitting skirt that landed a conservative inch below her knees. Jack still had to reset his pulse.

"Hi." And apparently, judging from the amount of grit in the word, his vocal cords too.

"Good morning. I . . . are you looking for this?" Evie held up the mug that Lily had made him for Christmas.

"Actually, I was looking for you."

"Me?"

"I met with Pastor Keith this morning, and he suggested that I talk to you if I have any questions about the picnic."

"I left some notes for you."

"I saw them." Jack tried not to smile. "Which leads me to my first question. What does Harvey have against face-to-face communication?"

Evie blinked. "Nothing."

"Really?" Jack let his skepticism show as he moved closer to the sink. "Then why do you communicate through Post-it notes? Because nowadays most people prefer e-mail, or they just text each other."

"Harvey refuses to get a cell phone. He's kind of old school that way. The church hired me thirteen years ago, but Harvey has been here for twenty-five. My first week I ran all over the building whenever I had a question or wanted to tell him something. Harvey would see me coming and yell, 'I won't remember. Leave me a note.' So I did." Evie shrugged. "It turned out to be a great system."

"Uh-huh. There's only one thing wrong with it."

"What's that?"

"I'm not Harvey."

"I . . . I realize that."

Evie looked away and Jack wished he could rewind Saturday night. He still would have sacrificed his last cup of coffee but kept his hands to himself.

"I have another appointment in a few minutes." She carefully set his coffee mug down on the counter. "Was there anything else you wanted to know?"

"As a matter of fact, there is." Jack dipped his hand into his back pocket and extracted one of her now-wrinkled Post-it notes. "What the heck is bunting?"

Evie's eyes went wide, and then an honest-to-goodness smile lifted the corners of her lips. "It's not for the picnic. It's the red, white, and blue fabric we use to decorate the windows and the fence. I made a note of it because Harvey likes to put it up ahead of time, and this Saturday is the Fourth. The parade goes right past the church."

"Fabric."

"I can show you."

That smile was already burning its way into Jack's memory as he followed Evie down the hall.

And she thought *he* was the dangerous one.

CHAPTER 11

Evie watched a week's worth of groceries move down the conveyer belt toward the freckle-faced teenage boy who stood at the end of the checkout line. And realized that three-quarters of the items she'd put in the cart were the things that Cody liked.

The night before, she'd set the table for two.

It didn't seem like the Fourth of July without Cody either. They'd always attended the parade together, but Evie couldn't muster the enthusiasm to go alone.

Janice, a retired teacher who manned the cash register at Truitt's Supermarket on the weekends, scanned the coupons and handed Evie her change. "Have a great holiday weekend, Evie."

"You too, Janice."

"Would you like to drive up, Mrs. Bennett?" The teenager tossed a twenty-pound bag of kibble onto the bottom rack of the cart as if it were a box of tissues.

"I've got it, thanks." Evie pushed the cart toward the entrance just as Melanie Gibson and her daughter Taylor, who'd graduated in May with Cody, breezed through the automatic doors.

"Evie!" Melanie whipped off her tinted sunglasses and anchored them on top of her head. "I was hoping to see you at the parade this morning!"

Taylor, used to her mother's outgoing personality, smiled at Evie before drifting toward the magazine rack by the produce department.

"I didn't go." Evie angled the nose of her cart closer to the wall as the automatic doors slid open and a group of women walked in. "Sonya should be able to let you know about the flyers for the garden walk by the end of next week."

"That's great, but it's not what I wanted to talk to you about. One of the instructors at the Tech is offering a watercolor class on Wednesday evenings. I remember you mentioning that you'd taken one in the past, so I thought we could sign up together."

"That was years ago, Mel," Evie murmured. "And I wasn't very good at it."

"Well, that's what the class is for! To get better."

Never mind that Melanie was closer to forty than fourteen. There were times — like this — when Evie could still see the head cheerleader of the Banister Falls Bobcats shaking her green-and-white pom-poms.

"Wednesday evenings?"

"Six thirty — and it's only eight weeks, so it'll be finished before the Wednesday night programs start up at church in the fall. We could grab dessert and a cup of coffee at the bistro afterward." Melanie nodded at Taylor, who was holding up the latest issue of InStyle magazine. "Ray and Scottie have softball that night, and you have some extra time on your hands now, right?"

"Right." Evie worked up a smile. "I'll think about it and let you know."

"It starts next week and the registration form is online."

Melanie pursed her lips and kissed the air near Evie's cheek. "Girls night out! Fun, fun, fun!"

The cart seemed heavier as Evie pushed it out to the parking lot. Wrestling the bag of dog food into the backseat, she made a mental note to take advantage of the drive-up service next time.

The once-a-week trip to the grocery store had been part of Cody's and her Saturday mornings even before Max died. So was the stop at the bistro afterward, to pick up two of Marie's homemade cinnamon rolls.

Evie bypassed Main Street this time. She'd accidentally buy two cinnamon rolls and end up eating both of them.

The smell of fresh-cut grass drifted through the open window of her Jeep when Evie stopped at the intersection, still littered with the flotsam and jetsam of the morning parade. At the end of Perkins Street she spotted a lone black pickup parked near the front doors of the church.

Jack was working. On a holiday weekend. She'd seen him loading tools into the bed of the truck earlier in the week, so she knew the vehicle belonged to him. Their paths hadn't crossed since she led him to the storage closet on Monday and pointed out the bins of red, white, and blue bunting that now adorned the marquee by the road and the windows that flanked the double doors.

Not that she had purposely avoided him. Gertrude Fielding, who'd rocked Evie to sleep in the church nursery when she was a baby, had broken her ankle and needed surgery, so Evie had made several trips to the nursing home where Gertrude was having rehab. The rest of the time Evie had been holed up in her office, finalizing details for the family picnic and the garden walk.

"I'm not Harvey."

Jack's words circled back through Evie's mind as she took a right turn toward Rosewood Court.

No, he wasn't Harvey. Because Harvey didn't whistle while he mopped the floors or listen to jazz during his lunch break.

Harvey didn't fluster her either.

A veil of pale-blue smoke drifted over Evie's street, evidence that her neighbor was still on a mission to grill the perfect steak.

A light-blue Datsun was parked in the driveway. The car had belonged to Dan's brother Will, who'd sold it to Cody a few weeks before the wedding.

Which meant . . . her son was home.

The strap of Evie's purse tangled with the seat belt in her haste to get out of the vehicle.

The front door swung open, and Cody met her in the middle of the sidewalk. His exuberant hug lifted Evie several inches off the ground. Over his shoulder, she saw Raine waving from the doorway.

"You said you weren't going to be here until later this afternoon!" Evie managed to gasp when her feet touched the ground again.

"We got an early start." Cody's lopsided

smile was pure Max.

"We were anxious to get home," Raine chimed in.

Evie stepped forward and hugged her daughter-in-law. She and Cody had only been gone a week, but the baby bump underneath Raine's loose-fitting shirt seemed to have doubled in size.

"You stopped at the house first?"

Cody nodded, his hand seeking Raine's. "It looks awesome, Mom. I can't believe how much work you put into it while we were gone."

"I can't take all the credit. Angela rallied the troops. What do you think of the color Ginevieve and I picked out for the nursery? Do you like it?"

"It's perfect." Tears misted Raine's eyes. "Everything is perfect."

"I wouldn't have gone to the grocery store if I'd known you were on your way home." Evie backed toward the Jeep, remembering there was ice cream in one of the bags. "How long can you stay?"

"Not very long. We have to unpack, and I promised Raine we'd go to the fireworks tonight."

"We just wanted to stop over and say thank you." Raine bent down to pet Diva, who'd decided she had been ignored long enough.

"Let me put the groceries away, and I can help you load up the rest of your things."

"We'll help." Cody jogged toward the Jeep and popped the hatch. He handed Raine a gallon of milk. "No heavy lifting."

Raine grinned. "Then I better take the ice cream instead."

"Actually . . . you can take it with you." Evie had bought a gallon of Mackinaw Island Fudge, Cody's favorite. "And those two bags in the back. Consider it a house-warming gift."

"Really? Thanks!" Cody transferred the groceries to the backseat of the Datsun.

Evie held the door open for Raine and noticed the empty hallway. "You took the boxes already?"

"You weren't here, so Cody figured we'd have time to run them over to the house."

"It didn't take very long." Cody brushed past them with what remained of Evie's groceries on his way into the kitchen. "Besides that, we had to make room for the most important thing."

"We already discussed this." Evie rounded up the bags of frozen vegetables and began to deposit them in the freezer. "You can't cut a square out of our concrete driveway and take your basketball pole and hoop."

Cody grinned. "I'm talking about this furry critter." He reached down to ruffle the heavy cowl of golden-brown fur underneath Diva's chin.

A lump instantly formed in Evie's throat, making it difficult to breathe.

"I always wanted a dog, but we couldn't get one because we moved around too much." Raine dropped to her knees and wrapped her arms around Diva's neck. The dog leaned into her, the liquid brown eyes closing in bliss. "And Mom had this 'no pets, no houseplants' rule."

"Mmm." Evie rearranged the peas and green beans.

"Raine insisted we stop at the store and buy her a new toy before we came over."

"It's so cute . . . It looks like a pink high heel." Raine rocked back on her heels and smiled up at Evie. "Do you think she'll like it?"

"She . . ." How *old* was the chili in that storage container anyway? ". . . She hasn't had a new toy in a while."

"We'll be close to the park too." Cody snagged an apple from the wicker basket in the center of the table. "Raine, Diva's dishes are in the laundry room. Can you grab them while I put her dog food in the car?"

"Sure. Come on, girl!"

Diva's ears lifted at the word *food,* her plumed tail waving like a victory banner as she trotted after Raine.

Evie closed the freezer door and started to unload another grocery bag. Shampoo — the brand Cody liked. Paper towels. Dog biscuits.

"You'll probably want to take these too." Evie slid the box across the table. "The turkey and cheese flavor are her favorite."

"Diva will adjust okay, won't she, Mom?" Cody's voice dropped a notch, his expression suddenly uncertain. "I mean, this is the only house she's ever lived in."

Tell him, Evie. Tell him that Diva should stay with you.

Tell him they'll be busy with a newborn in a few months and a dog will be one more thing demanding their attention.

Tell him the house is already too quiet. Too empty.

"I think . . . Diva will be fine if you're there, Cody. She really missed you."

Relief snuffed out the worry in Cody's eyes. "You won't have to vacuum as often or take her for walks. You'll have tons of free time."

"Tons." Evie smiled even though the word burned the back of her throat. "I'll meet you and Raine outside in a sec. You're going to need her leash."

CHAPTER 12

Evie had just finished e-mailing a copy of next year's projected budget to Pauline when a piercing shriek shattered the comfortable silence of a Wednesday afternoon.

She stepped through the doorway of her office as another one erupted.

A thin young woman in a tank top and denim shorts was trying to coax a golden-haired toddler to come out from behind the coffee center and relinquish the small basket of sugar packets clutched in her hands.

A few feet away were two more children so close in age it was difficult to tell which one was older, the boy or the girl. The boy was sifting through the canned goods in a donation box marked for a local food drive while the little girl, barefoot and wearing a crooked pair of butterfly wings over her sundress, spun pirouettes.

Gloria, who played keyboard for the worship team, hovered at the perimeter of the chaos. Evie could tell she wasn't sure if she should wade into the fray or maintain a safe distance.

One of the cans hit the floor and rolled underneath the counter.

The young mother twisted around and shot a frazzled look at the older children. "Ava and Luke! Put those back right now. They don't belong to you."

"Nicki?"

The woman glanced over her shoulder, and the sheer relief that flooded her eyes propelled Evie forward. By the time she reached Nicki's side, the little girl had scrambled out from behind the counter and attached herself to her mother's leg.

"She's looking for someone named Jack." Gloria's wide-eyed gaze slid to Nicki's son, who was stuffing a can of chicken noodle soup into the pocket of his cargo shorts. "I told her that we don't have anyone here by that name."

"As a matter of fact, we do." Evie gave Nicki a reassuring smile. "Come with me. We'll track him down."

Tears shimmered in Nicki's eyes. "Thanks, Mrs. Bennett."

Evie suddenly felt a hundred years old. "It's Evie, remember?"

The boy and girl, sweet-faced copies of

100

their mother, trailed behind Evie as she led them down the hall.

Jack wasn't in his office or the sanctuary. She finally found him washing one of the walls in the youth wing, where the teens had gathered for a pizza party the night before.

Before Evie had a chance to say anything, Nicki's children released a loud whoop and charged toward him. Jack barely had a moment to drop the sponge in the bucket and brace himself for the impact. Even the toddler propped on the ledge of Nicki's hip squealed and stretched her arms toward him.

The little family knew him. Well.

Jack's gaze met Evie's for a moment before shifting back to Nicki. "What's going on?"

"I'll tell you what's going on." Nicki's voice stretched thin. "Cheryl promised to babysit while I picked up an extra shift at the diner, but she took off somewhere and her phone goes right to voicemail."

"What about Trav?"

"He wasn't home when I stopped over either. I called Mom, but she won't watch the kids." Nicki's eyes rolled toward the ceiling. "Carl is taking her to the casino tonight."

Something dark flashed across Jack's face. "Where's Lily?"

Lily. The name on the bottom of Jack's coffee mug.

Evie knew she should leave — give them some privacy — but her feet seemed to be stuck to the carpeting.

"She's in the car. I figured if worse came to worse . . ."

"Lily can't watch them all, Nic. It's way too much responsibility for a ten-year-old."

"Then what am I supposed to do?" Nicki set the squirming toddler down, and she immediately made a beeline for Jack. He scooped her up in one easy motion and settled her in the crook of his arm.

"I'll try and get ahold of Trav."

"Don't bother — he isn't answering his phone either." Nicki's fingers plucked at the ragged end of her ponytail. "I've been begging Sue for more hours. She's going to fire me if I leave her shorthanded tonight."

Jack glanced at the clock on the wall. "I can leave a few minutes early and watch the kids, but it's going to have to be at my apartment."

"That's okay —"

"And you're going to have to drop them off. I don't have enough seat belts in my pickup for the whole crew."

"But I'm already late!" Nicki's wail was only a few decibels softer than her daughter's had been in the foyer.

Evie took a step forward. "I was about to leave for the day too. I can drive."

Jack wasn't sure who was more surprised by the offer. He or Evie.

Before the polite refusal forming in his head had a chance to become actual words, Nicki jumped at the opportunity.

"Really? That would be great! Thanks, Evie!"

Jack scrubbed a hand across his jaw in order to stifle a groan. "Pull around to the back of the church, and I'll transfer the car seats. Tell Lily we'll be out in a few minutes."

"Okay." Nicki shot out the door.

Leaving Jack, once again, to deal with the fallout from someone else's choices.

And Evie.

He could only imagine the thoughts running through her mind when Luke and Ava attached themselves to his legs like barnacles. Grace played shy, tucking her face into Jack's shoulder.

"I didn't realize you and Nicki knew each other." Jack shifted Grace to his other hip.

"Ginevieve introduced me to Nicki at the

diner a few weeks ago, but I didn't get to meet the rest of the family." Evie smiled at Luke and Ava. The same smile that had surfaced when he'd asked her about the bunting.

The one he hadn't been able to stop thinking about.

"Luke, Ava, and this little peanut" — Jack removed the toddler's finger from his ear — "is Grace."

Evie bent down until she was eye to eye with Ava. "And how old are you?"

Ava carefully pressed her thumb into her palm and wiggled the remaining fingers.

"Four." Evie looked impressed before she turned to Luke. "And what about you?"

"I'm almost six. Lily can stay in the car by herself 'cause she's ten."

Luke sounded a little envious, but Jack's lips tightened.

A few nights ago he'd stopped over and found Lily making a grilled cheese sandwich for supper. She'd told Jack that her mom had had to work a double, so Jack had stuck around until Travis finally came home.

"Something came up. It was only for a couple of hours." His brother had brushed off Jack's concern about leaving his niece alone in the house. "Lily's a responsible kid."

Who needs a responsible adult at home, Jack had wanted to say.

Instead, he'd told Trav that Lily could hang out with him on the nights when "something came up."

But why had Cheryl bailed on Nicki if she'd promised to babysit? Jack deliberately shut down the possible scenarios before they could take root in his mind.

"Can we have spaghetti again?" Luke tugged on Jack's pant leg. "I like it the best."

Jack knelt down, careful not to dislodge Grace as he wrapped his arm around the boy's shoulders. "Well, you're in luck," he said in a low voice. "Because it happens to be the only thing I know how to make."

He was rewarded with a giggle.

"I can sprinkle the cheese on it," Ava offered. "I know how."

"That's great because I can always use an experienced cheese sprinkler." Jack gave Ava's wings a gentle tug.

Nicki returned and slung a diaper bag roughly the size and shape of a VW Beetle at his feet. "I'll see you at nine. Thanks, Evie." She blew kisses at Grace as she jogged backward out the door. "Be good for Jack, you guys."

The door snapped shut and Ava pressed against Jack's side.

"Mommy was crying."

"She cries a lot." Luke was a just-the-facts kind of guy.

"Mommies cry when something hurts, just like you do." Jack angled his head away from Grace, who was trying to poke her finger in his other ear. "Tears wash away all the bad stuff inside, and then you feel better."

"Ice cream makes me feel better," Luke said.

"I think we can rustle up some of that." Jack pulled the ring of keys from his pocket and jingled them in front of Grace's nose. "But first I have to put some things away and lock up my office."

"I can do it!" Luke's and Ava's voices and hands collided as they reached for the key ring.

"Whoever picks the right key gets to pick the flavor of ice cream too." Jack herded them toward the door. "How does that sound?"

"Tee!" Grace shrieked.

Jack winced and glanced over his shoulder at Evie.

Last chance to change your mind . . .

She'd already picked up the diaper bag. "I'll meet you in the parking lot."

CHAPTER 13

Evie walked toward Jack's dusty black pickup, the only vehicle with three car seats lined up on the hood.

A little girl with a shoulder-length tangle of strawberry-blonde curls sat in the front seat, her attention focused on something in her lap.

"Lily?"

A pair of wide silver-gray eyes met hers, and Evie's heart rose and fell with a little thump, like she'd just hit one of the speed bumps in the parking lot.

Jack's eyes.

He didn't wear a wedding ring, hadn't mentioned a family, but it was another reminder of how little Evie knew about the new custodian.

"I'm Evie. I thought I'd keep you company for a few minutes until your . . . until Jack gets here. If that's all right with you."

"Okay." The girl flashed an engaging

smile. "I like your necklace. Did you make it?"

"No. It was a gift." Evie traced the thin gold chain to a single pearl resting in the hollow of her throat. Max had given her the necklace after Cody was born — and promised he would add another pearl to the strand every time they added to their family.

"You should have picked out a longer chain then," Evie had teased. An only child, she'd always dreamed of having a large family like Dan's, but Max had put all the money into the house on Rosewood Court, and he'd asked her to wait until he got a promotion before they provided Cody with a baby brother or sister. Evie hadn't realized it would take more than a few years, but she'd tried to be patient. Whenever she brought it up, Max would say the same thing. *We're young. We have plenty of time . . .*

"I know how to make my own necklaces and bracelets and stuff. I made a collar for Bitsy too . . . Do you want to see it?" Lily held up a bright-eyed guinea pig with a patchwork coat.

Evie moved closer to admire the animal's braided collar. "Very pretty. I love that shade of pink."

"Me too! Ms. Hadley, my science teacher, asked me to take care of Bitsy until school starts." Lily rubbed her cheek against the top of the guinea pig's head. "Otherwise she'd get lonely."

"I'm sure she would. My son volunteered to take care of the class pet one summer, but it was a lizard." Evie wrinkled her nose. "Not nearly as sweet and cuddly as Bitsy."

Lily's giggle was lost in the stampede as Ava and Luke charged up to the truck.

"Sorry. That took longer than I expected." Jack lagged a few steps behind them, holding Grace's hand as she tried to keep up with her siblings.

"That's all right. Lily and Bitsy and I were getting acquainted."

"Hey, Peanut." Jack reached through the open window and tweaked Lily's nose. The afternoon sun cut through an opening in the clouds and ignited gold threads in their hair, drawing Evie's attention to another similarity. "How are you and Bitsy doing today?"

"Hungry," Lily said promptly.

"Let's see what we can do about that." Jack grabbed Grace's car seat and opened up the backseat. In less than sixty seconds he snugged it into place with the seat belt, buckled the toddler in, and stowed the diaper bag on the floor behind the seat.

"Ava and Luke, you two can ride with Evie, okay?" Jack flicked a glance in her direction. "If you're still good with this. No appointments or meetings on your list?"

"No." Was it her imagination, or was there a glint of amusement in Jack's eyes when he mentioned her list?

The watercolor class was scheduled to start that night, but Evie hadn't filled out the registration form yet. She hadn't given Melanie a definite yes yet either, but if she decided to go, there would be plenty of time to change her clothes and drive to the technical college.

"My address is 620 Fairview." Jack picked up the other two booster seats and tossed them into the back of Evie's Jeep. "Do you know where that is?"

Evie nodded, even though she hadn't ventured into that part of town for years. When she was growing up, Fairview had been considered part of Main Street. But the value of homes had plummeted when the neighborhood was rezoned so the Leiderman factory could build an addition and expand its parking lot. The handful of small, family-owned businesses had eventually closed their doors when the city council focused their attention on revitalizing the downtown area.

"Okay, you two." Jack threaded the seat belts through the booster seats and snapped them into place with the practiced ease of someone who'd done it a thousand times. "In you go."

Evie went around to the other side to make sure Ava's wings didn't get tangled in the seat belt. Which brought her face-to-face with Jack again, who was in the process of buckling Luke in.

As he reached across the booster seat, the sleeve of his T-shirt rode up, offering Evie a fleeting glimpse of an intricate tattoo on his upper arm.

She fumbled with the buckle.

What are you doing, Evie?

A split second before Jack closed the door, she saw the same question reflected in his eyes.

Evie slid into the driver's seat. Her hand trembled as she slid the key into the ignition. She glanced in the rearview mirror. "Ready?"

Two small heads bobbed in unison.

"Okay." Evie summoned a bright smile, trying to match their confidence.

She followed Jack's truck as he cut through the heart of the town, zigzagging through a maze of stop signs that seemed to mark the division of neighborhoods as well as the intersections.

He turned onto Fairview and pulled up in front of a run-down three-story building a few blocks from the house on Brewster Street where she and Gin had dropped the groceries off for Nicki.

Evie was tempted to keep driving. She couldn't believe how much the neighborhood had deteriorated over the years.

Country music seeped underneath the door of a bar that had replaced the dry cleaners on the corner.

Thomsen's Bakery, a favorite Saturday morning destination for her and Max and Dan during their summer vacations, was abandoned. One of the windows was cracked, the other two were hollow eyes fixed on the vacant lot across the street. Evie couldn't remember when the bakery had gone out of business. She'd stopped going there when Marie had opened the bistro.

The houses that lined the other side of the block weren't in better shape. Faded siding, blistered paint, and spaced so close together it looked like a strong gust of wind would send the whole row toppling like dominoes.

Evie slid out of the car, and something crunched under her foot. The jagged remnants of a beer bottle, scattered like confetti along the curb.

"Be careful." She lifted Ava out of the booster and didn't set her down until they were safely on the sidewalk.

Jack was already there, Grace's diaper bag slung over one broad shoulder. "Grace conked out on me two stop signs ago. I'm going to try and get her inside without waking her up. Can you open the door?"

"Of course . . . which one is it?"

"That one." Jack tipped his head at the building behind them. "First door on the left at the top of the stairs."

"I thought . . ." Evie glanced at the row of houses again.

Compared to the run-down three-story building, they suddenly appeared downright charming. "I-I'll need the key."

"It's not locked."

Why? was the first word that sprang into Evie's mind.

Lily was cradling Bitsy's cage in her arms, but Evie took the two younger children's hands, forming a chain as they climbed the covered staircase to the platform on the second floor. The doorknob wobbled, and Evie half expected it to fall off in her hand.

"It's this one!" Lily ran over to one of the doors that lined the carpeted hallway.

It was unlocked too.

Ava and Luke wiggled free, and Evie followed them inside.

It was like stepping into the mouth of a cave. The shades on the windows facing the street were pulled down, shrouding the room in darkness. Evie ran one hand along the wall in search of the light switch.

"I've got it." Jack had come up behind her, close enough that his breath whispered against her ear.

It took a moment for Evie's eyes to adjust to the light that flooded the cavernous room. Another moment to adjust her heart rate when Jack's wry smile surfaced.

"It's kind of a work in progress."

Jack watched Evie's gaze travel around the room.

A grown-up, blue-eyed Alice who'd fallen down the rabbit hole.

He tried to see the apartment through her eyes.

The sun had scorched the hardwood floor, and tiny fault lines split the plaster walls. The previous tenant had painted one of them a startling shade of tangerine, the rest a dull cherry-cola brown.

A stack of wooden crates doubled as a bookshelf, and the only thing that separated the living area from the kitchen was a table fashioned from two old doors Jack had found buried underneath a stack of moldy cardboard in the basement.

He'd sanded through three layers of paint before finding the treasure underneath: the shifting variations of light and shadow that identified the wood as solid hickory.

Most people preferred steel doors over wood because they didn't require any maintenance, but Jack never understood that mentality. If you took care of things, they had a tendency to last longer. And if it required a little extra attention now and then, so be it.

Jack slanted a look at Evie. From the expression on her face, she thought his entire apartment needed attention.

"Harley!" Ava spotted the gigantic black-and-white cat curled up in a nest of tarps beside the paint cans.

The cat didn't belong to Jack, but like the rest of the tenants in the building, it somehow managed to find its way into his apartment on a regular basis.

Ava cut between the ancient plaid couch and the black walnut coffee table Jack had rescued from the curb the week he'd moved in.

Evie gasped when a head — decorated

with multiple piercings — popped up from underneath the pile of blankets.

"That you, Jack?" The blanket slipped another notch, and bloodshot eyes squinted in his direction.

"Yup." Andy was one of the reasons Jack didn't lock his door. "Time to rise and shine."

The young man pushed a lank strand of ink-black hair from his eyes and yawned so wide his jaw cracked. "What time is it?"

Jack glanced at his watch. "Almost time for your shift to start."

Andy yelped and rolled off the couch. "Catch you later." He charged past them, leaving the faint scent of motor oil in his wake as he bolted out the door.

Evie watched him go, her hand still pressed against her heart. "Who —"

"That's Andy. Sometimes he catches a nap before his shift starts."

"On your couch?"

Jack shrugged. "It's more comfortable than the backseat of his car."

Evie stared at him. Probably trying to figure out if he was joking.

He wasn't. "His wife, Serena, runs an in-home daycare, so he can't sleep there in the daytime."

The first time Jack had met his upstairs

neighbor, Andy had been tossing a pillow into the backseat of the rusty Oldsmobile parked in front of the building. Jack recognized the signs of an all-night bender. Andy's red-rimmed eyes and slow speech were collateral damage brought on by long shifts, the kids that Serena took care of for a little extra cash, and Amber Lynn, the young couple's colicky infant. Jack told Andy his couch was available during the day, but this was the first time he'd taken Jack up on the offer.

And of course it had to be the first time Evie visited his apartment.

Grace stirred in Jack's arms and her eyes fluttered open. He shifted her to the other hip and noticed the telltale damp spot on his T-shirt.

Evie saw it too.

Jack shook his head. "Wardrobe malfunction."

A smile bloomed in Evie's eyes, and Jack felt that strange tug again. The one that occurred whenever he caught a glimpse of the current flowing underneath her tranquil surface. It drew him. Made him want to get to know her better.

But that meant Evie would get to know *him* better too.

Jack could only imagine what her reaction

would be if she found out how closely the apartment resembled his life at the moment.

Not really a work in progress though. More like a construction zone.

A little loud, a little messy, and a whole lot of unpredictable.

It would be better — safer — if Evie stayed where she belonged.

And something told Jack it would be safer for him too.

CHAPTER 14

"Thanks again for your help."

Jack didn't bother to wait for Evie to respond.

He just strode away with Grace and disappeared through a doorway on the opposite side of the room.

The fluorescent light on the ceiling flickered. A little natural light might brighten the place up. Evie made her way over to the window, on the lookout for anything that might be considered a potential hazard for small children.

Luke and Ava didn't seem to think anything of Jack's abrupt departure. Ava sat on the floor with the cat draped across her lap, its lime-green eyes half closed, purring like a rusty chainsaw. Luke was a few feet away, constructing a tower from pieces of wood he'd found in a box underneath the window. Evie was about to suggest he put them away when she noticed that all the edges had been sanded smooth.

She began to pull up the window shades, one by one. They were so old and brittle she was afraid they would crumble in her hand.

Late-afternoon sunlight chased the shadows into the corners but didn't do anything to improve the overall look of the apartment. If anything, it magnified the deep gashes that marred the surface of the hardwood floor and the nails that sprouted from the walls, marking the spots where pictures had hung.

"Will you hold Bitsy while I get her some fresh water?" Lily deposited the guinea pig into Evie's arms before she could answer and dashed into the kitchen.

"Where's Jack?"

Evie almost dropped Bitsy. She hadn't heard the door open — or seen the elderly man shuffle in. But then, maybe *he'd* been hiding in the furniture too.

At least a head shorter than Evie and as thin as one of the spindles on the staircase, the man had wizened features, accentuated by a pointed chin and piercing blue eyes. He reminded her of a garden gnome.

"Jack," he repeated, a bit louder this time. "Is he here?"

"He's . . . busy at the moment."

Instead of leaving, the man claimed one of the threadbare chairs arranged around the coffee table.

"I can take her now." Lily returned, holding a shallow dish of water. "Hi, Mr. Ron."

The man responded with a noise that sounded more like a snort than a hello, but it made Evie feel a little better knowing Lily had encountered the visitor before.

"Mission accomplished. Grace fell back to —" Jack strode back into the room barefoot, and shock registered briefly in his eyes.

Evie's gaze bounced from Jack to the man in the chair and back again. "You have company."

"I see that." Jack's smile surfaced again.

He'd changed into a dry T-shirt, and a few strands of tawny hair dipped over his forehead. Evie felt a tiny curl in the pit of her stomach. It was close to suppertime. Her blood sugar was probably crashing.

"Ron . . . how is it going?" Jack veered into the kitchen and turned on the faucet. The pipes rattled and shook for a few seconds before a stream of light-pink water appeared. "I missed you yesterday."

"I had an appointment at the VA." A bone-rattling cough ripped through the man's body. "Took 'em three hours to tell me what

121

I already knew." He looked at Evie. "I'm dying."

Evie wasn't sure how to respond, but Jack didn't appear the least bit shocked.

"Ron" — he informed Evie calmly — "is always dying."

"Well, I'm one day closer than I was yesterday," the man retorted.

"Why didn't you tell me you had an appointment?" The water finally turned the color that water should be — no color at all — and Jack stuck a pan underneath it. "I would have driven you to the hospital."

"Heard you got another job. And I don't expect you to haul my carcass around. Not when you got someone like Blondie here to keep you company." Ron wiggled his eyebrows at Evie. "She's a whole lot prettier than I am."

"Definitely prettier." Jack coaxed the tiny blue flame underneath the burner into full bloom. "And she smells better too."

Prettier. Evie didn't have time to process the compliment because Jack finally got around to making the introductions.

"Evie, this is Ron. Ron, Evie."

"It's nice to meet you."

"I live in 3C." Ron jerked a thumb toward the ceiling.

"Are you sure about that?" Jack lifted a

brow. "Because every time I turn around, you're sitting in my chair."

Instead of looking offended, Ron's cackle echoed around the room. "Someone has to make sure you don't drop a ceiling on your head."

"Give me a break. That was *one* time."

Jack grinned, and the curl in Evie's stomach unfurled and traveled all the way down to her toes.

Nothing seemed to rattle the man. Not people sleeping on his couch. Not wet diapers or neighbors who wandered into his apartment without knocking first.

"Lily?" Jack waved a white dishcloth to get her attention. "Will you set the table, please?"

The girl bounded into the kitchen, but Jack stopped her before she opened the drawer. "Hands."

Lily obediently reached for the soap dispenser on the counter and thumped the handle in rapid succession until a drop of liquid appeared. "How many forks?"

"I'm not sure."

He wasn't *sure*? How could you not know how many people would be eating dinner at your table?

Jack opened the cupboard door. On the shelf, boxes of spaghetti were stacked like

123

cordwood. Apparently he hadn't been teasing when he told Luke it was the only thing he knew how to make.

"I saw this on TV." Lily folded one of the white paper napkins into an envelope and tucked a fork inside. "I think they look prettier this way, don't you?"

Jack stopped to admire her work. "I agree."

"Gracie's waking up." Luke paused in the middle of his building project, one ear cocked toward the hallway.

"I'll be right back." Jack reached for a towel and wiped his hands. "The marinara sauce is in the cupboard. Second shelf from the bottom."

It took Evie a moment to realize he was talking to her.

Jack had heard Ron come in. The person he hadn't expected to see in his living room was Evie.

Spine straight, hands curled at her sides. Poised to flee.

So why hadn't she?

And why hadn't he politely escorted her to the door instead of putting her to work?

Over the past few days he had caught fleeting glimpses of Evie in motion. Gliding through the day, her schedule divided into sections as neat and organized as the Post-it notes she left in the custodian's room. Completely comfortable in her surroundings. Completely confident in her routine.

Jack couldn't teach her the steps to this crazy dance. At the moment, he was making them up as he went along.

Which was why he experienced a sudden disconnect between his mouth and his brain when Evie skirted around him and reached for one of the boxes in the cupboard.

He hadn't been lying to Ron. She *did* smell good. A delicate floral scent layered with an intriguing hint of something — vanilla, maybe — that made Jack want to bury his face in the curve of her neck and solve the mystery . . .

"Jack?"

Oh. *Man.*

The expectant look on her face told Jack she'd asked him a question.

"Sorry. I got distracted for a second."

"What do you think?" Evie repeated.

"I —" *Nope.* Couldn't tell her truth.

Lily, God bless her, came to his rescue.

"Evie wants to know how much spaghetti she should make."

What was it? Wednesday? Jack made a quick calculation.

"All of it."

"All . . ." Evie looked down at the box. "This would feed the entire neighborhood."

"Yup." Ron's chuckle turned into another wrenching cough that made Jack's lungs hurt just listening to it. "That's about right, isn't it, Jack?"

Jack shot him a look. "If there are leftovers, I'll send them home with Nicki."

He retreated to the spare bedroom to retrieve Grace. She was sitting in the center of the bed, peering at Jack over the hedge of pillows he'd built around her.

"Da!" Grace managed to shout the word around the thumb tucked into the side of her cheek.

"Hey, Amazing Grace." Jack squeezed out a smile as he scooped her up. "It's Uncle Jack, remember?"

He and Nicki's children weren't related by blood, but Cheryl and Travis's wedding had merged their two families together, for better or for worse. Jack wasn't about to get bogged down in technicalities. Luke and Ava heard Lily refer to him as Uncle Jack, so that's what he'd become. To all of them.

"Da." Grace melted against Jack and patted his shoulder.

Moments like this, Jack thought, should be enough for a guy to get his head on straight. Unfortunately, Victor, Grace's dad, was a look-out-for-number-one kind of guy.

Nicki's first marriage, at the ripe old age of eighteen, had lasted long enough to produce Luke and Ava, but Victor had convinced her to move in with him when she'd found out she was pregnant with Grace.

Jack had only met Nicki's controlling ex-boyfriend once, when he'd shown up at Cheryl and Travis's house the day after Nicki left him. But he had seen the bruises the guy had left on her face . . . and her soul.

Cheryl and Travis had reluctantly let Nicki and the kids stay with them until she got back on her feet, but even now, when she was out on her own and struggling to put the past behind her, Victor didn't want to let go.

A crash came from the direction of the living room, and Grace's thumb popped out of her mouth. "Uh-oh."

"Uh-oh is right. I think your brother's tower came down."

Or — Jack tried not to cringe when he stepped through the doorway — all the mismatched plastic storage containers on the top shelf of the pantry did.

Evie stood in the center of the debris field, clutching a plastic colander.

"Sorry. I should have warned you the conditions were right for an avalanche." Jack moved to help, but Ava intercepted him before he reached the kitchen.

"Twirl me, Uncle Jack!"

Ava loved to dance. And who was strong enough to resist the plea in those big brown eyes?

"A question for heaven, Luke." Jack settled Grace against his hip with one hand and spun Ava in a slow circle with the other. "Why did God give an octopus eight arms, but people only get two? I mean, think of all the things I could do with eight arms. I could make spaghetti and twirl your sister and paint the wall and talk on the phone —"

"And pet Harley," Ava giggled.

"And pet Harley."

"And play the saxophone!" Lily flew to Jack's side. "Twirl *me* now!"

Jack lifted Ava off her feet and gently swung her onto the couch. Ron was thumbing through a rumpled copy of last week's newspaper, oblivious to the chaos going on around him.

Grace's chortle of laughter sent the black-and-white cat diving for cover as Jack took his niece by the hand.

When he finally released her, breathless

and laughing, Lily pointed at Evie. "Now it's her turn!"

CHAPTER 15

Jack made the mistake of looking at Evie.

What would she do if he took her hand and twirled her around the living room?

And why was he even *thinking* crazy stuff like that?

He'd invaded Evie Bennett's personal space once before, and it could have cost him his job.

"I really should be getting home." Evie's hands locked together at her waist.

Jack didn't have to be an expert in reading people's body language to know what that meant. No twirling for her.

"Aren't you going to stay for supper?" Lily looked puzzled. She'd visited Jack's apartment frequently enough to know that everyone who walked through the door after four o'clock ended up sitting at the table.

The newspaper dropped an inch. "There's plenty. Not always edible, but plenty."

And just for that . . .

"Here." Jack deposited Grace in Ron's lap. His neighbor immediately started to protest, shaking and sputtering like the building's outdated copper pipes. "You can keep Grace occupied while I finish making supper."

Someone rapped on the door, and Lily dashed to open it, Luke and Ava on her heels.

Evie had the Alice look on her face again when Bernadette Fraser marched in.

"The change machine in the laundry room isn't working again. I lost fifty cents." Bert, one of the tenants who lived on the third floor, walked like a soldier and wore Hawaiian-print housecoats that ended where the wrinkled folds of her nylon stockings began. "And someone broke the light in the back stairwell again. I swept up the glass, but I can't reach the fixture without a ladder."

Bert updated the building report on a daily basis.

The items she'd mentioned were easy enough to fix. If Jack didn't have four little helpers until Nicki's shift ended.

"I'll have everything fixed before I leave for work in the morning."

Bert acknowledged Jack's promise with a cautious smile, proof that after years of being ignored by the landlord, she was finally beginning to believe *him.*

"Here." Jack mined a few quarters from the front pocket of his jeans. "This'll cover what you lost."

The change disappeared into the stained pocket of the floral housecoat. "Something smells good." Bert's nose twitched underneath her tortoiseshell bifocals. "Manna again, Jack?"

"That's right." A gift from heaven . . . and double coupon day at Truitt's Supermarket.

"No, it isn't! It's spaghetti!" Ava, Luke, and Lily folded over on themselves, laughing.

"Spaghetti." Bert hummed the word like she hadn't eaten it before.

Hadn't eaten it the last three evenings she'd shown up at his door.

"You're welcome to stay."

"I don't know." Bert might not be shy about letting Jack know when something in the building required his attention, but she hesitated every time he focused his attention on *her.* She would rock in place, as if weighing his sincerity. Or maybe, weighing her worth.

"There's more than enough," Evie said.

And Jack suddenly remembered his manners. "Evie, this is Bernadette —"

"Bert," she interrupted. "My mother only

called me Bernadette when I was in trouble."

"Bert," Jack amended. "This is Evie Bennett."

"It's nice to meet you, Bert." Evie held out her hand, but Bert ignored it and hugged her instead.

"Now I know why Jack has been whistling the past few days. A man always whistles when he's in love."

Jack had assumed that playing in clubs with Travis's band once in a while had permanently disabled his ability to blush, but no. He felt the heat wash over his jaw.

"Evie and I work in the same building, Bert." Same building, different job descriptions. Different everything. "She drove Nicki's kids over because there wasn't enough room for everyone in my truck."

"Glen and I met at work too —"

A noise in the kitchen snagged Jack's attention, and he glanced over just in time to see water cascade over the side of the kettle and flood the burner underneath.

Evie got to it first.

She'd turned the heat down and was already blotting up the overflow with a towel by the time Jack reached her side.

"You should have run when you had the chance." Steam rose from the sink as Jack poured the pasta and what was left of the water through the colander. "Things can get a little hectic around here at dinner-time."

Another knock at the door proved it.

Evie took one look at the lanky adolescent boy who followed Jack into the apartment and hoped she hadn't been lying when she'd told Bernadette — *Bert* — that there was plenty. When Cody was that age, he could practically eat his weight in pasta.

She stole another glance at the odd collection of people gathered in the living room. Ava and Lily were stretched out on the floor, watching Bert and Luke build another tower. The black-and-white cat had wandered over and was batting at one of the silk ribbons dangling from Ava's butterfly wings.

Ron from 3C was entertaining Grace by reading the sports section out loud, but she seemed more interested in watching the boy unload the contents of his backpack onto the coffee table.

Jack returned and grabbed the dishrag from the sink. "I'm sorry."

"I have a son, remember? I'm used to cleaning up spills."

"I'm sorry because you can't leave now."

Evie's head snapped around. "Why not?"

Jack transferred the spaghetti from the saucepan into an enormous glass bowl. "Because you strike me as the kind of person who understands iambic pentameter."

Evie narrowed her eyes. "What *kind* of person understands iambic pentameter?"

"The kind of person who keeps a book of poetry on her desk."

Evie knew that Jack cleaned her office, but it was a little unsettling to discover that he'd taken an inventory of the contents. What else had he noticed?

"Josh is in summer school, and English lit wasn't exactly my best subject. I was hoping you could help him out."

Evie's cell phone began to vibrate in her purse. Melanie, no doubt. Wondering if she planned to go to the watercolor class.

A heavy sigh from the boy on the couch made up Evie's mind.

"I can take a look at it."

"Great . . . but you have to eat first. Like you told Bert, there's more than enough." Jack dropped a wooden spoon into the kettle of marinara sauce and clapped his hands together. "Okay, everyone, supper's ready. Come over here and wash your hands before you sit down."

Evie couldn't help but notice that Ron was the only one who grumbled as he handed Grace off to Bert and took his place at the end of the line.

She moved to the side while Jack supervised the washing and drying of little hands.

"Is there anything else I can do?"

Jack held Ava up to the sink. "There's a gallon of milk in the fridge. Plastic cups in the cupboard."

Evie found it hidden in the door next to a bottle of ketchup, checked the expiration date, and began to measure it into the glasses.

"Lily, can you get the tablecloth out of the drawer?"

"I've got it, Jack." Bert stepped around Evie and pulled out a piece of blue-and-white checkered fabric.

It wasn't until Evie smoothed down one of the corners that she realized the tablecloth was a crisp, twin-size bedsheet.

Lily circled the table, carefully centering a paper plate in front of every chair. Jack followed, depositing a small mountain of pasta on each one.

Ron shuffled over and dropped into the folding chair at the head of the table. Jack took Grace from Bert's arms and eased her into the chair across from Evie.

"You don't have a highchair?"

"No." Jack's wry smile — the one that never failed to make Evie want to smile back — surfaced. "I'm kind of winging it here."

It didn't appear that way.

"I'll show you something my mother taught me when Cody was that age." Evie went back to the kitchen and pulled a large flour sack towel from the drawer.

Jack had anticipated her next move and grabbed one of the pillows off the couch while Evie folded the towel into a triangle. Grace threaded her chubby fingers through Evie's hair while she secured her into the chair.

"Uh-oh!"

Jack's husky laugh rumbled through Evie as she carefully extracted her hair from the toddler's grip. "I think Grace is trying to tell you that if she's stuck here, so are you."

I don't feel stuck.

The thought unfurled, surprising Evie.

Jack surprised her.

Nothing seemed to throw him off. He switched gears with patience and humor, teasing one moment, serious the next.

There were no awkward silences during dinner because there was no silence at all.

A cacophonous melody played in the background. Upstairs, the creak of the floor

137

was synced to someone walking back and forth and the sharp, unhappy bleats of a baby crying. Outside Jack's building, a steady hum from the factory was punctuated by horns honking and the occasional burst of laughter from the group of men loitering in the doorway of the bar. The volume of both the music and the laughter increased as the sun started to set.

Ron left shortly after they finished eating, clutching a container filled with leftover spaghetti. There was no television, so Nicki's children sprawled on the floor in front of the window and made houses from a deck of cards.

Evie helped Josh decipher one of Tennyson's poems while Bert and Jack washed the dishes. She experienced one moment of panic when a dog's mournful howl filtered through the window.

Diva would be ready for supper and a walk —

Except she wasn't waiting patiently for Evie to come home. Cody and Raine were taking care of her.

"Thanks, Mrs. Bennett." Josh flashed a shy, slightly self-conscious smile as he shoved the textbook into his backpack.

"You did great."

The thin cheeks flushed pink. "I still think

algebra is easier."

"Don't tell anyone" — Evie lowered her voice to a whisper — "but so did I."

Jack walked Josh to the door, and even though Evie couldn't hear their conversation, she saw the grin that spread over the boy's face when Jack cuffed him on the shoulder.

All these people, pieces of the puzzle that was Jack. Evie wasn't sure where — or how — they fit.

She tucked a crocheted blanket around Grace, who'd fallen asleep beside her on the couch, and stashed her cell phone back inside her purse. Melanie had tried to call — twice — and Cody had left a text, letting Evie know that he and Raine wanted to help out at the picnic on Saturday.

"Bert, do you mind holding down the fort for a minute? I'm going to walk Evie down to her car."

"Not at all." Before Evie could blink, Bert had reeled her in for another hug. "It was nice to meet you, Evie. I'm sure I'll see you again."

"It was nice to meet you too," Evie murmured into the bright-red hibiscus splashed across the woman's shoulder.

By the time Bert released her, Jack was already waiting in the hall. The unexpected shiver that skated down her spine left her feeling a little off-kilter.

"I parked right underneath the window. It isn't necessary for you to walk me to the car."

"I wish that were true." Jack followed her down the stairs.

"This is Banister Falls, not Chicago."

"The size of the population doesn't matter. There are always people who are . . . willing to take advantage of a situation."

The grim look on Jack's face hinted that he was personally acquainted with some of them.

Evie stepped out from the covered staircase and was immediately pelted with a burst of whistles and catcalls from the group of people loitering in the vacant lot across the street.

"Try not to let all that attention go to your head," she whispered.

Jack's eyes went wide and then he grinned. "I won't."

Evie couldn't explain why, but she had a feeling she'd surprised him too.

He walked around to the driver's-side door. "Thanks for playing chauffeur this afternoon. They're good kids, but put the four of them together and it's a little like herding cats."

"Uncle Jack?" Lily's voice floated down to them through the screen. "Can I take Bitsy out of her cage for a while?"

"As long as you keep her away from Harley," Jack called back.

"Okay!"

Evie stared up at him. "Lily is your . . . niece?"

Jack nodded. "My brother, Travis's, daughter. Trav and his wife rent a house on Brewster Street."

Brewster Street. Some of the pieces began to fall into place. "The house —"

"You were lurking around that night."

"We weren't *lurking*." Blessing burglaries always took place after the sun went down, so the "burglars" could remain anonymous. That was kind of the whole point.

"It was dark. You had a paper bag —"

"With *groceries* in it."

"I didn't know that right away. Some of Trav's neighbors prefer a liquid diet."

It took a second for Evie to understand what Jack meant.

"But Gin and I were under the impression that *Nicki* lived on Brewster Street."

"She did — at the time. Travis's wife, Cheryl, is Nicki's older sister. Nic had broken up with her boyfriend and needed a place to stay. She has her own place now."

"But I thought —" Evie stopped. If she'd been wrong about Lily being Jack's daughter, was it possible she'd misinterpreted his relationship with Nicki too?

"Thought what?"

"That you and Nicki were . . . together."

"Together." Jack went completely still. "Why would you think that? Nic is . . . She's a *kid*."

"She came to you when she needed help. And you seemed so comfortable with her children." *With their mother.* "I assumed you were a couple."

Some emotion Evie couldn't define skimmed through his eyes.

"Yeah," Jack said softly. "I guess you would."

CHAPTER 16

"Where were you tonight, Trav?"

Jack waited until Lily went to her room to get ready for bed before he confronted his brother.

Cheryl was nowhere in sight, but Travis had been sitting on the couch, strumming his guitar, when Jack dropped Lily off.

Travis scowled. "Don't start on me, big brother."

"Cheryl promised Nicki she would babysit."

"Nic needs to find someone else to take care of her kids. We have a life too."

Jack tried not to let his frustration show. "That's true, but she was counting on you."

"Cheryl and I were only gone for a couple of hours. I wanted to take a drive. Clear my head."

When it came to his brother, Jack had gotten pretty good at reading between the lines. "Did you lose your job at Leiderman?"

"Why do you even ask me things like that?"

So the answer was yes.

"What happened?" *This time.*

"Someone stole an air compressor, and the shift supervisor figured it was me. He didn't even search our lockers. Anything turns up missing, blame it on the new guy, right?"

"Did you talk to him?"

"Why bother?"

"Because you have bills. A family who needs you."

"Cheryl knows I didn't like working the line." Trav shrugged. "You and I both know I could run that entire operation with my eyes closed. I'll find something else."

Travis had been let go from his last two jobs. Without a glowing recommendation from his employer, it would be difficult for his brother to find another job in a town the size of Banister Falls. The fear simmering behind Trav's forced bravado told Jack that he knew it too.

"You could always go back to Milwaukee."

"And pound nails with you?"

"You wish. You have to work your way up the ladder, buddy. No pun intended."

His brother grinned, and for a split second Jack saw a glimpse of the old Travis. And

144

made the mistake of pushing.

"We could go back together. Coop has more than enough work for both —"

"That's your thing, not mine," Travis interrupted. "So maybe you're the one who should go back to Milwaukee. There's nothing keeping you here."

It sliced deep, knowing his brother actually believed that.

"Sorry. You're stuck with me awhile." Jack strove to keep his tone light. "I have to finish the repairs so Phil can sell the building, and Hope Community Church needs a custodian for a few more weeks."

"Church." Trav plucked at the guitar strings, a sharp F chord harmonizing with his snort of disdain.

"They're having a picnic this Saturday. Free food and carnival games for the kids."

"Sounds like fun."

Jack let the sarcasm roll off him. "Lily would probably think so."

"Now you're telling me how to raise my kid?" Travis went from smirking to surly in the blink of an eye.

"No, I'm telling you about something she would enjoy."

Travis rolled to his feet. "I'm tired, bro."

Jack took that as his cue to leave.

He let himself out through the back door

that opened onto the porch. The breeze carried fragments of a muffled conversation in the alley. A raccoon raiding the trash can slipped through a hole in the fence and disappeared in the shadows as Jack walked to his truck.

He's tired? Well, I'm tired too, God. Tired of the accusations and the complaining and the anger and the indifference.

Tired of not *seeing* a difference.

Jack drove back to his apartment building, following the same route he'd taken earlier that afternoon. With Evie.

He'd sensed a change in her as the evening progressed. Moments when she'd seemed to accept the chaos even if she hadn't joined in.

But he and Nicki dating? Under any other circumstances, the thought would have made Jack laugh — if he hadn't realized Evie was completely serious.

That should have been a clue right there what she thought of him.

A shadow detached from the steps and took on the bulky form of the high school dropout who lived down the street.

"Hey, Zach." The kid was probably Cody Bennett's age, but that was the only thing they had in common. Zach had a reputation for being a hothead. He knew the local police so well — Jack had heard him greet the officers by name when they cruised down the street.

"I wasn't sure you'd be back tonight." Zach turned his head a fraction of an inch to the right and spit into the curb. "Looked to me like you had a hot date."

A date. With Evie. Now Jack did laugh. "I'm too busy to date."

"You working on that wall again tonight?" The question was thrown out casually, like he really didn't care, but Jack knew better. Over the past few months, he'd watched the number of guys in Zach's posse begin to dwindle. The neighbors weren't the only ones who'd been on the receiving end of Zach's hair-trigger temper.

But all Jack could see was the chip on Zach's shoulder.

The one that reminded him of Travis.

Zach had started hanging around when Jack was working on the first floor, the project he'd actually been hired to do. When Phil, Cheryl and Travis's landlord, had found out that Jack knew his way around a construction site, he'd hired Jack to renovate the first-floor storefront of a building he owned to make it more sellable.

What the guy had failed to mention was that there were people living in said building. People who'd started showing up at the door of Jack's second-floor apartment at all hours of the day and night. The list of needs would use up an entire block of Evie's Post-its. Mice. Leaky sinks. Hollow stomachs and empty hearts.

Keep your eyes open, Jack, Coop had told him on more than one occasion. *God brings people into your life for a reason.*

Jack just hadn't expected there to be so many of them.

What he really wanted to do was go upstairs, take a nice hot shower — if there *was* hot water — and crash.

Didn't you just hear me say a few minutes ago that I'm tired, Lord?

Waiting for God's answer, Jack felt a trickle of energy begin to flow through his veins.

And even though he hadn't known God as long as Coop, Jack had known him long enough to recognize the answer. Those moments when Jack felt like he had nothing left to give, God gave him just what he needed.

"I thought about taking a crowbar and knocking out a few walls. Want to help?"

A grin creased Zach's face, making him look about twelve years old. "Really?"

"Come on."

Jack figured that busting out walls was better than busting windows. Or heads.

And it might be a really good way to forget that Travis had lost another job and tended to fill the gaps in his life with alcohol.

And maybe — if Jack tried really hard — he'd forget his last conversation with Evie too.

"Evie, thank goodness you're here! I was afraid you hadn't gotten my message."

Actually, it had been six messages — and all within the space of an hour — but Evie smiled as she held up the tapestry overnight bag. "I've got it right here, Gertrude."

Visiting members of Hope Community at local nursing homes and the hospital was something Evie did on a regular basis, but Gertrude Fielding held a special place in her heart. Gertrude had rocked Evie when she made her debut in the church nursery at the age of two weeks, and in spite of the forty-year gap between them, they'd been friends ever since.

Gertrude plucked at the sleeve of her robe. "I was advised never, *never,* to wear this shade of lavender. I'm a summer, you know. We look better in vibrant tones."

Which explained why Gertrude's hair had matched the color of Dan's ladder truck for as long as Evie could remember.

Across the room, the young CNA in Minnie Mouse scrubs caught Evie's eye and winked. "I'll be back with your medication in a little while, Mrs. Fielding. Enjoy your visit."

Evie scooted the chair closer to the bed and unzipped the bag she'd retrieved from Gertrude's house on her way to the nursing home. The woman's eyes began to shine like a child's on Christmas morning when Evie pulled out a gold-trimmed peignoir and helped her slip it on.

"Much better." Gertrude sank against the pillow with a contented sigh. "I almost feel like myself again. Dr. O'Malley stopped in while I was eating breakfast. He said if I make good progress in my physical therapy, I should be able to go home in a few days."

Evie refilled Gertrude's water glass from a pitcher on the nightstand and straightened the stack of get-well cards. "Are you still in a lot of pain?"

"Everything hurts when you're my age, dear." Gertrude waved away Evie's question with a hand as pale as the bedsheets. "Now, tell me all about the wedding! I'm sure Raine was a beautiful bride."

Evie had come prepared. She slipped a photograph from the side pocket of her purse. "See for yourself."

"Oh . . . look at them." Gertrude's eyes misted over. "You look beautiful too, Evie. And Cody . . . so tall and handsome. The spitting image of his father."

Evie's throat tightened. "Yes, he is."

"Were your parents able to make it?"

"They don't want to leave their village until the new church is finished, but Mom Skyped with Cody and Raine before they left on their honeymoon. They're planning a visit in October."

"To meet their first great-grandchild." Gertrude nodded her approval. "I suppose Angela is thrilled there's going to be a new baby living next door."

Evie smiled. "Not just a new baby. She and John are excited to have Cody and Raine living next door. They moved the rest of their things in after they got back from their honeymoon."

"I'm thinking about moving too."

Gertrude said the words so matter-of-factly that it took a moment for them to sink in. "Moving?" Evie repeated.

"My sister, Corinne, and her husband have an extra bedroom, and she's been pestering me to move in with them."

"Corinne lives in Texas."

"That's right. Galveston. She and Robert

have lived there for almost fifty years."

And Gertrude had lived in Banister Falls for seventy-five.

"But what about your house?" Gertrude's home, a stately Victorian built at the turn-of-century, had been in her family for almost a hundred years.

"I would have to sell it, I imagine." Gertrude took a sip of water. "Either I'm getting old or that house is getting bigger, because I get tired just walking from the kitchen to the living room."

"The house must be getting bigger," Evie said promptly.

"You're sweet to say so, Evie, but there's no getting around it. I can't keep up with things the way I used to. I've got dust bunnies taking over the house and real bunnies taking over my garden, and together they're taking up more time than I'm willing to give."

"I'll talk to Pastor Keith. I'm sure there are people who would be more than willing to help."

"I know they would. But I've been laid up for over a week, asking God to show me what He wants me to do, and I realized I'm not quite ready to start asking for help . . . not when I've still got some help left in me. A woman who attends Corinne's church owns a salon, and twice a month she hosts a spa day for women undergoing cancer treatments. Manicures, facials, even help choosing the right wig. Whatever a woman needs to lift her spirits. They're looking for volunteers, and even though it's been a long time since my pageant days, I still know what to do with a makeup brush."

"I know you'd be wonderful serving that way, but it's still a big change, Gertrude. You've lived in Banister Falls your whole life. You've put down roots here."

"Every adventure starts with one step."

"Is that what God told you?" Evie asked cautiously.

Lines bracketed Gertrude's faded-green eyes and scored her pale cheeks, but Evie saw the smile that had made her the reigning queen of the pageant circuit when she was a young woman.

"No, you did."

"Me?"

"At the spring retreat a few years ago." Gertrude reached out and patted Evie's hand. "I take very good notes."

CHAPTER 17

When Hope Community hosted a picnic, it didn't just break out the hot dogs and lemonade. Two white tents took up most of the grassy area that bordered the parking lot — one a refuge from the heat of the sun and the other to hold the casserole dishes dropped off by a steady stream of women the day before.

Jack had taken a peek in the refrigerator before he'd left work on Friday afternoon, and the multitude of things a person could do with cold macaroni and Jell-O made his own set of skills seem a little inadequate.

The official kickoff for the event wasn't until eleven o'clock, but Jack had arrived at eight to take care of a few last-minute details. He still had to fill up the kiddie pool for the fishing game and hook the speakers up to the generator for the music that would give the midway a more authentic carnival-like feel.

Dan Moretti sauntered into the custodian's room while Jack was thumbing through the most current stack of Post-it notes, which Evie had stuck on the wall when he wasn't looking.

"How many of those things does she go through in a week anyway?"

"A lot." Enough that out of concern for the environment, Jack had started to recycle them.

Evie had arrived shortly after Jack but gone straight to the kitchen. Jack hadn't seen her since. In fact, he hadn't seen much of her at all since Wednesday night.

It might have been easier to determine if Evie was avoiding him if Jack hadn't been avoiding *her.*

"Evie likes things organized." Dan shook his head. "When we were kids, she was the only one I knew who got more excited about shopping for school supplies than opening presents on Christmas Day."

Jack bent down and picked up the box of prizes for the fishing game to hide his smile. "Nothing wrong with that — and it makes my job easier."

"How is the job going, by the way?"

"Most of the time it's going great." Jack pressed down a little on the first word. Moretti was a smart guy — he'd figure it out. "I better take these outside and finish setting up the game."

Dan grabbed the sheaf of old-fashioned cane poles propped up in the corner and followed Jack into the hall. "That was Cody's favorite game. If I was working it, I'd make sure he got one of those little plastic soldiers with a parachute. I don't know why he liked them so much. Those things never worked right."

"The parachutes are too light." Trav had liked them too. "If you tape a dime in the center of it, it helps distribute the weight."

"I didn't know —" Dan stopped abruptly, and his expression changed.

The only way Jack could describe it was it looked like someone had hooked Moretti up to a twelve-volt battery and plugged it in.

Jack braced himself, expecting to see Evie walking up behind them.

"Good morning."

It was Ginevieve Lightly who smiled at Jack — right before she stepped into Dan's arms and planted a quick kiss on his lips.

The guy didn't look the least bit shocked. Only slightly irritated . . . at him.

Because you're staring, Vale.

"Dan!" One of the teenagers in the youth group sprinted out of the kitchen and veered toward them. "Are you busy?"

"What's up, Logan?"

"We were wondering" — the boy cast a furtive glance over his shoulder — "where you, um, keep the fire extinguishers?"

Dan handed off the fishing poles to Gin. "I'll be right back."

"Do you think he needs help?" Jack watched them disappear through the doorway of the youth wing.

"Dan's got this." Gin started down the hall. "He warned me that a firefighter is always on call."

"I didn't know he was a firefighter."

"You didn't know we were dating either, did you?"

Jack slid a sideways glance at Gin as he opened the door. "Was my shock that obvious?"

"Actually . . ." Gin's smile held a hint of mischief. "It looked more like relief to me. Care to explain that?"

Jack couldn't . . . so he decided not to say anything at all.

People were already beginning to arrive, and a haze of smoke hung over the line of grills set up in the parking lot.

Gin set the poles down on the grass next to the inflatable swimming pool at the end of the midway. "I'm working in the food

tent this morning. If you need anything —
coffee, funnel cake, a clue — feel free to
stop by."

Jack liked Ginevieve. And maybe yes, he'd
felt a small, completely inappropriate stab
of relief knowing Moretti liked her too.

He emptied a bucket of plastic fish into
the pool, each one marked with a number
that corresponded to one of the prizes he
then clipped to the pegboard wall.

"Uncle Jack!"

"Hey, Lily." Hope flared inside of Jack
until he saw Nicki, not Travis, walking
toward them. "I didn't expect to see you
here."

"Gin convinced Sue to schedule me for
the afternoon shift so I could bring the kids
to the carnival for a few hours." Nicki
parked Grace's stroller in a strip of shade.
In a short denim skirt, tank top, and her
hair caught up in a messy ponytail, Nic
looked about sixteen years old. The little
sister Jack had never had.

And Evie had thought they were a couple.

The memory of that conversation still
stung.

"Are Cheryl and Travis with you?"

"Cheryl called last night and asked if Lily
could spend the night. I haven't talked to
her yet, but she promised she would stop by

and pick her up before I have to leave. My friend Tracey is going to watch the kids while I'm at work."

"Hopefully she and Trav will drop off my truck. Their car wouldn't start again so I let them borrow it." Jack had had to walk to the church. Not a big deal, but he hadn't had time to unload the lumber he needed for the apartment.

"I'm going to get my face painted, Uncle Jack." Lily tugged on his hand.

Nicki glanced over her shoulder. "Ava and Luke are over there now, but Lily wanted to come over and say hello first."

"Can you watch me?" Lily tugged on his hand. "I'm going to get a butterfly. Or maybe a heart."

"For a few minutes. Then I'll have to get back to work." The overtime would cover the parts Jack needed to fix Trav and Cheryl's car.

"Thanks, Jack." Nicki grabbed the handles of the stroller. "I'll take Grace over to the bounce house and meet you there in a few minutes."

"Bounce!" The whole contraption began to move as Grace demonstrated the word.

Nicki's laughter drew an appreciative glance from one of the guys flipping burgers on the grill. She bit her lip, and her gaze dropped to the ground.

Jack didn't know what to do with that kind of pain. He knew what she'd been through over the past few months, trying to get away from Victor. It had taken a restraining order to convince her ex that she wasn't going to take him back.

Cheryl was struggling with her own stuff too much to offer her sister much help.

But maybe . . .

Jack's gaze strayed to Evie again. She stood behind a table weighted down with homemade pies. Most of the people were dressed casually in shorts and T-shirts, but Evie wore a white sundress and strappy little sandals.

Lily broke free and scampered toward one of the booths.

Ginevieve's daughter, Raine, sat knee to knee with Ava, carefully painting a heart on the little girl's cheek. Cody stood behind her, making a balloon animal for Luke.

He looked up and smiled as Jack approached. "Hey, Jack."

"Cody. How's it going?"

"Great. Have you met Raine? My wife?" He practically hummed the last word.

Evie was right. They were young.

"It's nice to meet you." Jack had seen her posing for the photographer on the couple's wedding day, but they hadn't been formally introduced.

"Okay, who's next?" Raine leaned over and reached for the bucket of paintbrushes as Ava hopped down from the chair.

"This is my niece, Lily." Jack gave her a gentle nudge toward the chair. "She likes peanut butter sandwiches and guinea pigs and butterflies."

Raine grinned. "We should probably stick to butterflies, Lily. Is that okay? I'm kind of new at this, and I'm afraid my guinea pig would end up looking like a peanut butter sandwich with ears."

Lily grinned back and climbed into the chair.

The music filtering from the speaker in the corner of the tent suddenly stopped, and Jack heard a chorus of groans from the women in the food tent.

"Sounds like they blew a fuse." Cody set a white balloon crown on Ava's head. "Happens every year."

"Probably because they've got enough Crock-Pots plugged in over there to drain the national power grid," Jack muttered. He looked at Lily. "Will you guys be okay for a few minutes?"

"Butterflies take time." Raine flashed a warm smile as she dipped the brush into a container of yellow paint. "Don't worry — Cody and I will keep an eye on them for you."

"There's been a rush on potato salad already, Evie." Belinda held up the empty bowl as proof. "I'm going to make a quick kitchen run and grab some more out of the fridge."

"Thanks." Evie took a quick inventory of the food on the table. "It looks like we're going to need another jar of pickles too."

"Got it! Be right back!"

Evie was about to check the ice in the coolers when a shadow fell across the table.

"Hi, Evie." Nicki stood in front of her, a shy smile on her face and Grace teetering on the ledge of her hip.

Reminding Evie of the mistake she'd made.

But wasn't Jack's response — his quiet *"Yeah, I guess you would"* — an indication that he'd made some assumptions about her too?

That was the thought that had been chewing at the edges of her mind over the past few days. But she smiled at Nicki and tapped a finger against Grace's button nose.

"It's nice to see you here."

"Gin invited us." Grace was straining

toward the bowl of baked beans, so Nicki shifted her to the other hip. "How much does a hamburger cost?"

"There's no charge for lunch. All the activities are free too."

"Really?"

"Really. I can hold Grace while you make up a plate."

Nicki hesitated a fraction of a second before transferring her daughter into Evie's outstretched arms. The toddler grinned up at her. Today she wore a red sundress with a ladybug appliquéd on the pocket and a smudge of grape jelly on her chin.

"How are you today, Amazing Grace?" Evie tickled her bare toes.

"Jack calls her that too sometimes." Nicki tipped a spoonful of baked beans onto a paper plate. "He said it's the name of his favorite song."

"It's my favorite too." Strange that they had that small thing in common.

"I've never heard it." Nicki added a few wedges of ripe watermelon to the plate and looked around for a place to sit.

"The sun is pretty warm. Why don't you and Grace sit back here in the shade for a few minutes?" Evie suggested. "You can have my lawn chair — I'm not going to need it for a while."

"Thanks." Nicki sat down, balancing the plate on her lap as she reached for her daughter.

"Have you heard about the Moms' Day Out ministry we have here?" Evie poured a glass of lemonade and set it on the corner of the table for Nicki. "On the third Tuesday of the month during the summer there's free babysitting while the mothers with young children get together for an activity."

"I usually work on Tuesdays . . ." Nicki's plate suddenly slid off her lap, scattering the contents all over the grass.

Evie's first thought was that Grace had knocked it out of her mother's hand — until she saw the expression on Nicki's face.

"Nicki? What's wrong?"

Grace let out a squawk of protest as Nicki vaulted to her feet. "N-nothing."

"Are you sick? You're white as a sheet." Evie followed the direction of Nicki's gaze to a young man standing at the edge of the parking lot. Without breaking eye contact, he tossed his cigarette onto the pavement and slowly, deliberately, ground it out.

"Who is that, Nicki?"

The girl's mouth opened and closed, but the only thing that slipped out was a soft whimper that chilled the blood running through Evie's veins.

"He isn't supposed to be here." Nicki hunched over Grace as if she were trying to shield the toddler from view. "I filed a restraining order a few weeks ago."

Evie's heart began to hammer in her ears. "What do you want me to do?"

"Can you find Jack?"

"Stay here." Evie called over her shoulder. "I'll be right back."

There was no sign of Jack anywhere on the grounds, so Evie went back inside the church. The low murmur of masculine voices drew her down the short hallway that branched out from the foyer.

Relief weakened Evie's knees when she recognized the uniformed police officer talking to Jack and Keith in the pastor's office. She and Ryan Tate had gone to school together, and he'd been a close friend of both Dan's and Max's while they were growing up.

"Ryan." Evie pushed the door open without knocking first. "Thank goodness —"

"If you could give us a minute, Evie." Ryan's brows pulled together in a frown.

"But he's out there *now* and Nicki looks terrified. Don't you want to arrest him?"

"Who's out there?" Jack started toward her, but Ryan stepped between them, a blue polyester wall that almost completely

165

blocked Jack from view.

"I'm not sure . . . but Nicki said she'd filed a restraining order against him."

"Victor." Jack lunged toward the door, but Ryan anticipated the move and put his hand on Jack's arm.

"I'll have someone check it out."

"Aren't *you* going to check it out?" The words were out before Evie could stop them.

"I think we should give Officer Tate and Jack some privacy," Keith murmured.

Officer Tate? Ryan had attended Hope Community almost as long as Evie.

"I don't understand." Evie didn't budge. "Didn't Jack call Ryan and ask him to come down here?"

She'd directed the question at Keith, but it was Jack who answered it.

"Officer Tate came here to talk to me, Evie."

"You?" Evie glanced at Ryan for confirmation, but she'd never realized an unreadable expression was part of the uniform.

"If you'll come with me." Ryan tipped his head toward the door.

Evie couldn't believe this. "You're taking *Jack* to the police department?"

"It's okay, Evie," Jack murmured.

It didn't look okay. *Jack* didn't look okay.

"Don't worry about cleaning up after the

picnic, Jack," Keith said. "We've got it covered."

Evie knew the pastor was trying to be helpful, but the shadows in Jack's eyes deepened.

"Evie, will you tell Nicki that I'll get in touch with her as soon as I can — and that she's going to have to take care of Lily today? Make sure she knows she can't drop her off at the house until she hears from me."

"All right." Evie followed him to the door. "Is there anything else I can do?"

Jack's lips twisted in a smile that stopped short of his eyes. "Give me the name of a good lawyer?"

CHAPTER 18

Consider it pure joy, my brothers and sisters, whenever you face trials of many kinds, because you know that the testing of your faith develops perseverance.

When Jack had opened his Bible that morning, he hadn't realized that the apostle James had been speaking directly to him.

Jack turned to stare out the window. Joy seemed a little beyond his reach at the moment, but he was thankful that Officer Tate had let him sit in the front seat of the squad car. Anyone who'd seen them leaving the church together wouldn't automatically assume that Jack was being arrested for something.

Was he being arrested for something?

Ryan Tate didn't volunteer any information, and Jack wasn't ready to ask. He would find out what had happened soon enough.

The officer turned onto Main Street, and a group of people waiting at the crosswalk stared at Jack as the squad car cruised past.

"You've been working at Hope Community a few weeks?"

Jack suspected there was more to the officer's question than a polite attempt at conversation.

"That's right."

"Long enough to get to know Evie Bennett."

Jack wasn't sure he knew Evie at all. He'd been stunned when she'd charged into the pastor's office and all but demanded that Ryan do something about Victor.

"Are you avoiding the question?"

"No disrespect, but I didn't realize you'd asked one."

The officer took his eyes off the road long enough to toss a speculative look in Jack's direction. "I've known Evie since we were kids."

It was the same thing Dan Moretti had said the first time they'd met. Funny how both men had made it sound more like a warning than a simple statement.

The officer parked behind a brick building and left the engine running as they got out of the squad car.

"I'll see if the interview room is available, otherwise we can talk in my office." Tate punched in a code on the door and ushered Jack inside. "Make yourself at home. I'll be right back."

Jack nodded but he could feel his patience stretching thin.

At least the officer didn't see him as a flight risk.

But then again, how far could he get without his truck?

Jack blew out a sigh.

Trav, what kind of mess did you get yourself into now?

Jack had ignored that brief stirring of unease when Nicki had told him that Cheryl and Trav had asked her to keep Lily for the night. What did it say about his family, that he hadn't pictured the couple going to dinner and a movie? Right away, Jack had imagined them gravitating toward a place with loud music and cold beer.

A place that reminded Trav of home.

Whatever his brother had gotten mixed up in, he had somehow pulled Cheryl in too. Or maybe she'd gone willingly.

Jack paced the length of the tiled hall and looped back toward the door Officer Tate had disappeared through. A bronze plaque centered on the wall above the bench caught his eye.

IN MEMORY OF SERVICE AND SACRIFICE

Jack's heart plummeted toward his feet when he recognized the name on the raised shield underneath the photograph of a firefighter.

MAXWELL JOSEPH BENNETT

Evie's husband.

Jack sucked in a quiet breath. The guy didn't look much older than Cody.

A door opened and Ryan stepped back into the hall, noticing what had snagged Jack's attention.

Busted again.

"Max Bennett." Ryan walked over, his tone softening as he stared at the plaque. "He died in the line of duty. I thought for sure we were going to lose both of them."

"Both of them?"

"Max and Dan."

"Dan Moretti?" *"He was my best friend . . . more like a brother,"* Jack remembered him saying.

Ryan nodded. "Max and Dan were searching the house for a little boy when the roof collapsed. Dan barely made it out in time —" The officer's voice thinned. "Max didn't."

171

Jack stared at Max Bennett's picture. Clean-cut. Confident smile. The perfect match for a woman like Evie.

"They must have been married young."

"Right out of high school. Max and Evie started dating their freshman year and got married about a month after graduation. That was Max though. If he wanted something, he went after it, no holds barred. No one else could compete with him."

"And Evie never remarried."

The comment earned a sharp look from the officer, one that Jack figured signaled the end of the conversation.

"No," Ryan said after a moment. "Max was always larger than life. He would have gotten a kick out of being called a hero, that's for sure."

Max Bennett was a hero.

And Jack?

Best case scenario, the owner of an alleged stolen vehicle.

The worst?

A suspect in a drug deal.

Evie had been expecting Nicki to pick up Lily when her shift at the diner ended, but it was Jack who appeared at her front door.

"I'm sorry," he said without preamble. "I had no idea you'd brought Lily home with you until I called Nicki. The bowling league showed up at the diner a few minutes before closing, so she didn't have time to give me anything but your address."

He looked tired. Tired and rumpled, and Evie felt an overwhelming urge to reach out and smooth a wayward strand of hair off his forehead. She smoothed a wrinkle from her shirt instead. "The friend who'd offered to babysit for her has two children of her own. Nicki didn't want to ask her if she'd watch Lily too."

"How is Nic doing?"

"A little shaken." Evie didn't mention Nicki had seemed more upset when she'd told her that Ryan Tate had taken Jack to the police department. "Her ex-boyfriend left before the police got there. Nicki still doesn't know why he showed up at the church. The officer thought he wanted to scare her."

"Maybe." A muscle worked in Jack's jaw, and Evie wondered if he had another theory.

A car slowed down and Samantha Bellevue, one of Evie's neighbors, almost clipped the mailbox because she was staring at the tawny-haired man standing on Evie's porch.

"Why don't you come inside? Lily fell asleep watching a movie."

"Already?" Jack frowned at the shadows

pooling on the lawn as if he was just noticing them for the first time.

"We had a busy day." The door closed behind them, and the foyer suddenly seemed to shrink in size.

"I'm sorry," Jack said again.

"Don't apologize." With Cody at that age, it had been all about building blocks and Hot Wheels. Evie hadn't had a little girl who wanted her fingernails polished and ribbons in her hair. "I enjoyed having Lily over."

"Yeah, about that. How did it happen that Lily ended up with you? I assumed Nicki would take her over to her grandmother's house."

Evie had been hoping he wouldn't ask.

"When I talked to Carl, he said Lily's grandma left early this morning for a bus trip with some friends and he didn't expect her back until ten or eleven."

"You talked to Carl?"

"Shhh." Evie put a finger to her lips as Jack followed her into the living room.

Lily stirred in her sleep when Jack walked over to the sofa.

"I'll bet she loved this." He gently traced the lavender ribbon that Evie had woven into Lily's braid.

"We painted our nails too." Evie held up her orange fingertips as proof. "Caribbean

174

Sunrise. Lily picked out the color. It's a little bright —"

"I like it." The husky timbre of Jack's voice rumbled through Evie, making the words sound more intimate than they should have. "I better wake Lily up. It's getting late and I still have a few stops to make after we leave."

"Lily was a little concerned about her guinea pig."

"Bitsy. I totally forgot about her." Jack raked his hand through his hair, and Evie wished she could say something — do something — to erase the lines etched on his brow.

"Are you sure you want to get involved, Evie? Jack is a hard worker, but we really don't know anything about his personal life."

Evie hadn't been able to refute the pastor's statement, but even as she'd watched Ryan and Jack get into the squad car, something inside of her had quietly rebelled.

Keith hadn't seen Jack twirling his nieces around the living room. Hadn't seen him teasing Ron and coaxing Bert to stay for supper. Grabbing an extra plate and piling it high with spaghetti for Josh.

Jack didn't seem to shy away from getting involved. He cared about people. And right now, that was all Evie needed to know.

"Did you get a chance to eat anything for

supper? I could warm up some of the leftover lasagna that Lily and I made."

Jack was silent for so long Evie didn't expect him to nod.

Didn't expect him to smile either, but it stripped some of the fatigue from his eyes.

"That sounds good. Thanks."

She led the way to the kitchen, her legs only a tiny bit steadier than her pulse.

"You have a nice home. I didn't realize this subdivision was here."

"It's not very old. Max bought the first lot, and the other houses kind of sprang up around ours." Evie flipped on the light in the kitchen, uncomfortably aware of the differences between their kitchens when she saw the flash of disbelief in Jack's eyes.

Max knew how much she enjoyed cooking, so the spacious gourmet kitchen had been a splurge, a secret between him and the builder. Hardwood floors, custom-made oak cabinets, and a breakfast nook overlooking the patio.

Jack stopped in the middle of the room. "Can I help with anything?"

"You can sit down." Evie opened the fridge and pulled out the fixings for salad. She had a strong suspicion Jack hadn't eaten anything over the course of the day, so she put the entire casserole dish in the microwave and began to slice up another loaf of French bread.

One tawny eyebrow lifted. "This is what you consider leftovers?"

"I'm used to cooking for Cody. Like most eighteen-year-old boys, he eats about every two hours." Evie transferred the bread to a wicker basket and set it down in front of Jack.

But instead of tucking into it, he bowed his head. No flash or fanfare, just a simple gesture that seemed as natural as someone taking his next breath.

Evie realized she'd been caught staring when Jack held out a slice of the bread. "Did you want some?"

Butterflies — *where had those come from?* — took wing inside of Evie's stomach.

"No . . . thank you." She hoped Jack would attribute the color in her cheeks to the steam that rolled out when she lifted up the ceramic lid.

"That smells delicious."

"Thank you." Evie slid a generous portion onto a stoneware plate. "Lily said it was *almost* as good as your spaghetti."

"Aren't you going to sit down?"

She should. Except the things she thought were butterflies felt more like a flock of birds swooping around inside of her.

Dan had sat in the chair across the table from her at least a thousand times, and Evie hadn't thought anything of it. Why was it different with Jack?

Because Jack *is different.*

The thought whispered in Evie's mind.

He wasn't someone Evie had known from childhood. There were no unspoken rules governing their relationship. She and Jack couldn't reminisce about the past because they didn't have one.

"Evie?" The chair moved toward her, guided by Jack's foot underneath the table. "Please sit down."

She sat.

"Now you can tell me why you talked to Carl."

Carl.

It was all Evie could do to suppress a shudder. She really didn't want to relive that part of the afternoon.

"I spoke with Nicki after you left, and she was under the impression that her sister wouldn't be able to pick up Lily. She wasn't sure what to do, so she was hoping her mother would be able to keep an eye on Lily until she got off work."

"Okay, but that still doesn't explain how Lily ended up here."

"Nicki wanted to leave after we saw Victor,

but Lily had really been looking forward to playing some of the games. I offered to drop her off at her grandmother's house after the picnic."

What Evie hadn't realized until Lily got into the car was that the child didn't want to go there. She'd sat beside Evie on the front seat, her small fingers laced tightly together in her lap.

"When is Uncle Jack coming back?"

"I don't know, sweetheart." Fortunately, Cody had been fashioning a balloon crown for Lily so she hadn't noticed her uncle leaving the church parking lot in Ryan's squad car.

"I'm old enough to stay home by myself. I know the rules." Lily held up two fingers. "Don't turn on the oven, and don't answer the door if someone knocks."

"Those are good rules to remember, but wouldn't you rather spend the rest of the afternoon with your grandma and grandpa?"

"I don't have a grandpa," Lily said matter-of-factly. "Just Carl. He doesn't like noise when he's watching TV. It makes him grumpy and then he yells."

"What kind of noise?" Evie couldn't imagine a child as well mannered as Lily being a problem.

"Any kind." Lily sighed. "And he watches TV *a lot.*"

It was Just Carl who'd flung open the door when Evie knocked.

"Who are you?" he'd demanded.

"I'm . . ." Evie wasn't quite sure how to answer the question. "Evie Bennett. I'm a friend of Nicki's."

Carl's eyes raked over her. "You from that church she's been yammering about? I told her we weren't interested."

"I attend Hope Community, but that's not why I'm here. Is Lily's grandmother home?"

"No — and if you would have called first, you'd know that."

"I'm sorry." Evie wanted to tell him that Nicki had tried — several times — but no one had answered the phone. "She told Nicki that she'd be home today."

"Roxanne changed her mind. Those girls of hers don't run her life, you know. Where's Cheryl?"

"I don't know." All Evie could tell him was the truth. "But Nicki had to work this afternoon, so she was hoping Lily could stay with her grandma for a while."

Carl's face twisted in a scowl. "Those two are always looking for a free babysitter."

"Do you know when Roxanne will be home?"

180

"She went on one of them bus trips to the casino and won't be back till midnight."

Evie hadn't expected that.

"What's your daddy doing today that he can't watch you?" Carl glowered down at Lily. "I heard he got fired again."

"I don't know."

Tears welled up in Lily's eyes, and Evie decided to put an end to the conversation. She slipped her hand into Lily's, giving the little girl's fingers a reassuring squeeze and Carl a polite but completely insincere — *I'm sorry, Lord* — smile.

"Thank you for your time. We'll figure something out."

"Leave her here," Carl grumbled. "Just let me get back to my show. Nascar's on this afternoon and I already missed the start of the first race."

Lily's shoulders drooped.

"I . . . I appreciate the offer, but I think I'll take Lily back to my house until Nicki gets off work."

"Fine." Carl shrugged. "Doesn't matter to me."

The door snapped shut in Evie's face.

She and Lily had walked back to the Jeep in silence, but while Lily had a bounce in her step, Evie felt as if someone had poured wet concrete into her shoes. No wonder Lily hadn't wanted to stay with Carl. The man was about as warm and welcoming as barbed wire.

"Am I really going to your house?"

"If that's all right with you."

"Yes!"

"Then we'll stop by the diner and let your Aunt Nicki know that's where you'll be."

On the way to My Place, Evie struggled to keep her feelings about Carl to herself. It explained Nicki's reluctance to give Evie her mother's address.

And why she'd turned to Jack when she needed help.

"After the way Carl acted, there was no way I could leave Lily there," Evie told Jack. "He didn't even acknowledge her when he answered the door. *Nothing.* Not a smile or a hello."

"I don't know Carl very well, but according to Cheryl he was a bachelor before he and Roxanne eloped to Vegas last year, and he doesn't particularly like having kids underfoot."

Cheryl's name stirred up another set of questions in Evie's mind.

Were Lily's parents in some kind of trouble? Was Jack?

Their eyes met across the table.

"You can ask me, Evie."

Her mouth dried up, making it difficult to form a word at all.

"What happened today?"

"Travis and Cheryl were arrested this morning. According to the police report, the charges are possession of prescription drugs with the intent to deliver and fleeing the scene." Jack closed his eyes. "In *my* truck. I let Trav borrow it yesterday because he told me theirs was acting up again."

Evie remained silent, struggling to make sense out of what he'd just told her. Possession. Intent to deliver. Terms she'd heard on television but never translated into real life.

"Cheryl was already on probation for shoplifting when they moved to Banister Falls. Her mom and Nicki moved here a few years ago and the factory was hiring, so she decided this would be a good place to start over. Unfortunately, Cheryl can't seem to say no to the one thing that always drags her back down."

"Drugs?"

"My brother."

CHAPTER 19

Discouragement flooded Jack, and only a silent prayer for strength prevented it from pulling him under.

Evie leaned forward, her eyes never leaving his face, and Jack took that as his cue to go on.

"Officer Tate was the one who took Cheryl's statement, and she claimed she didn't know anything about the pills. Travis had told her that he was meeting someone who was interested in buying his guitar.

"She waited in the vehicle while Travis went inside. He came back out with his guitar case — and four bottles of oxycodone that had been stolen during a home invasion on Friday night. The police received an anonymous tip, and when they tried to pull Trav over, he decided to run a few stop signs instead. That's one of the reasons it took me so long to come back for Lily. I had to wait until they released my truck from the impound garage."

Jack had Ryan Tate to thank for that too. Not that he and the police officer were going to hang out and watch a Packers game together, but once Tate had decided that Jack wasn't guilty of anything but stupidity for believing Travis's claim that his car wasn't running, he'd been pretty decent.

The consequences of Travis and Cheryl's mistake didn't only affect them. Nicki would blame herself if she figured out what Jack realized — that Victor was the one who'd exploited Travis's weakness in an attempt to get back at her. And Lily . . .

"What's going to happen to Lily?" Evie voiced the one question that Jack actually knew how to answer.

"For now, she'll stay with me. Nicki has got enough on her plate, and Carl and Roxanne . . . well, let's just say I'm not inclined to leave Lily with them either."

"Travis and Cheryl have to spend the weekend in jail?"

"They have to appear before the judge on Monday. He'll set a bond, but your friend Ryan warned me that it might be high. Prescription drugs are becoming a problem in the area, and local law enforcement wants to crack down on it before things get out of control."

185

Evie was looking at Jack like he was speaking a foreign language. And maybe he was. She probably didn't meet too many people within the walls of Hope Community who struggled with addiction. Not that they weren't there, but for an hour once a week, it wasn't that difficult to hide it behind a smile.

"It's not your fault, Jack."

It was the last thing he expected Evie to say. And the one thing he needed to hear.

"I should have known Travis would start using again. He lost his job at Leiderman last week and he didn't handle it well. He's been clean for a while, but this is what happens. He'd rather dull the pain than deal with it. Cheryl does the same thing, but she admits she has a problem. My brother thinks everyone else is the problem."

"Do you believe Cheryl? That she didn't know anything about the drugs?"

"Yes." Jack had gone through all the possible scenarios in his mind, and his gut told him that Cheryl wouldn't knowingly take that risk. Not if it meant she could go to jail. "But what matters is what the judge believes. Cheryl was the one driving, so the police are treating her as an accessory.

"She got into some trouble before they moved to Banister Falls and ended up getting arrested. She didn't have a record, so she paid a fine and the judge sentenced her to a year's probation. By being involved in another crime, she broke the terms of her probation, so she might have to serve out the rest of that sentence until the trial."

"How long would that be?"

"January."

"That's six months from now." Worry clouded Evie's eyes. "Won't the judge take the fact that Cheryl has a child into consideration?"

"He did . . . the first time. And that was a different judge, so it's hard to predict what this one will do."

"And Travis?"

"Depending on what the district attorney decides to charge him with, he could be looking at some prison time. Possibly three to five years." Saying the words out loud made the whole situation seem real.

God, how can I help Travis if he's locked up in jail?

"I'm sorry." Jack pushed to his feet. "I didn't mean to dump my family's dirty laundry in the middle of your kitchen table."

"Uncle Jack?" Lily wandered into the kitchen, a colorful afghan draped around her shoulders like a cape, the ribboned braid that Evie had put in her hair slightly askew.

"Hey, Peanut." Jack swept her into a hug. "I'm sorry I missed out on all the fun today."

"I saved some cotton candy for you."

"The perfect dessert." He set Lily back on her feet with a wink. "Now, where are your shoes?"

"In the living room." Lily wiggled her bare toes. The tips were Caribbean Sunrise. "Do you want to see the pictures we drew? Evie drew a picture of Diva — she lives with Cody and Raine — and I drew one of Bitsy."

Jack had forgotten about Bitsy again. She and Harley were going to have to learn to get along.

"Lily, while you get your things together, I'm going to box up a few slices of lasagna for you to take along," Evie said. "There's too much for me, and you were the one who helped me grate all that delicious cheese."

"Did you like it, Uncle Jack?"

"It was delicious," Jack agreed.

He heard Evie's cell phone ring as Lily towed him down the short hallway to the living room.

After seeing her office at the church, the décor was a little more casual than he would have expected. The furniture comfortable, the kind built for relaxing instead of admiring from afar.

"Evie painted that picture too." Lily pointed to a framed watercolor above the fireplace mantel. A field of dandelions, tiny yellow splotches against a green background.

Jack wandered over for a closer look — and saw the photographs lined up on the mantle. Small snapshots of Evie's life.

Her husband, Max, wearing his turnout gear. Sitting in front of a Christmas tree, cradling a bald newborn in his arms. There were several photographs of Cody too.

But none of Evie.

Because she'd always been behind the camera? The one who recorded the memories instead of the one who made them?

"I'm sorry that took so long. Cody doesn't usually call me this time of night." Evie returned, holding one of those reusable grocery bags. "I put the cotton candy on top."

"Do you think I'll ever get to meet Diva?" Lily held up Evie's drawing, an impressive likeness of a sweet-faced golden retriever.

Evie hesitated — long enough for Jack to step in and save her from having to lie.

"Ready, Lily?"

"Uh-huh." Without being prompted, Lily threw her arms around Evie's waist. "Thank you for letting me come over."

"Thank you for the awesome manicure." Evie tucked a wayward strawberry-blonde curl behind Lily's ear. When she looked at Jack, her smile slipped a notch. "I'll see you Monday morning?"

"I'll be there." *Monday morning.* Less than forty-eight hours to figure out his new normal.

Lily was already buckled in when Jack hopped into the cab of the pickup.

"Rosewood Court." She twisted around and read the words out loud as Jack drove underneath the metal archway that divided Evie's neighborhood from the rest of the town.

Jack glanced in the rearview mirror. The two-story brick house, with its leaded glass windows and dormers that resembled miniature turrets, was smack-dab in the center of the cul-de-sac.

Max Bennett hadn't just bought Evie a house. He'd built her a castle.

"Do you think Mommy and Daddy are home yet? I want them to see my butterfly." Lily touched the glittery pink wings of the whimsical creature Raine had painted on her cheekbone at the picnic.

"You're —" Jack heard his voice crack and tried again. "You're going to be staying with me tonight, Peanut."

"Is it okay with Mommy and Daddy?"

Jack's hands tightened on the steering wheel.

You're supposed to be looking out for your family, Trav. Why am I the one who has to explain to Lily where you and Cheryl are spending the night?

"Yes, it's okay with them." Jack had no script for this. "Lil . . . I'm not sure when they'll be home."

"They did something bad, didn't they?"

"They did something bad." Jack's vision blurred. The street and the curb melting together, the way things looked after a hard rain. "But that doesn't mean your mom and dad are bad people. They love you, Lily, and what they did . . . It isn't your fault. Grownups make mistakes too, and when they do, there are consequences."

"Are they in jail?"

Jack didn't trust his voice, so he nodded.

"Can we get Bitsy? I don't think she wants to be alone tonight."

"That's going to be our first stop."

Jack glanced over at Lily, and the expression on her face just about wrecked him. Not the confusion or the fear he'd expected to see. Something even worse.

Relief.

Lily hugged her knees against her chest,

and out of the corner of his eye, Jack saw her release a long, shuddering breath.

Another question for heaven. Why did life have to be so hard down here?

The taillights of Jack's truck disappeared, but Evie stood at the window for another five minutes.

How would Jack even know what to say to Lily? How did you explain to a little girl that her parents weren't going to be there to tuck her into bed? Make her breakfast in the morning?

And Jack . . . his apartment wasn't exactly set up for a child. What was he going to do with Lily when he went to work every day? Nicki worked at the diner and was raising three small children on her own.

"Knock knock!"

The front door opened, and Evie heard the familiar sound of Diva's toenails clattering against the tile floor in the foyer.

She knelt down, and the retriever barreled into her arms. Evie rocked back on her heels and examined the paisley bandana tied around Diva's neck. "It looks like someone had a spa day."

"Raine gave her a bath yesterday." Cody sauntered in behind her, carrying two large plastic cups from Quigley's Drive-In.

"Okay . . ." Evie eyed the shake. "What are we celebrating?"

"She knows me too well." Cody grinned at Raine.

"We brought one for you too." Raine offered one of the cups to Evie.

The handle of the plastic spoon was embedded in a concoction of Play-Doh blue ice cream, marshmallow cream, and multi-colored sprinkles. Lots of sprinkles.

Evie blinked. "I have no words."

"It's not a vanilla announcement, Mom."

"Now you've really got me curious." Evie felt her smile fray a little at the corners.

Had Jack told Lily yet? Did he have a bedroom set up for her? How would Lily react when he told her?

"I'm sorry it got a little melty on the way here."

She'd been staring at the shake. Evie rerouted the direction of her thoughts and focused them on Cody and Raine. "It looks delicious. And it's a nice night . . . Why don't we sit out on the patio?"

Cody spotted the dishes on the table as they filed through the kitchen. "It looks like you already had a party."

"Jack came over to pick up Lily a little while ago, and he hadn't had time to eat supper. I warmed up some leftovers."

"Wow."

"What's wow?"

Cody and Raine exchanged a look that Evie couldn't quite interpret.

"I didn't realize she was going to be here that long, that's all."

"Neither did I." Evie flipped on the porch light. "But we had fun. You never let me braid your hair."

"There wasn't enough to braid," Cody shot back. "You cut it once a month, remember?"

"You should have called. I would have helped you entertain Lily." Raine patted her belly as she slid onto the bench of the picnic table. "I could use the practice."

Evie sat down on the other side. "Okay, what's going on? Don't keep me in suspense."

"John came over a little while ago and told me there's an opening at the lumberyard. I can start on Monday, and he's even willing to work around my schedule when I start classes at the Tech in the fall."

"Will you be working in the office?"

Cody laughed. "Gosh, I hope not, Mom. John said depending on how fast I get the hang of things, he'll teach me to drive the forklift."

He made it sound like that was a good thing.

"Raine and I have been praying that God would provide a job, and this one is perfect. It will cover the rent and it's like a free gym membership." Cody flexed his arm. "I have to get in shape if I want to pass the test at the end of the training program."

"That is great news, Cody."

Evie knew about the couple's five-year plan. At his high school commencement ceremony, Cody had received the memorial scholarship set up in Max's honor for a senior pursuing a career as a firefighter. If they were careful, they could live on the funds Evie had set aside for college and the income Cody would earn from a part-time job. Raine planned to stay home with the baby and start her degree program online, a few classes at a time.

"But wait, there's more." Cody bumped Raine's shoulder. "Now it's your turn."

"Cody talked me into signing up for an online creative writing class. I got an e-mail from the professor and I've been accepted, but the downside is that it doesn't start until September. I'd like to get a job too, but I don't think anyone will hire me when they find out I'll only be able to work until the baby is born."

"That's okay." Cody gave Raine's ponytail a playful tug. "Taking care of me and Diva is a full-time job, isn't it, Mom? *Mom?*"

Evie realized that was her cue to laugh, but she smiled at Raine instead. "I think I might know someone."

"Someone . . ." Cody waited for Evie to fill in the blank.

"Who will hire Raine."

Raine's spoon hit the table, spraying bits of blue ice cream and sprinkles everywhere. "Really?"

"If you meant what you said about needing the practice."

CHAPTER 20

On Monday morning Evie knocked on the door of the custodian's room. When there was no response, she eased it open.

"Jack?"

Lily sat at the table by the window, drawing on a piece of yellow construction paper.

Just as she'd suspected, Jack had had to bring his niece to work.

A smile swept the worried look from Lily's pearl-gray eyes as Evie walked in, followed by Raine.

"Hi!" Lily glanced at Raine, and Evie was thrilled when the girl's smile grew even wider. "I remember you. You painted the butterfly on my cheek! Uncle Jack made me wash it off before I went to bed though."

"I can do another one," Raine offered.

"Really?" Lily hopped down from the chair. "When?"

"First we have to talk to your Uncle Jack." Evie felt an unexpected surge of emotion when she saw the lopsided lavender bow tied around Lily's ponytail. "Do you know where he is?"

"He's right here."

Jack stood in the doorway behind them, and the guarded look on his face wasn't exactly encouraging.

Evie suddenly began to doubt the wisdom in her plan. "Can we talk a minute?"

Jack flicked a glance at Raine and nodded. "Sure."

"I'll take Lily outside." Raine took the little girl by the hand, and the two of them skipped down the hall together.

"I thought you might have to bring Lily to work with you this morning."

"I didn't know what else to do." Jack shoved his hands into his front pockets. "I'm probably breaking a few rules, but there wasn't time to make other arrangements."

"That's why I brought Raine with me. She'd like a part-time job, but she's afraid no one will hire her when they find out she has to quit at the end of the summer. I talked to her on Saturday night, and she would love to watch Lily during the day."

The lines in Jack's forehead eased slightly. "Really? Lily said she doesn't mind hanging out in here until I get off work, but I'm sure she'd much rather be playing outside."

"Raine claims it will be good practice. And John Moretti, Dan's dad, hired Cody at the lumberyard, so I think Raine would enjoy Lily's company. She doesn't have many friends in Banister Falls yet. If you don't mind though, Raine would like to watch Lily at her house. She and Cody have a big backyard and their house is within walking distance of the park."

Evie waved at Pauline as they walked through the foyer. The secretary waved back and then did a double take when she saw Jack at Evie's side.

"Lily would love that." Jack held the door open for Evie and followed her outside.

"Uncle Jack!" Lily's laughter flowed over them. "Look what Raine is teaching me how to make!"

She and Raine were sitting in the grass, making chains out of long-stemmed dandelions. Lily already wore one in her hair like a crown.

Jack didn't even have a chance to ask Lily what she thought about the sudden change in plans. She vaulted to her feet, scattering flowers everywhere.

"Can I go to the park with Raine and Diva today, Uncle Jack? Please?"

"I guess that answers my question." Jack

smiled at Raine. "I really appreciate this."

"No problem. Evie told me how much fun she had with Lily on Saturday, and I could use something to take my mind off the fact that I can no longer see my feet."

"We're going to get ice cream cones at Quigley's too!"

"You know she won't want to come home with me."

Raine grinned. "I'll give you my cell phone number. You can call anytime for an update."

Jack bent down until he was eye to eye with his niece. "Have fun and be good for Raine. I'll pick you up at four o'clock."

"Okay." Lily pressed a limp bouquet of dandelions into his hand and linked her arm through Raine's. "Can we go now?"

"I'll race you to the car." Raine pointed to the light-blue Datsun and Lily took off.

Jack looked a little uncertain as he watched Raine waddle after his niece.

"Don't worry," Evie said softly. "Lily is in good hands."

"It's not that." Jack turned to look at her. "I don't know what to say."

"You don't have to say anything. If it doesn't work out for some reason, Raine will understand. She knows there have been a lot of changes in Lily's life."

A shadow passed through Jack's eyes. "That's true."

"How is she doing?"

"A lot better than I expected."

"Isn't that a good thing?"

"It makes me wonder what was going on between Cheryl and Trav before they got arrested." Jack saw her expression and shook his head. "Trav isn't like Nicki's ex. He would never lay a hand on Cheryl, but when things aren't going well, they tend to argue a lot. That kind of environment is hard on someone as sensitive as Lily."

Evie imagined it must be hard on Jack too. "How are *you* doing?"

"I'm fine." A smile edged up the corners of Jack's lips, and it took Evie a moment to realize he was repeating the answer she'd given him after Betty had confronted her on Cody's wedding day.

Evie smiled back. "Should I take it that means you need a cup of coffee?"

"You probably should." Jack's gaze dropped to her lips a split second before he looked away, but it didn't matter. Evie's memory made the leap from the comforting warmth of the coffee mug to the warmth of Jack's fingers tracing the curve of her jaw.

And the warmth it ignited inside of Evie . . . hurt. The kind of sweet, prickly heat when the blood began to flow through your veins after a long time spent outside in the cold.

Something Evie had never expected to feel again.

She and Max had started dating when they were fifteen. Max had been her first love. Her first everything. After he died, it felt like her heart had died too. Evie had never been attracted to another man. Couldn't imagine being held in someone else's arms.

Until now.

She looked away.

Not because she was afraid of what she might see on Jack's face, but because of what he might see on hers.

Evie didn't recognize the petite brunette who stood outside her office, studying the posters pinned to the bulletin board that advertised upcoming events.

All Pauline had been able to tell her was that someone named Maggie McClain had called and wanted to meet with her at noon if she was free. Evie had cut short her early lunch date with Gertrude Fielding to make it back to the church on time.

"Are you Maggie?"

The young woman, who looked to be in

her midtwenties, whirled around.

Evie couldn't help but wonder if the woman's outfit — a crisp button-down shirt, navy skirt, and matching blazer — wasn't a deliberate attempt to downplay her pixie-like features.

"That's me! And you must be Evie." The lilt in the woman's voice complemented the sparkle in her blue-green eyes as she shook Evie's hand. "I know I'm a few minutes early. A client canceled at the last minute so I thought I'd come over and take a look around until you were available."

"That's fine. Please come in." Evie ushered Maggie into the office. "You can sit anywhere you like."

Maggie sank into one of the chairs by the window and kicked off her shoes. Her sigh of relief made Evie smile.

"I have to wear heels on the days I appear in court." Maggie wiggled her bare toes. "Even though I happen to know for a fact that Judge Bernhardt wears flip-flops underneath her robe."

Evie sat in the chair across from Maggie's instead of the one behind her desk. "What can I do for you?"

"A friend invited me to the picnic on Saturday, and I overheard some of the women talking about a garden walk. I wanted to know more about it, so one of them gave me your name."

"It's an event we put on every summer, usually the last weekend in July. We have several master gardeners who love to share their gardens with the community, as well as some women who just enjoy growing flowers as a hobby. Afterward, Marie's Bistro sets up an old-fashioned ice cream social for the women who sign up. We sell tickets, but all the money is given to a women's shelter in India."

Maggie's forehead puckered. "I wish I'd heard about this sooner."

"The tickets are available right up until the day of the event, so you have plenty of time to get one."

"But you have all the gardens lined up?"

"We typically schedule five, but at the moment we're still waiting on a response from one of the past hostesses. Do you know someone who might be interested in putting their garden on the tour?"

Maggie grinned. "That's why I'm here."

There was something infectious about the woman's enthusiasm, and Evie decided she liked Maggie McClain.

"Well, then I'll get a form for you to fill out." Evie rose and walked back to her desk. "The tour starts here at nine o'clock on

Saturday morning. We have coffee and pastries available and hand out a brochure with a map and a description of the gardens on the tour. If you have a photograph, we can include that too."

She pulled up the document on her computer and tapped the print button. "We try to offer a variety of different types of gardens to keep things interesting. Last year, we had a water garden and someone who had turned their entire front yard into a natural prairie. Does your garden have a theme?"

Maggie shifted in the chair. "It's not quite a garden . . . yet."

"I know we haven't had a lot of rain this summer, but by the end of the month, most of the flowers are at their peak. I'm sure your garden will be beautiful."

Maggie expelled a long breath. "I meant it's not quite a garden because it's still in the planning stages. I'm hoping that next summer it will be a reality."

"I'm afraid I don't understand." The printer spit out the last page of the form, but Evie ignored it as she turned to look at Maggie.

"I can tell you this because I know you won't look at me like I'm crazy . . . but I believe that God wants me to start a community garden in Banister Falls. Last week He provided the perfect spot. An abandoned building burned down a few years ago, and the owner didn't have insurance. He turned the land over to the city, and they ended up having to cover the cost of the cleanup. The lot was finally cleared in the spring, and I found out the city officials are willing to lease it out for the cost of the taxes."

Now Evie was beginning to understand. "You need donations."

"And volunteers." Maggie flashed an engaging but completely unrepentant grin. "But first I need people to catch the vision."

"I can bring it up to the women on my team, but I'm not sure it would be appropriate for the garden tour," Evie said slowly. "The women who attend have a certain expectation. If your committee has some literature, a flyer or a brochure explaining the program, we could certainly make it available for women to take home with them to read that day."

Maggie's smile slipped a notch. "I don't have anything like that yet. I'm not part of a committee, Evie. I was hired last year to oversee New Horizon, the local women's shelter, but I've been pursuing this on my own time. Every day I meet senior citizens . . . single moms . . . teenagers . . .

who are struggling. Financially. Emotionally. Spiritually. I spent a summer with my grandmother when I was thirteen, and she told me that a garden was God's classroom. 'You have to get on your knees, Maggie. Get your hands into the soil and work it. Sweat a little in the tending and the weeding . . . and then you'll see things grow.' " Maggie leaned forward. "That's what I want, Evie. I want to see things grow. Good things."

Evie felt the air around them practically hum, sparked by Maggie's vision. Which made it that much more difficult to state the obvious. "But right now it's a vacant lot, not a garden."

And in the spirit of the event, the women who attended dressed up for the occasion. Straw hats. Flowing dresses. Evie tried to picture Victoria picking her way through a vacant lot wearing her Kate Spade heels.

"Would you be willing to take a look at it before you make a decision?" Maggie asked. "I've already signed a contract with the city, so it's definitely moving into the planning stages. I've been going over there in the evening to pick up the debris."

"I thought you said the lot was cleared."

"It was . . . but it's a work in progress. There's always going to be something that needs a little TLC."

"A work in progress."

Evie heard Jack saying the same thing. No explanations, no apologies. Just a simple acceptance of the truth.

"What's the address?" she heard herself say. "I can drive by the lot and take a look at it."

"Thank you, Evie —"

"But I can't promise anything," Evie interrupted. "Some of the women who sign up for the tour are quite elderly. The lot would have to be safe to walk around."

"It will be." Evie's caveat didn't dim the sparkle in Maggie's eyes. "It's a few blocks from the Leiderman plant. Fairview Street. Do you know where that is?"

Evie managed a nod.

"The lot is right in the middle of the block."

"I've seen it."

Right across the street from Jack's apartment building.

CHAPTER 21

Jack heard a familiar giggle as he got out of his truck. He followed the sound to the backyard.

Lily was running around the sprinkler with two girls who looked to be around Ava's age.

Raine was perched on the picnic table next to a stack of towels, watching the girls play. A golden retriever was sprawled in the shade of an oak tree, a safe distance from the splash zone.

"Uncle Jack!" Lily broke away from the circle and ran toward him. She was soaking wet, but Jack let her plow into him anyway. "That's Amanda and Emily. We're chasing rainbows."

Jack envied a child's ability to live in the moment. A world focused on what *was* — blue sky, sunshine, a rainbow in the grass — not regretting what had been or longing for what could be.

"Did you catch any?"

"Nope." Lily took off again, and Jack walked over to the picnic table.

Raine handed him a towel. "I'm sorry! I meant to have her dried off and ready to go when you got here, but Emily and Amanda came over and I totally lost control."

The admission made Jack smile.

"No big deal." He pressed the towel against the wet spot on the front of his shirt. "It looks like she's having fun."

"There's a story time for kids at the library tomorrow morning. Do you mind if I take Lily? Ms. Davenport, the librarian, has a craft and a snack afterward."

"I'm sure she'd love to go, but only if you don't mind."

"Are you kidding?" Raine grinned. "Glitter and a glue stick? I'm in."

The screen door swung open and Cody jogged up to the picnic table, waving a spatula. "Can you stay for supper, Jack? I can throw another burger on the grill."

For a moment Jack was tempted. But the backseat of his car was loaded down with some of Cheryl and Travis's things. He'd used his half-hour lunch break to check on the house and found Phil, their elusive landlord, prowling around the living room.

He'd seen the article featuring Travis and

Cheryl's arrest on the front page of the newspaper and told Jack it was his "civic duty" to search the premises for the local police. He'd also informed Jack that because the lease went month to month, he wanted all of Travis and Cheryl's personal possessions out of the house by August first.

Jack had silently added that to the list. From the rate it continued to grow, he'd be forced to reevaluate his priorities and give something up. Like sleep.

"I appreciate the invite, Cody, but we should get home." Jack felt a small, wet hand slide into his.

"We have to be there 'cause people are coming over for supper," Lily said matter-of-factly. "But Uncle Jack makes spaghetti, not hamburgers."

Raine made a humming noise. "Spaghetti sounds really good."

"Now I know what we'll be having for a late-night snack," Cody said in a pseudo-whisper.

"You can come over to our house. Everyone does."

"Everyone?" Raine looked a little bemused as she draped a beach towel around Lily's shoulders.

"Mostly." Lily nodded. "Sometimes Uncle Jack puts it by their door —"

"Don't you want to say good-bye to Emily and Amanda before we leave, Peanut?"

"And Diva!" The red-and-white striped towel unfurled like a banner as Lily ran back to her new friends.

"Can I drop Lily off at quarter to eight tomorrow morning?" Jack opened his wallet and pulled out the money he owed Raine. Balanced against his peace of mind and Lily's shining eyes, it didn't seem like nearly enough.

"That will work. I get up early so I can spend some time with Cody before he leaves for work."

"She makes pancakes." Cody tucked his arm around Raine's waist. "I'm going to be the only firefighter at Second Street Station who won't be able to climb a ladder."

"It's not fair that I'm the only one who's gaining weight."

"You're beautiful," Cody whispered in his wife's ear.

Envy streaked through Jack. His one not-so-long-term relationship, with a college student named Julie Powers, had crashed and burned when Jack found out she'd started dating him so her dad would agree to let her study abroad for a year. In those days he'd been as wild as his brother. If the situation was reversed and Jack had had a daughter — a grown-up version of Lily — he wouldn't have wanted her to date him either.

Jack's perspective on dating had changed roughly about the time God had changed his heart. He was no longer interested in spending an hour or two with a woman in some shadowy corner of a club, hours that ended up leaving shadows on his soul the next day. Jack's parents hadn't exactly been the poster couple for happily-ever-after either, although once in a while he met a couple, like Coop and Anne, who made him wish he'd done things differently.

God had forgiven his past mistakes, but Jack wasn't sure a woman would be as understanding.

Especially one like Evie.

Jack couldn't think about Evie. Not like that anyway.

"I'll see you tomorrow, Raine!" Lily returned after round two of the good-byes.

The golden retriever escorted them down the sidewalk to Jack's truck. Lily scrambled into the cab, twisted around to find the seat belt, and spotted the boxes lined up along the backseat.

"That's my mushroom chair."

Jack's first thought was that he'd messed up. Lily hadn't seemed upset when they'd boxed up her clothes and some of her stuffed animals after church on Sunday. But she looked upset now.

God, you're going to have to help me out here. I can restore houses, but I have no idea how to fix the broken things inside of a person.

"I thought you might want to put it in your room."

"Where is my room going to be?" Lily whispered.

Jack finally understood the source of her fears.

"With me, Lily. I don't know when you're going to be with your mom and dad, but I'm your family too. You aren't alone, and I want you to think of the apartment as home. It's not my place . . . It belongs to you, too, and I want you to be comfortable there."

"Can we paint it pink?"

"The apartment?"

"No." Lily's low giggle was music to Jack's ears. "My room."

"We'll stop at the hardware store to get paint tomorrow when I get off work."

Jack would paint rainbow stripes on every wall in the building if it would make this easier on his niece.

He turned onto Fairview Street. No fancy metal archway here — just a misshapen

214

street sign separating Jack's neighborhood from the rest of the town.

"There's Evie!" Lily pointed to a woman standing on the sidewalk across from his building.

"No, it —" *Can't be,* is what Jack had been about to say.

But it was.

Evie had been staring at the vacant lot for the past fifteen minutes, and she still couldn't see a garden.

How could Maggie McClain take on a project this size on her own?

The low rumble of an engine raised the hairs on Evie's neck. The driver of the last car that had slowed down had invited her over to his place for a drink . . .

"Evie!"

She whirled around at the sound of a familiar voice. Lily jumped down from the passenger seat of Jack's pickup and ran over to her.

"Hey, you." Evie caught her up in a hug. "Did Raine take you to the pool today?"

"I was playing in the sprinkler with Emily and Amanda." Lily flipped her damp ponytail over her shoulder. "They're my new friends. I got to play with Diva too."

"It sounds like you had a busy day."

Jack reached into the backseat of the truck and pulled out a large cardboard box. The gingham quilt stuffed inside made a snug cocoon for a white lampshade with pink tassels. He anchored the box against his hip and strode over. "I didn't expect to see you here."

It hadn't occurred to Evie that Jack would think she'd been waiting for him.

"I'm trying to catch the vision."

His lips quirked in a smile. "You're going to have to explain that."

"How much time do you have?"

Evie had been joking but Jack didn't respond in kind.

"Enough." His gaze locked with hers over Lily's head, and Evie felt that shimmer of awareness again.

The one that told her to get back into her car and drive back to Rosewood Court. She could talk to Jack at church in the morning and find out what had happened when Travis and Cheryl appeared before the judge. If the cardboard boxes in the back of his truck meant that Lily's stay would be longer than a few days.

"You should stay!" Lily clapped her hands. "We're having spaghetti."

"Again?"

"Yes, again." Jack's smile expanded to a

216

full-blown, heart-stopping grin. "But I'm using the noodles shaped like little seashells this time, just to shake things up a bit."

The thoughts forming in Evie's head didn't match the words that came out of her mouth.

"All right."

"Yay!" Lily danced down the sidewalk. "Don't forget my mushroom chair!"

"Don't ask," Jack murmured. "It's the kind of thing you have to see to believe."

A heavyset young man wearing black jeans and a T-shirt with the sleeves shorn off intercepted Jack before they reached the stairs.

"You need some help with that wall to-night, Jack?" He flexed his arm. "I'll bring my own crowbar."

"Not tonight, Zach, but thanks."

"Got other plans, huh?" He cast a sly grin at Evie.

"You and Lily can go ahead." Jack clapped Zach on the shoulder. "I'll be right up."

On the way up the stairs Lily launched into a brief but entertaining recap of the day.

Diva had found a dead bird in the back-yard and *rolled* in it, so they had to give her a bath with the hose and Raine's shampoo and now she smelled like strawberries.

They'd had grilled cheese sandwiches for lunch, and Raine cut the bread into hearts. She'd let Lily put the sprinkles on the ice cream sundaes for dessert. Emily and Amanda both had pink bicycles, and Emily promised to let Lily ride hers the next time they came over.

Jack caught the last part of the conversation as they reached the top of the landing.

"Raine is going to be a tough act to follow," he murmured. "She asked if she could take Lily to the library for story time tomorrow."

"Ms. Davenport, the librarian, does that every summer. I took Cody there until he informed me that he could read books all by himself. I think I missed it more than he did."

Lily let go of Evie's hand and raced for the door. "I'm going to check on Bitsy."

"Change into —"

"Dry clothes! I know!" Lily finished the sentence as she dashed ahead of them.

Late-afternoon sunlight streamed through the windows of his apartment. The painting supplies in the corner were gone, the dark cherry-cola brown walls now a soft shade of blue. As busy as Jack was, Evie had no idea how he'd found time to paint.

Interspersed among the mismatched

pieces of furniture were some of Lily's things. A heart-shaped pillow edged in sequins. A stuffed rabbit draped over the back of the sofa. Girlish touches that brightened the space like a smile.

"I like what you've done to the place."

Jack gave her a quick glance, as if trying to gauge her sincerity. "I call it the pink tide," he whispered.

"When Cody was that age, I couldn't walk barefoot through the house unless I wanted a building block embedded in the bottom of my foot."

Jack moved a stack of papers aside and set the box with the lampshade down on the counter.

"You brought the rest of Lily's things over."

"I thought she'd need them. To make it feel more like home."

"Did you make it to the hearing today?"

"After Raine and Lily left, I called the clerk of courts to find out what time Travis and Cheryl were scheduled to appear before the judge. She told me they were the first ones on the docket and they'd already been sentenced. Cheryl's probation agent revoked her parole. She'll remain in jail until her trial. Trav" — the name rolled out in a ragged sigh — "he went back to jail too.

The judge set his bond so high, Travis would have to sell everything he owned to come up with the money. I went over to the jail on my lunch break and talked to the person in charge. Cheryl had already added my name to her visitors list so I can let her know how Lily is doing."

The shadow in Jack's eyes told Evie that his brother hadn't. She could only imagine how much that must have hurt.

"I'll be right back." He pivoted toward the door. "There are a few more boxes in the car. And the mushroom chair."

"Do you need some help?"

"One trip." Jack was out the door before she could argue.

Evie crossed over to the window and opened the curtains. On the street below, Jack was talking to the young man — Zach — who'd offered the use of his crowbar.

Realizing she'd been staring, Evie retreated to the kitchen. Two enormous boxes of generic pasta flanked an equally enormous can of marinara sauce like bookends. She turned on the faucet and waited for the water to run clear before she slid the kettle underneath it.

The door swung open and Ron clumped in. "Hey, Blondie."

Evie set her hands on her hips. "If you

remember what time Jack starts dinner every night, I know you remember my name."

She wished she could take back the words when Ron's eyes went wide and he began to sputter. Maybe Jack was the only one who was allowed to give his upstairs neighbor a hard time. But then she realized the sputtering wasn't indignation. It was laughter.

Jack chose that moment to return, and Ron pointed at her.

"You better keep an eye on this one, Vale. She's a spark plug."

Evie could honestly say she'd never been described as a spark plug. Oddly enough, she kind of liked it.

Ron collapsed into the chair next to the coffee table, and Harley materialized from underneath the couch. The cat jumped into his lap and began to purr.

"Walking flea trap, that's what you are." Ron scraped his knuckles under the cat's chin.

Lily skipped back into the living room. She'd changed into shorts and a T-shirt and was tugging a brush through the tangles in her hair. "Do you want to play checkers, Mr. Ron?"

"Cats and kids," Ron muttered. "Can't

get a moment of peace when they're around." He reached for the board. "I'm red this time."

Evie folded a white dish towel into a triangle and knotted it around her waist while Jack grabbed a skillet, three times larger than the one she had at home, from underneath the cupboard.

They settled into an easy rhythm, weaving around each other as if they'd made supper together a hundred times before.

A sharp knock on the door announced Bert's arrival.

"Hello, Evie." Bert didn't look the least bit surprised to see her in Jack's kitchen.

"Hi, Bert."

Jack stopped what he was doing and gave the woman his full attention. "What's the report?"

"The ceiling fan in Andy's apartment is making a funny noise. He wanted me to tell you when the baby isn't keeping him awake at night, the fan is."

"I'll give him a call after supper."

"And he was hoping you could put a washer and dryer in their apartment. Serena switched to cloth diapers to save money, and it's hard for her to run up and down three flights of stairs every day."

"I'll see what I can do." Jack added another plate to the stack on the counter.

"Won't happen," Ron barked from the living room. "Landlord makes more money with the ones in the basement. They take more quarters than a slot machine, and half the time they don't work."

"Can you heat up the sauce, Evie?" Jack shook a loaf of French bread roughly the size of a baseball bat out of a plastic bag and began sawing it into thick planks.

Evie wrestled the can onto the opener and tried to hold it in place as the blade sheered through aluminum, sending tiny pieces of the label drifting onto the countertop like confetti.

She poured it into another saucepan, turned on the burner, and opened the refrigerator.

"What are you looking for?" Jack opened the drawer beside the sink and pulled out a wooden spoon.

"Something . . . green."

"I've got just the thing." One of Bert's stockings pooled around her ankle as she strode toward the door. "Come with me."

CHAPTER 22

Evie followed the woman up a narrow flight of stairs to the third floor. Until Bert had mentioned Andy's wife running up and down three flights of stairs, she hadn't realized there wasn't an elevator somewhere in the building. A wicker basket filled with silk roses hung on the door, the yellow-and-white blooms as faded as the wallpaper that lined the walls of the landing.

"I've lived here almost fifteen years." Bert dipped her hand into the front of her housecoat and pulled out her necklace. A key and a gold ring, worn thin, dangled like charms on the end of it.

Her apartment was half the size of Jack's, but it reminded Evie of the thrift shop on Bird Street. Floor-to-ceiling shelves sagged under the weight of a collection of hardcover books and old encyclopedias. Porcelain figurines crowded every inch of space in an old curio cabinet. Two lace doilies embellished the red velvet sofa, pristine white cuffs against the smooth wooden arms. Another dozen or so hung from a satin cord stretched across the window.

"This way." Bert led Evie through a doorway and into a room not much bigger than her bedroom closet at home. "The landlord had to bring the building up to code a few years ago in case there's a fire, so he added on a balcony."

And what, Evie thought, was an elderly woman who suffered from arthritis supposed to do with a balcony if there was a fire? Tie a sheet onto the railing and rappel down the side of the building?

"Go on." Bert pressed her back against the wall, allowing Evie access to a narrow door that looked like it had been an afterthought. "Take a look."

Evie took a tentative step onto the balcony because a step was all she *could* take. Terracotta pots filled with tomato plants, emerald-green lettuce, and living bouquets of fragrant herbs took up all the available space.

"Cut some of the lettuce." Evie was handed a pair of sewing scissors. "And a few of those cherry tomatoes. They're as sweet as candy."

Evie took another step onto the wooden

225

platform. If the balcony was strong enough to hold all those pots, it would probably hold her too.

Bert hovered in the doorway, supervising the harvest. "Don't forget the basil and oregano. That canned spaghetti sauce Jack buys is as boring as a pair of orthopedic shoes. Don't dare tell him that though. Might hurt the boy's feelings."

Evie choked back a laugh even while a thought ran through her mind. Even holding a mushroom-shaped chair covered in pink-and-lavender sequins, there was nothing remotely *boyish* about Jack Vale.

She snipped a fragrant sprig of oregano from the base of the plant. "I can't believe you grew all this in such a small space."

"It's my husband Glen's fault. He had the heart of a farmer, but his father wanted him to sell insurance. Glen was a good son — came home from work that first day and tilled up our entire backyard to plant a vegetable garden." The corners of Bert's lips curled in a smile. "I figured out early on that if I wanted to spend time with my husband, I'd have to pull weeds and pick beetles off tomato plants.

"Glen and I had some of our biggest fights between those rows of green beans, and some of our sweetest kisses too. After he passed away, our son and his wife asked me if they could move into the house. They have three children, and little ones need room to stretch their legs, so I didn't mind. The house . . . it was too much space for one person . . . but I sure miss that garden."

A lump the size of one of Bert's cherry tomatoes formed in Evie's throat.

"I know what you mean about the space. My husband died thirteen years ago, and our son got married last month. The house seems empty, but I don't know if I could ever sell it. It would feel like I was losing Max all over again."

Evie had gotten used to a look of stunned surprise when people found out she was a widow. Bert simply nodded. "You must have been very young."

"Twenty-five . . . we were only married for seven years."

Evie hadn't realized she'd been turning her wedding band round and round on her finger until Bert's speckled hand closed over hers.

"You know what I discovered, Evie? The memories can comfort us . . . or we can hold onto them so close, so tight, there isn't room for anything else."

Jack couldn't put his finger on it, but

something had changed after Evie raided Bert's garden.

He still didn't know why she'd been studying the vacant lot across the street so intently. A steady stream of neighbors had made it impossible to talk. Andy's wife, Serena, had stopped by to ask about the washing machine and accepted his invitation to stay for supper. Josh had shown up a few minutes later with his geometry textbook.

There were times — like tonight — Jack was tempted to turn off the lights and pretend he wasn't home. Because Banister Falls *wasn't* home. He hadn't planned to stay more than a month, and it had already turned into three.

And depending on what happened, Jack would have to make a decision before school started. Take Lily back to Milwaukee or fill out the enrollment forms for Banister Falls Elementary.

When you don't know what to do, do the next thing is what Coop would say.

Now that Josh had figured out the difference between a polygon and an equilateral triangle, Jack's "next thing" was drying the dishes collecting on the towel that Evie had spread out over the counter.

Jack hadn't expected her to stay this long. The rest of the guests had left right after he'd served dessert — ice cream sandwiches from the freezer case at Truitt's — and Lily was in her bedroom, unpacking the rest of her things.

He hunted for a dry towel and realized the one he'd been looking for was knotted around Evie's slender waist. The humidity in the room had put a glow in her cheeks, and a few strands of silver-blonde hair had escaped the confines of the yellow barrette she'd borrowed from Lily.

"I still can't believe Bert grew all this on a balcony about the size of a postage stamp." Evie rinsed out the salad bowl and handed it to him.

"I have one too, but I haven't done anything with it."

"Why not?" Evie flicked a glance at him. "You have so much free time on your hands."

It took Jack a moment to realize she was teasing him. His heart broke loose from its moorings and bumped against his rib cage.

If Evie was starting to feel comfortable with him, Jack didn't want to do anything to ruin that. Like telling her that he enjoyed spending his not-so-free free time with her.

"I sit out there in the evening and have a cup of coffee."

Not quite an invitation.

"That sounds nice."

Not quite an acceptance.

Jack released a quiet breath. Took two mugs out of the dish drainer, his hand suddenly as unsteady as his pulse.

A door slammed, followed by the heavy tread of footsteps on the staircase. Jack glanced at the clock. "Josh's dad. He works third shift at the factory."

"He was home this evening?" Evie frowned. "Why didn't he help Josh with his homework?"

"He was probably catching a few hours of sleep before he punched in."

"What about his mom?"

"She doesn't live with them. I'm not sure why, but Josh never talks about her."

"You mean he's *alone* all night?"

"Sometimes he stays with his older sister, but her new baby keeps him awake." Jack reached for the carafe and filled both mugs. "Josh knows he can always knock on my door if he needs anything. Is milk okay? I don't have any cream."

Evie nodded, but the troubled look remained in her eyes. She'd probably never been in a position where she'd had to leave her son alone at night.

Jack paused to check on Lily before they went out to the balcony. She'd already changed into her pajamas and was sprawled on the rug, sorting through a box of beads.

"I think Raine wore her out. I might have to pay her extra." Jack opened the storm door and waited for Evie to go first.

She lowered herself onto the narrow platform of the balcony, her knees forming a table for the coffee cup. Jack dropped down next to her and his leg bumped against hers. The balcony suddenly seemed smaller. A lot smaller.

Maybe this hadn't been such a good idea.

He shifted half an inch to the right and propped his feet on the bottom of the railing. The moon had already made its appearance, a perfect round pearl against an indigo sky.

Laughter drifted up from the sidewalk as a couple walked past. Someone — probably Zach — squealed his tires at the corner.

"It's not very quiet, is it?"

"It is compared to where I used to live."

"Where was that?"

"Milwaukee."

"A city boy."

"Born and raised. What about you?"

"Born and raised in Banister Falls. My parents live in Uganda now. It was always their dream, to serve on the mission field, but they waited until I graduated from high school. It was one of the reasons Max and I got married right away. I wanted Dad to walk me down the aisle. They left the day after the wedding."

Jack didn't want to talk about Evie's husband.

"Do they come back very often?"

"No. Africa is their home." Evie didn't sound angry or bitter. "They try to visit every three or four years. We e-mail and Skype, so they don't seem so far away. What about your parents?"

"Mom died when I was sixteen." And Jack didn't want to break the tenuous connection between them by talking about his dad. "You never told me what brought you to Fairview this afternoon."

Call him a coward, but it was either reroute the conversation to safer ground or wade into the deep waters of his family's history. Not exactly something Jack wanted to do, especially after Evie had just told him that her parents were missionaries.

"I met a young woman — Maggie McClain — today. She wants to turn the vacant lot across the street into a community garden."

If Jack had any lingering doubts that God was at work in the neighborhood, Evie's announcement settled them once and for all.

"You don't think it's a good idea?" She tipped her head to one side, and a wisp of hair slipped free from the barrette. Jack wrapped both hands around the coffee mug. Not because he was tempted to sweep it back into place — because he wanted to unclip that little piece of plastic and pitch it over the side of the balcony.

"I didn't say that."

"You didn't say anything . . . but I can tell you were thinking something."

"I think it's a good idea." And so was the community garden.

"Really?"

"There are a lot of elderly people in the neighborhood," Jack said slowly. "Their mortgages are paid off, but the property value has gone down so much they can't afford to move somewhere else. They're stuck on Fairview with roofs that need to be repaired. Siding that needs to be replaced. People like Ron and Bert . . . they're isolated. Lonely. They don't feel like they're contributing anything useful anymore."

Evie was staring at him in astonishment. "You know a lot about the neighborhood for someone who hasn't been in Banister Falls very long."

Jack shrugged. "I live here."

And Evie lived in Rosewood Court. In a

233

castle.

"But you wouldn't have to make spaghetti for everyone in the building or help Josh with his geometry or let Andy take a nap on your couch when the baby gets colicky."

"That's just life." Jack thought about the gold plaque hanging on the wall at city hall, a tribute to Max Bennett. "I'm no hero."

"You are to them."

CHAPTER 23

"So Maggie has a lot picked out for the community garden, and now she has to get people on board to help?"

Jack didn't want to talk about himself — or he didn't believe her. Maybe both. Whatever the reason, Evie took the hint.

"Right, but there's a little more to it than that. She asked if I would consider adding the lot to the garden walk the women's ministry team is hosting in a few weeks." Evie took a tentative sip of the steaming coffee. "I guess she's hoping it will get people excited about the idea."

Jack cocked his head. "You don't sound excited."

"I haven't had a lot of time to think about it. We sponsor the event every summer, and the women expect to walk through a *garden,* not an empty lot."

"But you told her you'd look at it."

"You've never met Maggie . . ." Evie

paused. "Do you hear that?"

Was it her imagination, or had Jack just winced?

"Hear what?"

"Someone playing the guitar." Evie leaned closer to the edge of the balcony and tried to peer through the railing. "Where is it coming from?"

"The building next to this one, I think."

The soft patter of bare feet against the hardwood floor told Evie that Lily had heard it too. The little girl appeared a moment later, hugging a large black leather case.

No question about it anymore, this time Evie did see a wince.

"Evie and I are talking right now, sweetheart."

"But you have to answer!" Lily set the case down next to Jack and popped the gold hinges.

"Answer?" Evie couldn't hide her curiosity.

"He and Uncle Jack talk to each other." Lily opened the lid and scuttled backward as Jack lifted a tarnished saxophone from the case.

"One song." He rose to his feet, fitted the reed into the mouthpiece, and slipped the strap over his head.

The guitarist was silent, almost as if he was waiting for Jack to make the next move.

Lily plunked down in Evie's lap and tugged the hem of her nightgown over her feet, her low giggle blending into the opening notes.

Evie wasn't familiar with jazz, but it was impossible to remain motionless when the fluid, bluesy notes of the saxophone blended with the music from the guitar and Lily's shoulders began to sway. Evie gave in and swayed along with her.

When the song ended, a scattering of applause erupted from the guys hanging out at the corner bar.

"Okay . . . time for bed." Jack bent down and pressed a kiss on top of Lily's head.

"Already?"

"Already. I told Raine I'd drop you off a few minutes early tomorrow morning, and she's got a busy day planned for the two of you."

"Okay." Lily's face lit up. " 'Night, Evie!"

"Don't forget to brush your teeth." Jack eased the saxophone over his head and put it to bed too. "I'll be there in a little while to tuck you in."

Lily disappeared into the apartment, leaving them alone again.

"Sorry about the interruption." Jack

exhaled a laugh as he sat down next to her again. "You were telling me about Maggie."

"Who was playing the guitar?" Maggie could wait a moment. "A friend of yours?"

"I have no idea. We've never met." Jack shrugged. "Lily asked me to play when she was over here a few weeks ago, and all of a sudden someone joined in on the guitar. Once or twice a week we go back and forth. Play a few songs together."

Evie wasn't a musician, but judging from the quality of Jack's performance, he wasn't an amateur.

"How long have you been playing?"

"Since middle school. Mom gave Travis and me an ultimatum. Pick an extracurricular activity or she would. She worked a lot of evenings and weekends, so she wanted to make sure we didn't have time to get into trouble.

"There was a guy in our apartment building — Jefferson — who played the trumpet, and it kind of sparked our interest in music. I wanted to play the drums, of course, but Mom said we'd get evicted. We found a used alto sax at Goodwill, so I joined the jazz band. Trav announced it wasn't cool enough and talked one of Jefferson's friends into giving him guitar lessons."

"Did you ever play professionally?"

Jack hesitated. "It depends on what you mean by professionally, I guess. Trav and I messed around, wrote a few songs together. He was more serious about it than I was though. Started a rock band when he got out of high school, and they did pretty well in the clubs. Once in a while, he talked me into playing a set or two with them. I didn't really fit the whole rock-and-roll thing they had going, but it was a way to stay connected to my brother."

"I never thought of you as a jazz musician."

"Let me guess." Jack cocked his head. "Professional baseball player?"

Evie couldn't help it. She started laughing. "Truth?"

Jack pressed one hand against his heart. "I'm ready."

"Biker gang."

"*What?*" Jack looked stunned by Evie's confession. "No leather jacket. No do-rag. And — this is kind of important — I drive a *pickup* truck."

"I didn't know that at the time." Evie's gaze dropped to his arm and bounced back up again.

"What are you . . ." Jack glanced down. "Oh, I get it now. The stereotypical biker tattoo."

Evie's laughter died when he pushed up the sleeve of his T-shirt. "It's a sword. And a reminder."

"That the decisions you make when you're young can't always be erased?"

"I suppose that's true." Jack looked like he was trying to keep a straight face. "But I got it right before I moved to Banister Falls."

"What does it remind you of?"

"I'm in a battle."

"You're going to have to explain that."

"How much time do you have?"

Evie realized Jack was repeating the words she'd said to him when he'd found her on the sidewalk in front of his apartment building, staring at Maggie's vacant lot.

And there was something in his eyes — some dark memory — that should have prompted a swift but polite good night.

But what she said was, "Enough."

The muscles in Jack's arm seized up when Evie suddenly reached out and traced the outline of the sword with her fingertips.

"Have you read the book of Nehemiah?" Jack's airway was about to seal shut, so the words came out a little rough.

Evie nodded. Her hand fell away, but her eyes never left his face.

"He left the king's palace, where he was

comfortable, and returned to Jerusalem, even though everyone thought he was crazy for trying to rebuild the walls around the city. Nehemiah didn't care. He assigned certain groups of people to work on sections of the wall, but they were always under the threat of attack, so they had a sword in one hand and their cordless drill in the other."

Evie's lips tipped in a smile.

"When the people got discouraged, Nehemiah told them to fight for their brothers and sons . . . for their daughters and wives and their homes. I realize it was written a long time ago, but there was my answer. Trav and Cheryl and Lily, they're the only family I have."

"What happened to your parents?"

"Believe me, Evie, my family saga is never going to be featured on the Hallmark Channel."

"But it's *your* family," Evie said. As if that made all the difference.

And for some reason, it did.

"They divorced when I was four. Dad had an affair with a woman he met at work and walked out on us. Mom was pregnant with Trav at the time, and Dad didn't even put up a fight when Mom filed for full custody. He picked me up once in a while and took me out for a burger, but Trav was a baby, and what was he supposed to do with one of those, right? Dad wasn't even sure what to do with me for a few hours on a Saturday afternoon.

"Mom did her best, but she held down two jobs. We stayed with a neighbor until I was old enough to keep an eye on Travis while she was at work. When I was fourteen, she was diagnosed with ovarian cancer."

Jack let Evie draw her own picture of that. He couldn't begin to describe what it had been like. Standing by, helpless, while the disease slowly claimed its victory.

"Dad ended up with us anyway. Trav was so bitter by the time we moved in with him, he wouldn't cut Dad any slack. Couldn't forgive him for walking out on Mom. And on us."

"But you forgave him."

"Not right away. Dad's second marriage had already fallen apart and he worked a lot. When he was around, he and Trav butted heads constantly. I don't think they realized how much they were alike. After high school, I got a job at a construction company and Coop — the owner — took me under his wing. The crew called him Preacher behind his back, but the funny thing was, Coop never preached at all. He just lived what he believed."

Jack was under no illusions — he might have walked the same path as Trav if it hadn't been for Theodore Cooper. But it was a whole lot easier to talk about his brother's mistakes than his own. Especially when he was talking to Evie.

"I came home from work one day and found Trav packing a suitcase. He was moving in with a girl he'd met at a party."

"Cheryl?" Evie guessed.

"They had a lot in common at first — they both loved loud music and a cold bottle of beer — but Cheryl finally admitted she had a problem and joined a recovery group. She'd started hinting that she wanted to break things off with Travis, but then found out she was expecting Lily. She convinced Trav to get help, and for a while he did okay. He quit the band, got a decent job, and didn't party on the weekends. And then . . . our dad died."

Evie looked so shocked Jack was tempted to end the story right there.

She'd known loss, too, but Max Bennett had left a legacy behind that his son could be proud of.

"How?"

The question prompted Jack to turn the next page.

"A heart attack. Trav took it pretty hard. He'd rebuffed Dad's attempts to start over so many times . . . and then he ran out of time. He didn't show up for the funeral, and then I got a call from Cheryl at three o'clock in the morning. A sheriff's deputy found Travis's car upside down in the ditch a few miles from the cemetery. He was still in it.

"He had a ruptured spleen, a few cracked ribs, and a broken femur. The doctor prescribed pain pills, and Trav kept taking them. When he couldn't get a doctor to renew his prescription, he started looking on the street. He got into an argument with his boss and lost his job. Cheryl . . . The pressure got to her and she slipped up too. It was a wakeup call for both of them.

"A friend put in a good word for Cheryl at the factory and she accepted the job. She'd planned on it being just her and Lily, but Trav convinced her to give him another chance. New city, new start, right? But you and I both know that a change of scenery doesn't change a person on the inside. Only God can do that. And Trav hasn't figured out that he can't fill the empty places inside of him with drugs and alcohol."

"So you put your life on hold and moved here too?"

"I don't look at it that way." Jack smiled at the thought. "My life isn't on hold — I'm just living it *here.* Moment by moment. But sometimes you have to decide what's going to cost you more. The risk or the regret. I've read the pamphlets. I realize I can't fight my brother's battles for him. I just had to show him that he's worth fighting *for.*"

CHAPTER 24

When she got home on Wednesday afternoon, Evie found two packages on the front step, both of them addressed to Mr. and Mrs. Cody Bennett. Belated wedding gifts, most likely.

Anchoring them against her hip, she unlocked the front door and heard . . . nothing.

Ordinarily she liked the quiet. But today the weight of the silence settled over her, as oppressive as the humidity that thickened the air outside.

She tried to shake away the feeling as she set the packages down inside the door.

Cody and Raine sometimes walked Diva over for a visit in the evening, but Evie couldn't see them carrying the packages halfway across town — especially when it looked like a storm was brewing. The sun had disappeared, hidden behind the gray-and-black clouds that rolled together in a slow boil.

The perfect night to stay inside, make a batch of popcorn, and watch a movie.

After she dropped off the packages.

She changed into a pair of jean capris and threw on the light-blue camp shirt she'd bought on a shopping excursion with Dan's sisters to the Mall of America.

The packages went into the backseat, and Evie drove across town to Cody's house. She'd spent the majority of the day with Gertrude, helping her get settled in at home after the social worker at the nursing home signed her discharge papers. A week's worth of meals were tucked into Gertrude's freezer, and Evie had compiled a list of volunteers to do some light housekeeping until she regained all her strength.

Gertrude had fussed a little, but Evie could tell the woman was pleased by all the attention. And why wouldn't she be? The people who attended Hope Community loved Gertrude.

The only time she hadn't looked so pleased was when Evie revisited her decision to move to Texas.

Oh, that broken ankle was just a little setback, Evangeline. I've still got all my faculties about me, and if God hadn't wanted me to help those women learn the correct way to apply eyeliner, He wouldn't have given me such steady hands.

How could Evie argue with that?

Cody's car wasn't in the driveway, but Evie knew where they hid the spare key. She let herself in through the back door and almost tripped over a pair of pink sandals.

Lily's sandals.

Was she still here? It was almost five o'clock and Jack got off work at four.

"Hello?" Evie followed the low murmur of voices to the living room.

The three girls — Raine, Lily, and Diva — were curled up on the sofa.

"Evie!" Lily leaped off the couch and bounded toward her.

A curl of delight ribboned through Evie as she bent down and pulled her into a hug. "I didn't expect to see you here."

"We're watching a movie. Well, I was watching a movie. Raine fell asleep during the best part."

Raine's cheeks, still imprinted with the diamond pattern from the sofa pillow, turned pink. "Did I really?"

"Just for a few minutes."

"Jack called and asked if Lily could stay a little longer. When Cody gets back with the car, I'm going to give her a ride home."

"I can drop her off."

"Are you —" Raine stifled a yawn. "Sure?"

"I'm sure. You look like you could use a little nap."

"I think it's from carrying around all this extra weight." Raine's gaze dropped to her stomach. "I'm starting to walk like a penguin."

Evie remembered feeling the same way when she was pregnant with Cody. "This might cheer you up. Two packages addressed to you and Cody were delivered to the house today. I set them on the kitchen table."

The lights flickered and Lily let out a squeak of alarm. "Bitsy doesn't like storms."

Evie gave Lily's shoulders a quick squeeze. "Then we better go."

"Thanks, Evie." Raine pulled the blanket up higher, her eyes already beginning to drift close. "I'll see you tomorrow, Lilliputian."

"Those are little people," Lily whispered to Evie. "It's in a book."

"I think I remember Cody reading that one." Evie waited for Lily to stuff her belongings into her backpack, and then they slipped out the back door.

On the way to Fairview Street, Lily told Evie everything she and Raine had done that day. The park. The variety store, where they'd bought a knitting loom for Lily and a teddy bear for the baby. No wonder Raine was tuckered out.

Just as Evie parked the car, raindrops began to pelt the sidewalk. Lily squealed and crossed her arms over her head as she dashed for the covered staircase.

Jack was waiting for them at the top of the landing, a tool belt riding low on his hips. Tufts of pink insulation decorated his hair and clung to the long-sleeved cotton T-shirt he wore.

"You look like you got into a fight with a cotton candy machine."

Evie's laughter washed over Jack. A song he was going to hear in his dreams. Oh, who was he kidding? Evie had already invaded his dreams. And his thoughts.

In fact, Jack had been thinking about their last conversation when he glanced out the window and saw the silver Jeep pull up next to the curb. Her office had been dark most of the day, and he'd overheard Pauline telling someone that Evie was out for the day.

She hadn't even left a Post-it note in his office, sentencing Jack to eight hours of hard labor in the youth wing.

"I made a deal with the landlord." He tried to shake some of the pink stuff from

250

his hair. "I replace the cheap insulation in the attic with something a little more substantial, and with the money he saves on the heating bill in the winter, he's going to put in two more washers and dryers."

"Andy and Serena will appreciate that." Evie notched her voice above the rain as the heavens opened up.

Lily squealed again and pushed open the door leading into the hallway. Jack guided Evie inside as a gust of wind rattled the metal sheeting that covered the staircase.

"I hope you don't mind that I brought Lily home," Evie said when they were safely inside the building. "I had to drop something off for the kids, and Cody wasn't back with the car yet."

Mind? After revealing all the skeletons in his family closet, Jack was surprised she'd offered.

"I've got a few more things to finish up on the third floor, but it shouldn't take me more than an hour." Jack gave Lily's ponytail a gentle tug. "Can you wait that long for supper?"

"Uh-huh. Raine and I had bugs on a log for a snack when we got back from the store."

"Celery, peanut butter, and raisins," Evie whispered.

"Thank you for translating. And for bringing Lily home." Through the window at the
top of the stairs, Jack saw a shard of lightning slice through the clouds. "You can wait
out the storm in the apartment if you want
to. According to the weather report I saw,
it's supposed to pass over pretty quickly."

Evie's gaze slid away from his.

Or not.

Jack tried not to let his disappointment
show. "If you need anything, Lily, I'm right
upstairs. Just give me a shout."

"I will." His niece disappeared into the
apartment, but Evie didn't follow her.

Okay, then. The lady obviously had other
plans.

Jack's head told him that was a good
thing . . . but his heart was a little slower to
catch up.

The storm had rumbled on, the mountains
of cumulus clouds dissolving into a glorious
crimson sunset.

Jack loved it when God showed off.

The project had taken a little longer than
he'd expected, but he hadn't heard a peep
from Lily. Not that that was unusual. After
spending the day with Raine, she played
with Bitsy for an hour or two so the guinea
pig wouldn't feel left out.

Jack let himself into the apartment and headed straight for the bathroom. Although he'd worn gloves and a mask, the fiberglass insulation had still managed to work its way under his collar. He felt like he'd rolled in a patch of poison ivy.

"I'm going to take a quick shower," he called out.

Fifteen minutes later, in a clean T-shirt and jeans, he felt almost human again.

Light flowed into the hallway outside Lily's room. The door was open a few inches, far enough that Jack could see she wasn't alone.

Lily was perched on the sequined mushroom stool. Evie knelt on the floor behind her, combing the tangles from her hair. Lily started singing a song Jack vaguely recognized, and Evie joined in, laughing as they stumbled through the lines.

She looked . . . different. She'd discarded her sandals, leaving her feet bare . . . except for the Caribbean Sunrise nail polish on her toes. A gigantic purple flower Jack was sure he'd never seen in nature bloomed above her left ear.

A surge of longing crashed through him. Because this was the picture he wanted to see at the end of a long day. Jack had been so busy taking care of the people in his family over the years, he'd never let himself dream of having one of his own.

But this apartment didn't belong to him. Lily wasn't his daughter. And Evie . . . she didn't belong to him either.

He was about to duck out of sight when Lily spotted him lurking in the doorway. "Evie trimmed my bangs, Uncle Jack! And now she's going to braid my hair."

All he could do was nod. The storm outside might have subsided, but Jack could feel one brewing on the inside.

"Did you finish the insulation?" Evie drew a comb through Lily's hair and began to divide the long curls into sections.

"Almost." Jack tore his gaze away from her hands. "Bert pointed out a leak in the third-floor landing that I have to investigate. Taking care of this building is like playing Whack-a-Mole. Just when I think I'm making some progress, something else pops up."

Lily giggled at the image.

Evie wrapped a tiny elastic band around the end of the little girl's braid. "All done."

Lily leaped to her feet, presenting her back to Jack so he could admire Evie's handiwork. "Beautiful . . . and so is the braid."

Giggling, she swung around to face him again. "You need a haircut too, Uncle Jack."

Jack fingered the ends, a little surprised

that his hair practically brushed his collarbone. "I guess I do."

"Or you could put it in a ponytail." The tease in Evie's voice sent sparks of electricity shooting through him. "I'm sure Lily can spare one of her elastic bands."

"Mmm." Jack pretended to consider the notion. "I don't know . . . People might think I'm in a motorcycle gang. Better not risk it."

Lily wrinkled her nose. "You don't have a motorcycle."

"One would *think* that would be part of the criteria . . ." Jack feinted to one side, narrowly escaping the heart-shaped pillow that hurtled past his head. "I think Evie is trying to tell me it's time to start supper."

"We already ate."

"I found some chicken in the fridge and made a stir fry," Evie said.

"We saved some for you though, Uncle Jack. Bert gave us some stuff from her garden to put in it." Lily ticked off the ingredients on her fingers. "Spinach. Onions. Something yellow that looks like celery."

Evie smiled. "Swiss chard."

He must have been gone a long time. How many other people had wandered in while Evie held down the fort? "I'm sorry . . . You didn't exactly sign up for the whole evening."

"I don't mind." Evie rose to her feet. It was funny, how much grace there was in the simplest of movements.

Jack enjoyed just looking at her . . .

Stop looking at her.

He pivoted toward the hallway to put some distance between them.

Which would have worked if Evie hadn't followed him. Jack almost hoped he would see Ron sprawled in the chair or Josh at the table with his textbook. Because right now a page of geometry problems would be easier to analyze than his feelings for Evie.

But Harley, stretched out on the back of the sofa, was the only visitor taking up space in Jack's living room.

Evie echoed his thoughts. "I think the storm kept people inside this evening."

"Since you and Lily have already eaten, I better make sure there's no water coming in on the first floor."

"What are you doing on the first floor? I thought you were only in charge of maintenance."

"The landlord offered a break on my rent if I agreed to renovate it." Building maintenance, that was a freebie, a labor of love for Bert and the rest of the tenants, but Jack kept that little bit of information to himself. "When I'm finished, he's going to put the building on the market."

"He's *selling* it?"

"That's the plan. Nothing should change as far as the apartments are concerned, but this building was zoned for commercial, so I think he's hoping the downstairs space will be an added bonus to potential business owners."

Evie glanced at Lily to make sure the child wasn't in hearing range before she murmured, "Another bar?"

Jack didn't admit he'd been worried about the same thing.

"Thomsen's Bakery used to be on the corner, but it went out of business when I was in high school. I can't remember what was in this building."

"It's hard to tell now. The last guy who owned it pretty much gutted the downstairs." Jack smiled. "I actually prefer it that way. I'd rather work with a blank canvas."

"What are you doing to it?"

"The usual. Windows. Walls. Floor. Ceiling."

"Uncle Jack says the houses tell him secrets." Lily had moved close enough to catch the last part of the conversation. Close enough for Jack to reach over and hook his arm around her waist.

"And you're supposed to keep them, Squirt," he growled in her ear as she giggled and tried to escape.

"What kind of secrets?" Evie looked intrigued.

At least this was one Jack could safely share. "I guess you'll have to come downstairs and take a look."

CHAPTER 25

Lily held Evie's hand as they followed Jack downstairs.

Plywood covered the windows overlooking the street, and they waited on the sidewalk while Jack fished a key from the pocket of his jeans and unlocked the door.

"You can explore a little but don't touch any of the tools, okay? I don't want you to get hurt."

"Are you talking to me or Lily?" Evie murmured.

Laughter backlit Jack's eyes. "Both of you." He pushed the door open and turned on the light.

Gutted, Evie thought, had been a pretty accurate description. Sections of paneling were missing. In some places, there weren't any walls at all.

She turned a slow circle in the center of the room. "You've been doing this by yourself?"

"All that free time, remember?" Jack took a lap around the room, searching for water damage. "Zach helps me out once in a while."

"Zach?"

"You met him a few days ago."

"The one who offered to bring his crowbar." The one who'd implied that *she* was the reason Jack had refused his help.

"Uh-huh. The kid knows the difference between a hammer and a screwdriver, but we're still working on his social skills."

Evie would have dismissed the words as a joke if she hadn't remembered the way Jack had sent her and Lily upstairs so he could have a "minute" with Zach. "You've got your work cut out for you, that's for sure. With this room, not Zach," Evie added.

Jack frowned up at the ceiling, where a flap of metal had come loose. "That doesn't look good."

Evie followed his gaze. "Aren't you going to rip that one down anyway?"

"Rip —" Jack choked. "I spent about six hours researching that particular style and at least another four calling salvage yards, talking to dealers who might have some lying around. It dates back to the early 1900s, about the time Banister Falls was founded."

Evie didn't even know what year that

260

might be.

"The woodwork is original too." Jack squatted down and scratched the layer of white paint on the base of the counter. "Do you see the edges? No nails. You don't see this kind of craftsmanship anymore . . ." He stopped, shaking his head. "Don't even get me started. Coop says I get a little carried away sometimes."

The name sounded familiar. "Coop is . . ."

"He owns the construction company I told you about. I worked for him for about five years, and then he fired me." Jack saw Evie's expression and laughed. "It was Coop's way of forcing me to go out on my own. I still subcontract for him when he needs custom-built cabinets and finishing work done, but restoration is kind of my specialty."

His specialty.

But Jack didn't seem to mind that he'd walked away from something he loved because he loved his family more.

"My life isn't on hold — I'm just living it here. Moment by moment."

Evie didn't do the living-moment-by-moment thing very well. She preferred to plan ahead.

Except where Jack was concerned. Then Evie found herself saying things — *doing*

261

things — that were contrary to her nature.

"There's a kitchen back there, but I haven't done anything to it yet. I've been focusing all my attention out here." Jack ran one hand along the beveled edge of the counter, almost like a caress, before rising to his feet again. "The landlord may want me to leave it alone in case he turns the first floor into another apartment."

"There's a kitchen? Maybe it will attract someone who wants to open a coffee shop."

"Like Marie's Bistro?"

When Jack put it like that . . .

"Or a café."

"It's not big enough to be commercial grade, but I suppose someone who's motivated could knock out a wall and make it work."

"Uncle Jack! Come here! I found something!" Lily's voice drifted in from somewhere in the back of the building.

"I'm almost afraid to look." Jack strode toward the doorway his niece had disappeared through a few minutes before.

Evie didn't wait for an invitation. He'd offered her a tour, and she was going to take him up on it.

A narrow hallway branched out into two rooms. One was the kitchen, and Evie paused a moment to peek inside.

It was as small as Jack had claimed, with a two-burner stove and dorm-size refrigerator. The porcelain sink jutting out from the wall wore a faded gingham skirt. A shelf on the wall held a coffeepot, a loaf of bread, and a jar of peanut butter. It had the same dark paneling as the room that overlooked the street. A collection of plaques shaped like fruits and vegetables covered the walls.

In spite of the unusual artwork — or maybe because of it — the room exuded a certain amount of vintage charm.

Lily's squeal of laughter echoed through the building, and Evie went to investigate. A floor-length curtain hung across the doorway of the room opposite the kitchen. Evie swept it aside.

The first thing she saw was her reflection in the panel of mirrors that took up the entire back wall. Lily was in motion, arms lifted over her head, as she pirouetted around the room.

Jack was kneeling down, peeling back a corner of the stained carpeting. "Hardwood floor," he said without looking up. "Really. They actually *glued* a piece of indoor-outdoor carpeting to a hardwood floor."

The disbelief in his voice was tempered by a smile, giving Evie permission to smile back. "*They* being the same kind of people who would replace a tin ceiling?"

"Exactly." Jack rose to his feet and dusted his hands off on his jeans.

"Twirl me, Uncle Jack!" Lily flitted over to them. "This is a dancing room!"

Banister Falls had never had a dance studio, so Evie decided a seamstress must have rented out the space at some point in time. It made sense now that she thought about it. With the promise of lower rent, small business owners who didn't have the money to lease the more desirable space on Main Street would have tried to make a go of it in Jack's neighborhood, not realizing it would put them in a catch-22. Rent in the neighborhood was affordable because people didn't want to make a special trip to Fairview for the things they could purchase on Main Street.

But of course Jack didn't correct Lily. Just took her by the hand and made it a dancing room. When he finally released her, Lily collapsed in a heap on the floor, breathless and laughing.

And then Jack held out his hand to her.

Evie started to feel light-headed before her fingers tangled with Jack's.

She should have felt self-conscious. There was no sound in the room — no music except for the rapid thumping of her heart as Jack spun her in a slow circle.

"Is anyone here?"

Jack's other hand instantly settled at Evie's waist, steadying her. And then he stepped away a split second before Ryan Tate appeared in the doorway. In uniform.

Under different circumstances, the shocked look on Ryan's face would have been comical. "Evie?"

The question in Ryan's voice and the ones Evie saw rising in his eyes made her feel like she'd done something wrong.

"Ryan . . . What are you doing here?"

"I saw a light underneath the door. We've had a few burglary complaints around here lately so I thought I should check it out." Ryan's gaze cut back to Jack. "Do you live in this building?"

Instead of responding to the question, Jack reached out and drew Lily to her feet. "Lily, this is Officer Tate. Officer, this is my niece."

Lily ducked her head and melted against Jack's side, the perpetual sparkle in her eyes overshadowed by fear.

Ryan must have seen it too, because he whipped off his hat, and his entire face flexed in a smile. "It's nice to meet you, Lily."

Instead of responding, Lily locked her arms around Jack's waist.

Evie instinctively took a step closer to them and felt Jack stiffen.

"I live upstairs, but I'm doing some renovations for the landlord," he explained.

"Then you just saved me a trip." Ryan's smile didn't slip. "Because I planned to stop by Hope Community tomorrow and talk to you about . . . another matter. If you have a minute."

It wasn't posed in the form of a question.

Evie wanted to protest, but Jack gently pried Lily's hands apart. "It's okay, Peanut. Run upstairs and start getting ready for bed," he murmured. "I'll be there in a few minutes."

Lily's lower lip quivered and she cast an uncertain look in Ryan's direction. Evie was about to offer to go with her, but Jack didn't give her the opportunity.

"I'll see you tomorrow at church, Evie." His tone was polite. Distant. "Thank you for dropping Lily off."

Because they worked in the same building. Because helping people was part of Evie's ministry.

Evie wasn't sure if the carefully worded statement was meant for Ryan or for her. Or for himself.

But she knew when she was being dismissed.

■ ■ ■ ■

"You better be calling to tell me you're on your way back."

Jack wedged the phone between his ear and his shoulder, only slightly muffling Coop's rant as he reached for a hammer. "Not exactly."

"You're killing me, Jack. You know that, right? I distinctly remember someone telling me they were going to be gone a month or two."

"That was before Trav and Cheryl got arrested for drug possession last weekend."

Coop's sigh rattled through the line. "Aw, Jack."

It was one of the things Jack liked about Coop. He wasn't an I-told-you-so kind of guy.

"It sounds like they're not getting out anytime soon either. The judge set a five-thousand-dollar cash bond for Trav, and because of Cheryl's record, she won't get out until her trial."

"Where's Lily?"

"With me."

"Whoa."

Yeah. That about summed it up.

"Nicki is trying to raise three kids on her

own, and I wouldn't ask Roxanne and Carl to watch my pet goldfish for the weekend."

"When did you get a goldfish?"

The knot in Jack's stomach loosened a little. He should have called Coop right away. "Scratch the goldfish. But Lily does have a guinea pig."

"How is she doing?"

"Okay, considering she won't see her parents for a few months and she's stuck with an uncle who is better at hanging drywall than braiding hair."

"You pick things up pretty fast."

"So what's happening on your end?"

"I'm up to my eyeballs in the Waylon-Masters project, and we're not talking about me right now. How are *you* doing?"

"Confused." The wood splintered around the nail as Jack tapped it into place. Great. His third casualty of the evening. "I came here because I wanted Travis to know he's not alone. I know he's responsible for his own actions, but I also know he's trying to cover up a truckload of pain.

"He lost his job at the factory last week and I could tell he was struggling, but I couldn't get him to open up. I told Evie that I'm here because I wanted Trav to know he was worth fighting for, but how am I supposed to do that when he's locked up in jail?"

Silence stretched across the line. Jack waited. Unlike a lot of people, Coop wasn't one to talk until he had something to say.

"You're forgetting one thing."

"What's that?"

"Sometimes the best way to fight is on your knees."

Jack expelled a slow breath. "You're right."

"And if I remember correctly, God can get into places no one else can. Just because things don't look the way you thought they would doesn't mean that coming to Banister Falls was a mistake."

Jack wanted to believe that, but the "other matter" Ryan had wanted to talk about was Travis. The officer had been at the jail earlier that morning and heard from one of the jailers that Travis had gotten into a fight with another inmate. He'd returned from the hospital a few hours later with six stitches in his forehead.

The last time Trav needed stitches he'd been ten years old. He and a couple of friends had constructed a jump in the alley behind their apartment building, and Trav volunteered to be the first one to try it out. He ended up with a three-inch dent in the handlebars of his bicycle and another one in his forehead.

Jack had called their mother at work to tell her what happened, but her boss wouldn't let her leave.

"Take care of your little brother," their mom had said.

So Jack had been the one sitting next to Trav at the clinic while the doctor stitched him up. And the words had stuck with Jack long after the stitches healed.

"I feel . . . helpless, Coop."

"I've been there. But I have a feeling that God has Travis exactly where He wants him," Coop said. "It wouldn't be the first time He spoke to someone in jail, you know. Think about it. God's got your brother's undivided attention, and Travis doesn't have access to the stuff that's messing with his head."

"So you're reminding me to trust."

"That's what it all comes down to, right? Believing in God means we *believe* Him. Things may not look the way we want them to — or the way we think they should — but God sees the whole picture. If you hadn't been in Banister Falls, what would have happened to Lily?"

"I hadn't thought about that." But Jack knew the answer. She would have been shuffled back and forth between Nicki and her grandmother.

"Well, God did. Trust Him to take care of Cheryl and Travis, and you take care of the people He entrusted to you."

Jack's memory instantly downloaded an image of Evie sitting cross-legged on the floor, singing a silly duet with Lily.

He shut it down, afraid of where those thoughts would take him. Evie didn't need him. She had family, close friends, guys like Ryan Tate and Dan Moretti ready to protect her.

What did he have to offer that she didn't already have?

"I will." Jack rerouted his thoughts before they got him into more trouble.

"And don't be so bullheaded that you don't let me know when something happens. You're too used to doing things on your own."

"You're calling me bullheaded?" Jack grinned around the nails protruding from the corner of his mouth. "If it weren't for you, who knows where I'd be right now?"

Coop knew it was a hypothetical question. Without his intervention, they both knew where Jack would be right now. Sitting in a cell next to Travis.

"I promise I'll keep you in the loop."

"Good . . . because there's one more thing

I'd like to know."

"What's that?"

"Who's Evie?"

CHAPTER 26

Dan was sitting on Evie's front step when she got home from work the next day.

"Hey." Evie greeted him with a smile. "What brings you here?"

"My mother." Dan pushed to his feet. "She wanted me to extend a formal invitation to a cookout on Sunday."

"Formal?" Evie teased, aiming a pointed look at Dan's gray cargo pants and black T-shirt, the uniform the firefighters at Second Street Station wore when they were on call.

"Okay, maybe not so formal, but I just got her text about half an hour ago so I figured I'd swing by on my way home and ask you. She mentioned she'd tried to call you last night."

"I was gone for a few hours and I didn't realize my phone was on silent." Because she'd spent the evening with Lily and Jack and hadn't even checked for messages until she got home.

Until Jack had *sent* her home.

Evie still didn't understand what had caused the subtle shift in his mood. And because Jack had spent the majority of the day outside, mowing the lawn around the church and working on the landscaping, she hadn't had an opportunity to talk to him about the reason behind Ryan's visit.

"Eves?"

Oops. Dan must have asked her a question. "Sorry. Long day. What can I bring?"

"Nothing. You know that feeding people is my mom's spiritual gift."

And Sunday dinner at the Morettis' had been on Evie's calendar since she was a teenager, but her attendance had been sporadic the last few months. Evie enjoyed being with Dan's family, but she'd wanted to give them an opportunity to get to know Gin better.

"Will Cody and Raine be there?"

"*Everyone* will be there." A mysterious smile hitched up the corners of Dan's lips.

"I'll give your mom a call this evening." Evie unlocked the door and pushed it open a few inches. She expected Dan to say goodbye, but he didn't seem in a hurry to leave. "Did you want to come in for a few minutes?"

"Sure." Dan stopped just inside the foyer and looked around. "It feels . . . I don't know . . . *different* in here. Did you change something?"

"What's changed is that you aren't tripping over size-eleven shoes scattered in the hall." Evie smiled and looped the strap of her purse over one of the hooks on the wall. "And Diva isn't trying to lick you to death."

Dan didn't smile back. "I was kind of surprised when I saw Cody and Raine at the park with her last weekend."

"She belongs to Cody," Evie said simply. "His fifth birthday present from Max and me." She bypassed the living room and went into the kitchen. "Would you like something cold to drink? We can take it out on the patio."

"Sounds good." Dan grabbed two glasses from the cupboard while Evie opened up the fridge and took out the pitcher of iced tea she'd made the day before.

Dan was silent until they sat down at the picnic table, but from the troubled look in his eyes, Evie could tell there was something he wanted to say.

"Don't take this the wrong way, Danny, because I'm glad you stopped over, but is everything all right?"

"That's what I was going to ask you," Dan

muttered.

"What do you mean?"

"I mean, are you doing okay, Eves? It must be an adjustment with Cody being gone."

"I'm not the first parent who's had to face the empty nest. A good mom works herself out of a job." How many times had Evie said those exact words to women at Hope Community over the years? Now she wondered if the words had been an encouragement at all.

"That's true. But it doesn't answer my question."

"I'm fine, Danny."

Dan gave her The Stare. The one that said he didn't believe her.

"Really." Evie tried not to let her exasperation show. "Gin invited me to have lunch with her at the diner next week. Sue let her tweak the menu again, and she asked me to be her guinea pig."

"You're changing the subject."

"Yes, I am."

"Sue wants to make Ginevieve a business partner."

"That's great." Evie meant it. "Is she going to accept? Or do you plan to make her a better offer?"

"I'm not sure what you mean."

This time Evie gave *him* The Stare. "I

276

mean, when are you going to propose to the woman?"

"On her birthday."

"Which is . . ."

"Sunday." Dan grinned. "I invited Ginevieve to go hiking at the ridge right after church."

Maple Ridge, the locals' nickname for the county park, was a favorite place to while away a summer afternoon. A labyrinth of scenic trails the Youth Conservation Corp had made during the Second World War wound through the woods, the paths eventually converging at an old stone bridge that arched over the river.

It was beautiful. *Romantic.* And suddenly everything clicked into place. Everyone would be attending the dinner because Angela and John would be announcing their oldest son's engagement.

Tears stung the back of Evie's eyes as she reached across the picnic table and squeezed his hand. "Congratulations, Danny. I'm so happy for you and Gin."

Gratitude warmed Dan's hazel eyes. "Thanks, Evie. Your friendship means a lot to me . . . and to Ginevieve."

"You two are good for each other." Evie smiled, but inexplicably, Dan's smile faded.

"Eves —" He hesitated. "There is something else I wanted to talk to you about."

"Sure." Evie tried to squelch a stirring of unease. Did it have something to do with Cody? In spite of the difference in their ages, Dan was not only her son's friend but his confidante . . .

"It's about Jack Vale."

"Jack?" The air rushed out of Evie's lungs. "What about him?"

"I'm concerned, that's all. I saw the article on the front page of the newspaper, about that couple who were arrested on drug charges last week. The guy's last name is Vale, so I figured he and Jack must be related."

"Travis is Jack's younger brother."

"And Lily? The little girl that Raine is babysitting for during the day? Where does she fit in?"

"Lily is Jack's niece. She's living with him for a while."

"Until her parents get out of jail." Dan combed his fingers through his hair, a sign he was struggling to keep his emotions in check. "I'm just wondering why you took it upon yourself to get involved, that's all. Did Vale ask you for help?"

"Of course not. Raine was looking for a summer job, and I knew Jack couldn't bring Lily to work with him every day. It worked out well for both of them."

"He has a police record, Evie."

"I know, but you can't hold Jack responsible for his brother's actions."

"I wasn't talking about his brother. Jack was arrested for disorderly conduct. Granted, it was a long time ago, but he was involved in a fight and ended up spending a night in jail."

The words landed like a physical slap, and Evie reared back. "How could you possibly know that?"

"Ryan —"

"You asked *Ryan* to investigate Jack?"

"*Investigate* is a pretty strong word. But when it comes right down to it, we don't know much about Jack's past."

"Maybe you shouldn't be so concerned about the past. Isn't it more important what kind of person he is now?" Evie planned to have a little chat with a certain police officer. "Jack moved to Banister Falls because he knew his brother was struggling and he wanted to help. You can't blame him for that."

"And you can't blame us for being protective of you."

Blame them? Maybe not. They'd been doing it for years. If her car needed the oil changed, if she needed a lightbulb changed, all Evie had to do was pick up the phone.

She'd always felt safe, knowing people in the church and community were looking out for her. The love, the caring, wrapped around her like a cocoon. Made her feel safe. Secure.

But not right now.

"I don't understand you. When I met Ginevieve, you encouraged me to reach out to her. You knew Gin had a past, but you didn't hold it against her."

"You're getting pretty worked up over someone you barely know." Dan's eyes swept over her. Brief but intent, his firstresponder mode. If Evie didn't have her arms crossed, he'd be taking her pulse.

"I'm not worked up!"

Dan actually smiled. "Look, Jack may be a decent guy —"

"Then why are you warning me not to spend time with him?"

Dan's eyebrow shot up. "*Have* you been spending time with him?"

"We both work at the church. Raine has been taking care of Lily during the day. Our paths are bound to cross once in a while."

"I don't want to see you get taken advantage of, that's all."

"Because I'm a lonely widow?"

"*Lonely.*" Dan cringed. "That's not what I

meant, Evie. I know you wouldn't be interested in him like . . . like *that.* Jack Vale is nothing like Max. You've poured eighteen years of your life into raising Cody, and now he's married. He and Raine are going to have a child of their own. You're a caring person, Evie. I can see why you'd be drawn to Lily. Her mother is in jail and you're concerned about her. It makes sense that you're looking for something to . . . I don't know . . . fill the gap."

"I don't have a *gap,* Danny."

"You hold the memories so tight, so close, there isn't room for anything else."

Bert's words.

Evie hadn't been able to put them out of her mind.

She did care about Lily. But what about her feelings for Jack? Because it was time to stop denying they were there, swirling just below the surface.

Evie hadn't expected him to share his past with her. But while Jack had been telling Travis's story, Evie had been reading between the lines and learning more about him.

Jack, as the older son, would have taken care of Travis when their mother worked two jobs. He'd probably taken care of her, too, after she was diagnosed with cancer.

Everything Evie knew about Jack told her that he saw the value in things that other people would throw away.

"You're upset with me." Dan expelled a sigh. "Now Gin will get to say I told you so."

"You talked to Gin about this?"

"I've been worried about you," Dan muttered. "For the record, she said I was overreacting and that I should trust you."

One more reason she liked Gin. "And she would be right."

"Will you at least promise you'll be careful?"

Careful?

Evie almost laughed.

She didn't know how to be anything else.

CHAPTER 27

"When you said we were going to take a field trip this morning, I didn't think you meant it literally."

Evie silently thanked God for Belinda's sense of humor. Because right now she was the only one on the women's ministry team who was smiling.

Evie had stocked the church van with a thermos of Marie's French roast and a basket of scones and told them about her meeting with Maggie McClain on the drive over to Fairview Street.

"Maggie is going to meet us here in a few minutes, but I'm sure she won't mind if we take a look around."

Not that there was much to look at. Over the past few days, the temperature had inched into the eighties. The sun had baked the litter that washed over the curb during the storm right into the hard-packed ground.

But what Evie hadn't expected to see was the graffiti on the wall of the brick building next to the lot. Words at spray-painted odds with the bright, cheerful colors the "artist" had chosen.

Evie's cell phone chirped in the side pocket of her purse. She tapped the screen and a text from Maggie popped up. Sorry! Emergency meeting. Will be tied up the rest of the morning. God will provide.

Evie's heart sank. She'd been counting on Maggie's infectious smile and enthusiasm to counter any misgivings her team would have about putting the vacant lot on the tour. Not to mention that Maggie had promised to bring photographs of successful community garden projects to show everyone what the end result would look like.

"It looks like Maggie won't be able to make it after all."

The frown between Jill's eyebrows eased a little. "I guess there's no point in staying any longer then."

Belinda, who'd broken away from the group, returned with an armload of empty glass bottles. "I'll toss these into the recycling bin when we get back to the church."

"Are we leaving now?" Sonya, who hadn't ventured off the curb, took a step toward the van.

Evie glanced at Maggie's text again.

God will provide.

If You want this to happen — if Maggie is right and this is really Your idea — You're going to have to make it clear. Not just to me . . . but to everyone here.

"Evie . . ." Jill's gaze locked on something over Evie's shoulder.

She twisted around, expecting to see Bert, a person who would see the value of a community garden — or Maggie — because God had provided a swift answer to Evie's prayer . . .

"Hey!"

Zach was walking — no, *lurching* would be a better word — straight toward them. As if something — and Evie was pretty sure she knew what that something was — had short-circuited the connection between his head and his feet. And it wasn't all that straight either. More like a jerky start-and-stop momentum that reminded Evie of a carnival ride.

She'd asked God for a sign and He'd sent Crowbar Boy.

Jill's jaw dropped another inch when Zach stopped right in front of Evie.

"I thought that was you. How's it going?"

Funny you should ask, Zach.

"Fine. *Fine.*" Evie said it twice, just to see if it would stick.

"Sweet." Zach pressed closer and peered at the beer bottles cradled in Belinda's arms. "Did you get community service too?"

Belinda didn't look the least bit shocked by the question. "Just tidying up a little."

Zach pulled a beer bottle from the pocket of his hoodie. "You can have this one too."

"Thank you." Belinda tipped it upside down, shook the remaining drops of liquid onto the ground, and added it to the pile.

A squad car cruised around the corner, and Zach took a few stumbling steps backward. "Gotta go," he mumbled. "When you see Jack, tell him I'm going to be out of town for a few days, okay?"

"Okay." One look at her friends' faces and Evie had a feeling she would be explaining more than Maggie's vision for the garden on the way back to the church. "And thank you for letting me know. Jack would notice if you were gone."

"He's the only one." Some of the fog lifted in Zach's eyes, revealing a spark of amusement. "Pretty annoying if you ask me," he added cheerfully.

There were a few other words — Evie

wasn't sure if they would be considered nouns or adjectives — sprinkled throughout the sentence that any family-friendly television show would have bleeped out.

And then Zach lurched away in the opposite direction.

For a split second, Evie was tempted to go with him.

The squad car pulled up behind the van and stopped. When Ryan Tate got out of the vehicle, Evie practically heard the women's collective sigh of relief.

"Morning, ladies. What are you up to this morning?" Ryan whipped off his mirrored sunglasses and looked at Evie, revealing a pair of espresso-brown eyes that lacked their usual sparkle. Remembering her last conversation with Dan, she wasn't feeling very sparkly toward him either.

"We're looking over the future site of the community garden," Evie told him. "We might partner with the woman who's spearheading the project."

"Maggie McClain."

"You know her?"

Ryan rubbed his temple, as if he was trying to ward off a headache. "Everyone who works at the PD knows Maggie McClain. Someone complained — *mentioned* — that she'd been attending the city council meetings, trying to convince them to donate a piece of property. I had no idea it was this one."

The frown that scored his forehead told Evie what Ryan thought about Maggie's choice.

"She asked if we'd consider adding the lot to our garden tour next weekend," Jill said.

"You're kidding." Ryan eyed the beer bottles in Belinda's arms. "Does Maggie have any idea how often we respond to calls in this neighborhood?"

"I'm sure she does. In fact, that's probably why she chose it," Evie heard herself say.

She realized how that might have come across when Sonya and Jill exchanged a wide-eyed look. Evie hadn't meant to be disrespectful to an officer of the law. No, she'd been sharing her opinion with the boy who used to steal her jump rope during recess and turn it into a lasso.

"With the layoffs at Leiderman, we've been getting a lot of vandalism and alcohol-related complaints. The county jail is at capacity." Ryan's gaze held Evie's long enough for her to catch his meaning.

"Those kinds of crimes actually decrease in a neighborhood where there's a community garden."

"Did Maggie tell you that too?" Something in the way Ryan said the woman's name told Evie the two had been at odds in the past.

"I did some research after Maggie stopped by my office on Monday."

"Did the city actually agree to this, or is Maggie still pestering them?"

Evie took issue with his choice of words. "They agreed. She's trying to form a committee that will oversee it now."

"Are you against a community garden, Officer Tate?" Sonya ventured.

"No, but let's just say I'd prefer to see it in another part of the community." Ryan slid his sunglasses back on. "The building across the street is for sale, and I've heard rumors that a liquor store will be going in there at the end of the summer. If that happens, Maggie will be setting up a target, not a garden."

Three heads swiveled toward the building in question. The one Jack had been painstakingly bringing back to life. Had he heard the rumors about a liquor store? And what would it mean for the tenants like Bert who rented the upstairs apartments?

Ryan's radio crackled and he unclipped it from his utility belt. "Excuse me." He took a step away from Evie as the dispatcher rattled off a combination of letters and numbers. They must have made sense to Ryan because he frowned. "10–4. I'm on my way."

Evie tried to hide her relief. Thanks to Zach and Ryan, it was going to take more than coffee and scones to convince her team that the community garden was a good idea.

"If you'll excuse me now, I better get back to work." Ryan glanced at Evie. "If you have any other questions or concerns about anything, feel free to give me a call."

"I will." But the garden wouldn't be the only topic of conversation.

Ryan strode back to the squad car and drove away.

No one said a word until they got into the van.

"I can't believe how run-down the neighborhood has gotten." Jill pointed to Jack's building. "That was a fabric store when my grandparents lived here. The owner taught sewing classes on the weekends. My mother would drop me off with Grandpa every Saturday morning while she and Grandma learned how to quilt. Grandpa and I would walk down to Thomsen's Bakery and buy a dozen crullers. Most of the time, they were still warm when Mr. Thomsen put them in the bag."

"That was before Marie opened the bistro and started making these amazing scones." Sonya held up the white cardboard box. "The Thomsens didn't have room to set up tables and chairs. Customers want a place where they can linger over a cup of coffee."

"It's sad how some people don't take any pride in their neighborhood." Jill clucked her tongue. "I don't mean to sound harsh, but if they don't maintain their own property, what makes Maggie McClain think they would take care of a garden?"

"That's true," Sonya said around a mouthful of scone.

Evie's hands tightened around the steering wheel. "Sometimes people don't have the resources. I'm not just talking about money for improvements, but family or friends who are willing to help out."

"You saw the graffiti and the trash lying around. I'd feel terrible if I put all that time and energy into a garden plot, and someone came along during the night and vandalized it."

Jill nodded in agreement. "Maybe Officer Tate is right. The garden is a great idea, but I think it should be in a better part of town. The church bought that extra lot in case we expand again — maybe we should talk to Pastor Keith and see how the church would feel about turning *it* into a garden."

"I think we might be getting a little ahead of ourselves." Evie pulled into the church parking lot, noticing that the spot where Jack usually parked was empty. "Melanie wants to finish the brochures on Monday, so we should make a decision about whether to include Fairview Street in the garden walk."

The silence that followed Evie's suggestion wasn't exactly encouraging. And then Jill chuckled. "I thought we already had."

"The women have certain expectations," Sonya said slowly. "And one of those expectations is that they're actually going to tour a garden."

"Plus, we're not sure at this point that it's really going to happen," Jill added. "The city agreed to lease the land, but there's no guarantee that Maggie will be able to get enough volunteers interested."

"That's why Maggie asked us to include the lot on the garden walk. She's hoping the women who enjoy gardening would support one that benefits the community." Evie glanced at Belinda and was slightly encouraged by the fact that she was nodding.

Until she spoke her thoughts out loud.

"I love the idea, but I have to agree with Sonya. Maybe next summer we could do it

— when Maggie has everything in place?"

Again, something that required volunteers.

"We have to make sure that every event we offer for the women lines up with our purpose statement." Jill opened her binder. "I like the idea of the community garden too, but it falls under the category of outreach. The purpose of the garden walk is to provide a day of fun and fellowship. The women should be given a choice if they want to find out more about it . . . It shouldn't be something we force on them."

There was a murmur of agreement.

"All right." Evie respected their decision. "I'll let Maggie know."

No one asked Evie her opinion.

But why would they?

Jill had just quoted right from one of Evie's handouts.

Chapter 28

"Why can't we go?"

It was the fourth time — not that Jack was keeping track — that Lily had asked the question since they'd gotten home from church.

He pulled in a breath and prayed for patience. "I thought you wanted to go to the pool this afternoon. We can stop at Quigley's and get an ice cream cone afterward."

It was official. He was turning into the kind of person who stooped to bribery. At the moment, however, he was hoping the reason so many parents succumbed to the temptation was because it worked.

"I want to go to Raine's party instead. I helped her pick out the decorations for the cupcakes."

Jack wasn't sure why Raine had invited Lily to Ginevieve's birthday party, but she had to have known his niece couldn't

294

exactly borrow the truck and drive herself over there.

"We don't have a present." And Jack was running out of excuses.

"I made a bracelet for her last night while you were painting my room. I showed it to you, remember?"

"I remember." Only Jack assumed Lily had been making it for herself. She'd spent almost two hours carefully threading heart-shaped plastic beads onto an emerald-green ribbon.

"Raine said green is her mom's favorite color."

Jack made the mistake of looking into his niece's big gray eyes and caved. "I suppose we could stop over for a few minutes — on our way to the pool."

A smile lit up Lily's face — and those had been few and far between since she'd spent Friday with Roxanne and Carl.

Raine had had an ultrasound appointment at the hospital and Roxanne had been asking Jack when she could see her grand-daughter. Unfortunately, Jack couldn't come up with a reasonable excuse, other than the fact that Roxanne didn't hesitate to express her opinion of Travis even when Lily was within earshot.

"Pack up your stuff." Jack grabbed his cell

off the coffee table. "I'm going to call Raine and make sure they're expecting us."

Lily didn't have to be told twice. She disappeared into her bedroom, and Jack punched in Raine's number. It went straight to voicemail, and Jack sighed into the phone.

Party crashers it was.

Lily bounced all the way to the car, the gift-wrapped bracelet cupped in her hands. Jack, who'd mastered just about every power tool ever made, had discovered he was as inept at making bows out of curly ribbon as he was at French braids.

He'd bet Evie could do both.

Jack hopped into the cab of the pickup and made sure Lily was buckled before he pulled away from the curb. "You're sure the party is today?"

"Uh-huh. Two o'clock. But it's not at Raine and Cody's house."

Not — "Where is it then?"

"It's at the house right next door. Where Emily and Amanda's grandma and grandpa live."

Jack was starting to get a bad feeling about the whole thing. Especially when he turned the corner and saw vehicles lining both sides of the street.

"Lily, hold on a minute." Jack reached for his niece's hand, but he missed. She bailed out onto the sidewalk and scampered toward the group of people in the backyard.

Leaving Jack with no choice but to follow.

Lily was already attached to Raine's side as Jack made his way across the manicured lawn. Dan and Gin stood in the shade of an oak tree surrounded by people. Jack recognized some of them from the wedding. The slender, dark-haired twins. The older man Jack had seen handing out the boutonnieres. Ryan Tate.

The gang was all here.

The buzz of conversation subsided as Jack approached. He focused on Raine and Cody, who actually looked happy to see him, and then turned to Raine's mother.

"Happy birthday, Ginevieve."

A smile played at the corners of Gin's lips as she looked up at Dan. "Up until an hour ago, I thought that was what we were celebrating."

"Mom and Dan got engaged." Raine's approval of the match glowed in her eyes. "He proposed to her at Maple Ridge."

Jack wasn't familiar with the place, but he shook Dan's hand. "Congratulations."

"Dan picked today because he's getting old and he's afraid he won't remember their anniversary," one of the guys leaning against the picnic table said in a pseudo-whisper.

"Be nice, Will, or no leftovers for you." A striking brunette in her mid to late fifties set a platter of ham sandwiches down on the picnic table and turned to Jack. "We haven't officially met, but I've gotten to know Lily quite well over the past few days. I'm Angela Moretti."

"Jack Vale. It's nice to meet you, Mrs. Moretti. I didn't realize you were hosting the party." Or he wouldn't have come.

"Please, call me Angela. And there are so many people — Raine and I decided we would need both yards."

"And help yourself to the food." Ginevieve motioned to the table, and the sunlight glinted off the diamond ring on her finger. "There's plenty."

"Thank you, but Lily and I are going to the pool this afternoon. She wanted to drop off a gift for you on the way."

"Your niece is such a sweetheart." Ginevieve filched a carrot stick from a tray of fresh vegetables. "Nicki's kids talk about her all the time."

"Can we stay for a little while, Uncle Jack? Emily and Amanda want me to push them on the swing." Lily landed in front of him, holding hands with the blonde-haired girls who'd been playing in the sprinkler the first day he'd picked her up at Raine's. Jack

298

should have known they were tiny shoots of the Moretti family tree.

"Ten minutes . . . and then we're off to the pool."

"Okay!" Off they went again, leaving Jack stranded in the middle of what he now realized was a family get-together.

"Don't be shy, Jack." Cody handed him a paper plate.

Jack's gaze swept over the yard, searching the faces of the guests. Searching for . . .

"My mom went over to our house to get the cupcakes Raine and Lily decorated."

"I wasn't —" Jack's voice died in his throat. Because yes, he was. Jack hadn't seen Evie since the evening Officer Tate had shown up at the apartment building and found them together. Ryan hadn't said anything after Evie left, but the way he'd looked at Jack made him feel like he'd committed some kind of misdemeanor.

Kind of the way Tate was looking at him now.

"You should go over and say hi before you leave." Cody scooped up a handful of chips and deposited them on his plate.

"I should?"

Cody shrugged. "Why not?"

Jack could think of about a dozen reasons. Starting with the discreet glances he was getting from the people gathered around the picnic table. Not unfriendly. *Cautious.* The Morettis were the kind of people who would greet a stray dog that wandered into their yard, but that didn't mean they weren't wondering where it had come from and what it was doing there.

"Evie's in the house." Ginevieve handed Jack a glass of lemonade.

It suddenly occurred to him that *not* saying hello to Evie just might trigger a whole different set of questions.

"I'll be right back."

The faint tang of fresh paint hung in the air as Jack let himself into the house. Familiar with the floor plan of a Craftsman-style home, he found the kitchen without any problem.

A tray of cupcakes and a pitcher of lemonade were on the counter, but no Evie.

On impulse, Jack made his way up the stairs, the plush carpeting absorbing the sound of his footsteps. He stopped at the top of the landing, considered his options, and headed for door number two.

The door was open, but it took a second for Jack's brain to register what he was seeing.

Evie, stretched out on the floor, playing tug-of-war with a chunky, white-faced golden retriever. The dog growled low in its throat — all for show — and Evie giggled.

The sound arrowed through him, and Jack suddenly felt like an intruder. He stepped away from the door, but the retriever tattled on Jack with a cheerful woof.

Evie rolled to her feet. "Jack?"

Diva immediately trotted over to say hello, but it was difficult for Jack to tell if Evie was as happy to see him.

"Raine invited Lily to the party, so we stopped by for a minute on our way to the pool."

"Raine mentioned that, but I didn't think —" Evie glanced down, smoothing an invisible wrinkle from her skirt. "I'm glad you brought her."

"I didn't have much of a choice. Lily made a bracelet for Ginevieve's birthday."

"It *is* her birthday." Evie smiled. "She just didn't realize Dan's gift would be an engagement ring."

"I better go. Lily's waiting for me." Jack was fibbing. Lily would be thrilled if they canceled their pool date and spent the entire day hanging out with the Morettis. "Cody said I should stop over and say hello, but I think what he really wanted me to do was find out why the cupcakes haven't made their way to the picnic table yet."

Color flowed into Evie's cheeks. "Diva and I got a little sidetracked. Cody mentioned he'd set up the crib last night and I wanted to take a peek." She ran her hand over the wooden railing. "I still can't believe I'm going to be a grandma at the end of the summer."

She didn't look like one. In fact, Evie barely looked old enough to have a son Cody's age. Especially today, when she was wearing a knee-length denim skirt and a white sleeveless top that showed off smooth, sun-kissed shoulders.

Evie smiled. "I know parents say this kind of thing all the time, but it seems like only yesterday when Max and I put Cody's crib together."

A surge of emotion rushed through Jack and left a bitter taste in his mouth. He hadn't experienced it very often over the past thirty-six years, but he knew what it was. Envy.

He was envious of the man Evie had given her heart to when she was a teenager. The man who *still* had her heart.

None of us could compete with Max.

Isn't that what Ryan Tate had said?

Jack should have realized it was a warning.

Evie felt everyone's eyes on her and Jack as

they walked out of the house together. Side by side, but she could feel the distance between them.

Jack had made it clear that Lily was the only reason he'd accepted Raine's invitation to the party. He set the tray down on the picnic table and waved to Lily. "It's time to go, Peanut."

"The pool is going to be pretty crowded this time of day. You should take Lily to Sandy Point." Cody snagged a cupcake from the tray and handed it to Raine.

Jack's smile looked a little forced. "I'm not familiar with the local landmarks yet."

"It's not a landmark, it's a well-kept secret." Cody nudged Dan. "Dan and my dad discovered it when they were kids."

"Accidentally." Dan smiled. "Sandy Point is a secluded stretch of beach a few miles from the campground — accessible only by hiking a mile up an old logging road or by raft."

"Which one did you use?" Will asked. As always, Dan's youngest brother, the family prankster, loved to stir the pot.

"The raft." Dan glanced at his parents. "It worked a little better than we thought it would," he added in a whisper.

"They put up a rope swing too."

"That was a long time ago, Cody." Evie

tried to move the conversation to safer ground. "I doubt it's there anymore."

"The original one isn't." Cody grinned. "But Dan and I made another one a few years ago. We go there once or twice a summer."

"What?" Evie made a fist and cuffed Dan's shoulder. "You never told me that."

"What happens at Sandy Point stays in Sandy Point."

"Why am I only hearing these stories now?" Angela planted her hands on her hips, the look she tossed at her son a blend of amusement and exasperation. "I guess I should have asked more questions when you told me that you and Max were going swimming."

"Technically, it wasn't swimming. With a running start from the point, you landed in the middle of the river. The current kind of took you from there, right, Eves?"

"I don't know. You and Max wouldn't let me try it."

"Really?" Dan rubbed the back of his neck, frowning. "We probably thought you didn't want to. Besides, someone had to dial 911 if the rope broke."

"And you lecture kids on the importance of safety," Ryan chided.

"I was kidding." Dan didn't look the

slightest bit guilty. "The water is shallow in some places too, and it's peaceful out there. Max was the one who turned everything into an obstacle course."

Lily, who'd been listening to the conversation with wide-eyed fascination, tugged on Jack's arm. "Can we go there instead, Uncle Jack?"

"Not today, Peanut. I'm not sure how to get there."

"Evie can show us." Lily looped her arm through Evie's. "Cody said she used to go there too."

"I'm sure Evie wants to stay at the party with her friends a little longer."

"But —"

"I said no."

The words were sharp enough to make Lily flinch, and her grip on Evie's arm tightened.

"Let's stick with our original plan." Jack's smile softened the words. "The pool and Quigley's for ice cream, okay?"

Lily's chin dipped in a nod. "Okay."

"Good-bye, Lily." Ginevieve bent down and gave her a hug. "Thank you for coming to my party and for the gift."

Jack waited patiently while Lily said the rest of her good-byes. By the time she got to Evie, the sparkle was back in her eyes.

"You could come to the pool with us."

Evie glanced at Jack but he was shaking John's hand. Walking away.

"It's sweet of you to invite me, Lily, but you and your uncle have to stick to the plan, remember?"

A plan Jack obviously wasn't willing to change to include her.

CHAPTER 29

"You have to rescue me, Evie. I'm drowning in spinach and arugula."

The announcement, accompanied by Bert's throaty laugh, lifted Evie's spirits. Dan and Gin's engagement party wasn't officially over, but Evie had been getting into her car to leave when her cell rang.

"I'll trade you some for a piece of birthday slash engagement cake."

"Only if you have a glass of iced tea with me and explain what that is," Bert said.

"I'll be there in five minutes."

Evie made a U-turn in the middle of the street and drove across town to Fairview Street.

Disappointment waged war against relief when Evie saw the empty parking space in front of Jack's building.

She made her way to the third floor. Bert was waiting for her at the top of the landing. Today she wore a bright-orange housecoat with oversize buttons that looked like daisies.

"Come in. Make yourself comfortable. Jack put one of those little air conditioners in my window a few days ago." Bert side-stepped into the tiny kitchen. "I have to admit, it makes it a whole lot easier to breathe on a day like this."

Instead of taking a seat in the living room, Evie poured two glasses of iced tea while Bert peeled back the lid on a plastic storage container and removed two enormous oatmeal cookies studded with raisins and walnuts.

"Ron's favorite," Bert said. "I made a batch to cheer him up when he gets back from the VA."

"Did something happen? Is he all right?"

"It's just a few routine tests to make sure his lungs are clear from that last bout of pneumonia. Jack says that we should start worrying when Ron stops complaining."

Every time Bert said Jack's name, Evie felt a little pinch in the vicinity of her heart. She carried the glasses into the living room, and as she passed the window, she saw a VW Beetle the color of a McIntosh apple rolling up to the curb on the other side of the street. Maggie McClain hopped out of the driver's seat a second later, wearing denim overalls over her T-shirt and bright-green gardening clogs.

Evie had called her after the meeting on Friday and told her what the committee had decided. Maggie understood, but Evie could tell she was disappointed.

"I'm going to keep moving forward, Evie. If God wants this to happen, He'll give the right people a little nudge. I don't have to worry when I've got a man on the inside."

The unconventional comment sounded like something Jack would say. And made Evie feel worse.

"You're welcome to attend the garden walk as my guest, Maggie. I can introduce you to some of the women who might be interested in serving on your committee."

"I appreciate that, Evie, but I'll be spending every available weekend finishing up the plans for the garden. I ran into some . . . unexpected opposition . . . and I'd like to get to know the people in the neighborhood better so I can convince the naysayers that the garden won't be a target for vandalism."

A target.

Evie was glad they were talking on the phone instead of in person so Maggie couldn't see her expression. Because she had a strong hunch who the "unexpected opposition" was.

Their conversation was cut short when Maggie got an incoming call. Evie had taken a walk around the block to clear her head, but she couldn't shake the feeling they'd made the wrong decision. Not even when Victoria Kellan called a few hours later and told her she would be back in time for the garden walk.

"That car was parked here last night too." Bert paused to see what had gotten Evie's attention. "Do you think it's someone who's interested in buying the building?"

Bert had heard the rumors too. But in this instance, Evie could put the woman's mind at ease.

"Her name is Maggie McClain. She got permission from the city to put a community garden on the lot."

"What's that?" Bert took a step closer to the window, watching as Maggie popped the hatch on her car and pulled out a large plastic bin.

"Anyone who's interested in gardening can sign up for a plot. It's up to each person to decide what they want to plant, and then they're responsible for weeding and watering it. The way Maggie explained it to me, any extra produce" — Evie smiled — "like a bumper crop of spinach, for instance, is shared among the gardeners or donated to families in need. Maggie has big plans. She wants to designate an area for a children's garden and grow herbs in one of the plots."

"You have to be careful with herbs." Bert's brow furrowed. "Glen and I found out the hard way that mint will spread and take over everything if you don't contain it properly."

"So . . . would you be willing to tell Maggie that?"

"Me?"

"Maggie is looking for volunteers to help her get things started, and I think you'd be a great resource. You could introduce her to people who live in the neighborhood, plus you know a lot about growing things."

Bert didn't answer, but something in the rigid set of her shoulders told Evie she'd overstepped.

"I'm sorry, Bert. I didn't mean to push."

"You didn't."

"Then what's wrong?"

"I was." Bert fished a crumpled tissue from the pocket of her housecoat. "My son and my grandkids don't live close by, and they're busy with their own lives. I was starting to think everyone forgot about me. Even God. Then He sent Jack here and I could sleep better because I knew the building wasn't going to fall down around my ears. And now *this.*" Bert's eyes glowed. "It's

311

more than I can hold, Evie."

"You're going to get along great with Maggie. When you're ready, let me know and I'll introduce you."

"Do you think she likes oatmeal cookies?"

"You want to meet her now?"

"When you're seventy years old, you don't want to put things off very long."

The comment reminded Evie of something Gertrude Fielding would say. She had a feeling the two women would get along really well too.

"Then let's go."

Evie linked her arm through Bert's as they made their way down the flight of stairs. As they reached the second floor, Evie couldn't help but glance at the door of Jack's apartment.

"Jack must be gone this afternoon." Bert must have read her mind. "It's pretty quiet around here."

"He took Lily to the pool."

"Jack is sure good for that little girl. Good for all of us, I think."

Evie didn't say it out loud, but she thought so too.

"There's Evie's car!"

Lily's finger arrowed over Jack's shoulder as he turned onto Fairview Street. Sure enough, a silver Jeep was parked in front of his building. Jack pulled up behind it.

"Do you think Evie is waiting for us?"

"Don't forget your beach bag, Lil." Jack dumped the empty plastic cups from their ice cream sundaes into the cooler. By the time they got to Quigley's it was so close to dinnertime, they'd ordered burgers and fries before dessert. "Evie might be visiting Bert. She knew we were going to be gone today."

And after he'd released his inner jerk, Jack was probably the last person Evie wanted to see. He still wasn't quite sure what had gotten into him . . .

Or what got to you?

Jack pushed the thought away. Nope. Not going there.

"Can I —"

"Change out of your swimsuit? I think that's a great plan."

"Uncle *Jack.*"

Jack never ceased to be amazed how a little girl could turn three syllables into six. "How about this? The last person upstairs has to clean Bitsy's cage tonight?"

Lily squealed and Jack gave her a three-second lead when her feet hit the sidewalk.

One crisis averted.

Until he reached the bottom of the stairs.

At first glance, Jack thought one of Bert's

granddaughters had stopped by for a visit. But the petite brunette with Bert and Evie looked to be in her midtwenties instead of her teens.

Lily suddenly lost interest in the competition. "Evie!"

"Did you have fun at the pool?" Evie swept his niece into a hug.

"Uncle Jack and I ate at Quigley's too. We had a hamburger and French fries." Lily patted her stomach. "And hot fudge sundaes."

"I love Quigley's." The young woman smiled at Jack, and good manners dictated that he stop for a moment.

"Jack, this is Maggie McClain." Evie made the introductions. "Maggie, Jack Vale. He's restoring the first floor of the building."

Now Jack connected the name with the face.

"Garden girl." Jack held out his hand.

Maggie laughed, her grip surprisingly strong for a person who couldn't weigh more than a hundred pounds. "That works for me."

"This young woman has big plans, Jack," Bert announced. "She wants me to teach a class about cooking with herbs."

Jack glanced at Evie. One look at her face and he knew who was responsible for bringing the two women together.

"Bert is going to teach a lot of classes." Maggie began to tick them on her fingers. "How to preserve vegetables. Natural ways to get rid of cut worms. One hundred and one things you can do with a zucchini . . ."

"Bread is number one on the list, and I'm going upstairs to make a loaf right now." Bert smiled down at Lily. "I could use a helper."

Lily whirled around, a pleading look in her eyes. "Uncle Jack?"

"All right. I've got some work to do downstairs tonight anyway —" Jack paused until the squeal died out. "You have to change your clothes and hang your wet swimsuit . . ." He was talking to the air.

"Up."

Maggie chuckled. "Your daughter is adorable."

Jack didn't bother to correct her. "It was nice meeting you, Maggie."

"Same here. I'm sure we'll see each other again." Maggie smiled at Bert. "You inspired me! I'm going to go home, fire up my computer, and figure out where a potting shed will fit."

Jack wasn't sure how it happened, but suddenly he and Evie were standing on the sidewalk alone.

"Thanks, Evie."

"I didn't do anything but introduce them."

"This is going to be good for Bert. I knew she had a few plants growing on her balcony, but I had no idea we had a master gardener living upstairs."

"Bert mentioned that gardening was something she and her husband used to do together. She misses it."

And Evie missed Max.

"I better get to work." Jack took a step toward the door. "If Bert is going to keep Lily busy for a few hours this evening, I'll have time to put another coat of stain on the baseboards."

Evie didn't move.

"So . . . I'll see you tomorrow." Jack tossed the words casually over his shoulder as he walked away.

He could feel Evie watching him as he fumbled with the key and unlocked the door.

Forget the paintbrush. Where was his crowbar?

The door snapped shut and Jack expelled a breath he didn't realize he'd been holding.

"Jack?"

He closed his eyes.

Evie had followed him inside.

CHAPTER 30

Evie should have taken the hint and left. Especially after Jack's second not-so-subtle attempt to get rid of her.

He slowly turned to face her, his expression so wary that Evie blurted out the question that had been rolling around in her head the past few days.

"Did I do something to offend you?"

"No." Too quick. Almost as if Jack had anticipated the question. "I've just got a lot on my mind."

"The other night, when Ryan stopped by to talk to you, did it have something to do with Travis? Is that why you seemed uncomfortable at the party today? Because Ryan was there?"

A shadow passed through Jack's eyes and he pivoted away from her, leaving her standing there as he strode to the back of the room.

It was so unlike Jack that fear propelled

Evie forward.

"Why won't you tell me what's wrong? Did he bring up your record?"

Evie wished she could take back the question when Jack spun around. "My *record*?"

"Dan . . . told me that you were arrested a few years ago."

"Wow." Jack stared at her. "It wasn't a few years ago. It was *ten.* And the charges filed against me were dismissed the next day. Trav got into a fight after his band played in a club one night, and it turned into a free-for-all. I got there when the chairs and tables started flying around — which happened to be five minutes before the police showed up and hauled everyone to jail. Once they sorted out the lies from the truth, the charges against me were dismissed. But I suppose Dan didn't mention that, did he?"

"It doesn't matter." Evie wished she hadn't brought it up. "I told Dan the past is in the past."

"Is it, Evie?"

"What is that supposed to mean?"

"Nothing," Jack muttered. "And no — Ryan didn't bring up my brief but apparently memorable relationship with the Milwaukee PD the other night. He knew that all he had to do was tell Moretti and it would get back to you."

318

"Don't be upset with Dan. He's always been protective of me. He and Max —"

"I get it." Jack cut her off. "And I'm not upset with Dan either."

"Then . . . it's me you're angry with." Evie swallowed hard. "I did something. That's why you didn't want me to go with you and Lily to Sandy Point today."

Jack shoved his hands in his pockets and looked away. The tight set of his jaw a signal the conversation was over.

"All right." It was so not all right, but Evie gave up anyway. "I-I'll let you get back to work."

She turned to leave but suddenly Jack was there, in front of her, blocking her path.

"Do you really want to know why I didn't want to go to the river with you today?"

The turbulence in his eyes should have sent her running for the door, but Evie took a step toward him instead.

"Yes."

"You were born and raised in Banister Falls, Evie. There isn't one place in this town — in this whole *county* — you haven't been. Not one place that doesn't remind you of —" Jack's ragged exhale replaced whatever he'd been about to say.

Evie stood rooted in place as she silently filled in the blank.

319

"You're wrong." She managed to push the words out even though her mouth had gone dry. "There is one place I haven't been."

"And where is that?"

"Here."

"Here," Jack repeated. "In a run-down apartment building with stained carpeting and paper-thin walls and balconies that overlook the Dumpsters in the alley." He choked on a laugh. "Great. That's just . . . thanks for that, Evie."

Jack had talked about his past, about Travis's struggles with addiction, but this was the first time she'd ever heard bitterness taint his voice.

"I *like* it here," she whispered.

"Right."

"I don't care about the stains on the carpeting or the walls. I like making spaghetti and talking about things that mean something and laughing."

And twirling.

Jack frowned. "Max —"

"Worked a lot." The weight of that truth still felt heavy. "Do you know what the other firefighters called him? *Max Will.* He was the first one to sign up for overtime. The first one to volunteer for additional training. I'd promised Max that I would support his career, so I didn't want to complain.

"On the weekends he played basketball with the guys or worked out at the gym. Max had a stressful job, and I knew it was important that he stay in shape. He was always in motion. He lived for that rush of adrenaline, and you don't get that when you're pacing the floor with a newborn baby."

"You had Cody right away, didn't you?"

Jack's expression changed, softened, and Evie nodded.

"I found out I was pregnant two months after we got married. We hadn't planned on having a family so soon. It was a lot of pressure on Max. He was anxious to prove himself, and he wanted to be the youngest member of the crew to get a promotion. I knew why he put in extra hours at work. But sometimes . . ."

Max had been restless at home. He'd talked to Danny and the guys at the station more than he talked to her.

Evie had fallen head over heels in love with Max at the age of fifteen, but even when they were chasing each other around the neighborhood and sharing Popsicles in the Morettis' sandbox, she'd been drawn to his outgoing personality, so different from her own. If the old adage was true that opposites attract, they were destined to be together.

But there were times — times when Evie had been alone too many evenings in a row — when she'd wondered if Max regretted getting married so soon. Or if she was one more thing he'd conquered and then lost interest in.

"Evie?" Jack prompted softly.

"I know Max loved Cody and me, but sometimes I wish he would have enjoyed the 'nows' instead of always focusing on the 'somedays.' Like you."

Jack looked as stunned as if Evie had clobbered him over the head with a two-by-four.

Saying the words out loud, even if they were true, felt like a betrayal of Max's memory somehow. "I shouldn't have said that." Evie ducked her head and tried to get around him.

Jack was faster.

He caught her shoulders and turned her around, walked her backward, his hands forming a warm buffer between her and the wall. And then he was kissing her. Not a tentative first kiss. A kiss that was searching and sweet and a little untamed. A kiss that told Evie he'd been thinking about it for a long time.

She wound her arms around Jack's neck and felt the rapid beat of his heart. Heard a low groan catch in his throat when her fingers tangled in his hair.

And then, just as suddenly as Jack had taken her in his arms, he broke the kiss and his lips grazed a path down her neck. And then —

Thump. Thump. Thump.

Jack was pounding his forehead against the wall. The sound was so unexpected that a laugh slipped out before Evie could stop it.

"What are you *doing*?"

"That's a good question," Jack muttered against her hair. "I didn't mean for that to happen, Evie."

Didn't mean . . . Evie melted against the wall. Not that her knees would have been strong enough to hold her upright.

Maybe it *had* been an impulsive kiss.

Jack tucked a strand of hair behind her ear. "I'm sorry."

Even worse. Because Evie wasn't.

"It's okay. I . . . I understand."

No, Jack didn't think she did.

Evie was trying to let him off the hook. And by the time she got home, Jack knew she would find a way to blame herself for his total lack of control.

He hadn't planned to kiss her, but there'd

been moments — more than a few lately — that he'd imagined it. The real thing had been a hundred times better. The way Evie had melted against him, the scent of her hair, the taste of her lips.

But the reason Jack hadn't kissed Evie was because he was afraid that if he took her in his arms, Max would still be the one in her head.

Evie had shared something about her marriage that Jack suspected no one else knew. And by sharing a glimpse of her heart . . . maybe it meant there was room for someone else.

Room for *him.*

The thought blew him away.

Evie slipped underneath Jack's arm, but there was no way he was letting go when she'd just let him in.

"Evie . . . wait."

She pulled free, the fingers that had sifted through his hair a moment ago knotted together at her waist.

"I'm not sure what to do right now." Jack had thought apologizing was a good idea until he'd seen the stricken expression on Evie's face.

"Neither am I."

They stared at each other.

"I like spending time with you." Crown

him king of the understatement. "But I'm thinking I skipped a few critical steps. Like two or three dates before I finally scraped up the courage to kiss you good night." Jack blew out a sigh. "Do you have any idea how long it's been since I've even asked —"

"Yes."

"Yes you know how long it's been?"

A shy smile teased the corners of Evie's lips, and it took every ounce of Jack's self-control not to reach for her again.

"Yes, I'll go on a date with you."

CHAPTER 31

The first thing Evie saw when she sat down at her desk on Monday morning was the Post-it note stuck to her computer screen.

Parking lot. 4 o'clock.

It had been difficult to concentrate the rest of the day.

At three forty-five she finished her outline for an upcoming meeting with the women's ministry team from another church and spent the next fifteen minutes trying to subdue her rising panic.

A date. With Jack.

She rose and walked over to the window. Adjusted the vase of fresh flowers on the table.

"Those are pretty." Pauline poked her head in the doorway. "You don't usually see wild flowers made into a bouquet."

You did if the flowers had been picked from the field across the parking lot.

Evie felt her cheeks get warm. Maybe Pauline would attribute it to the sunlight streaming through the window.

"I've been swamped with phone calls or I would have popped in sooner. Do you have time to look over the agenda for the annual business meeting? Pastor wanted me to make sure everyone who's involved in ministry has enough time to present an update."

"Now?"

Pauline glanced at the clock on the wall by Evie's desk. "It should only take fifteen or twenty minutes."

"Tomorrow would work better."

"Oh." Pauline blinked. "Okay. I didn't see anything on your calendar so I assumed you were free."

"Not today. I" — Evie hesitated — "have plans."

"Tomorrow it is then." Curiosity burned bright in the secretary's eyes. "Does eleven o'clock work for you?"

"That will be great."

Two more people stopped Evie as she made her way to the parking lot. It was almost quarter after four by the time she slid into the front seat of her car.

Another note was attached to the steering wheel.

Jack was enjoying this. She just knew it.

327

Swimsuit. Shoes (no heels)

Swimsuit? The last time Evie had worn one in public, Cody had been in elementary school.

She turned onto Rosewood Court, expecting to see Jack's pickup parked in her driveway. It wasn't, so she unlocked the door and went upstairs to find her swimsuit. And shoes without heels.

The first mission was easier.

She pulled a pair of shorts and a T-shirt over her swimsuit, gathered her hair in a low ponytail, and bypassed the full-length mirror in the corner on her way out the door.

While she was debating whether she should pack something to eat, the low rumble of an engine outside drew her to the kitchen window. Jack hopped down from the cab of his pickup. He looked as good in a pair of charcoal-gray athletic shorts and a T-shirt as he did in paint-spattered jeans.

Heat shot through Evie. Desire was another emotion she'd thought had died with Max, but apparently it had only been lying dormant. Coaxed back to life when Jack had drawn her into the warm circle of his arms, his breath mingling with hers.

Evie opened the refrigerator and let the

rush of cool air strip the blush from her cheeks before she grabbed two bottles of iced tea and went outside.

Jack opened the passenger-side door. "Ready?"

"Where's Lily?"

"I arranged for her to stay with Cody and Raine a little longer. They said something about karaoke."

"I'm terrible at karaoke."

"That's not what I heard." Jack winked at her.

"I can't remember the last time I wore tennis shoes." Evie looked down at her feet.

"You make them look good." Jack walked around the front of the truck to the driver's side. He pulled the door shut, sealing them inside, and the butterflies in Evie's stomach made their presence known again.

A date. With Jack.

Evie spoke at conferences and retreats several times a year, sharing her story, and she never felt this nervous.

"Where are we going?"

Jack smiled.

"You'll find out when we get there."

Jack hoped this wasn't a mistake.

The breeze whispered in the leaves and there were golden places where the sunlight

329

breached the canopy above their heads as he and Evie followed an overgrown path through the woods.

Cody had given him directions when he'd dropped Lily off that morning, but suddenly Jack was questioning the wisdom of bringing Evie here. To a place where the memories of her husband went as deep as the roots of the oak tree that shaded the riverbank.

But he hadn't been able to get it out of his mind. The look on Evie's face when Dan had been talking about the rope swing.

Longing.

Evie hopped over a branch and set her ponytail swinging between her shoulder blades. "It's about fifty feet beyond those trees."

"What is?" Jack played dumb.

"Sandy Point." Evie tossed a look over her shoulder. "Unless there's a restaurant around here that I don't know about."

Because a restaurant is the usual choice for a romantic first date, Vale. You brick.

Fortunately, there was still time for that. Maybe more than he'd planned if this whole thing backfired.

He followed Evie through a break in the trees and sucked in a breath. She heard and a smile backlit her eyes.

"It's beautiful here, isn't it?"

Jack managed a nod.

You do like to show off, don't You, God?

Sapphire sky and trees a vivid, feed-the-soul green were more than enough, but all that beauty was painted on the surface of the water too.

"I wish I'd had access to a place like this when Travis and I were kids." In their neighborhood, the only thing green was the stoplight on the corner.

"Look." Evie pointed to a thick rope dangling from the branches of an enormous birch tree. "So much for hoping that Cody was teasing me about the rope swing."

"I wasn't."

Jack reached for the rope, and Evie reached for him. "You aren't really going to try it out, are you?"

"No."

"Thank good —"

"You are."

"Me!" Evie backed away from him. "No."

If Jack had seen disbelief, confusion, or even outright panic on her face, he would have let go of the rope. Let go of the whole idea.

But there it was again. The flash of longing Jack had seen the day before.

He'd guessed right.

"This is why you told me to wear my swimsuit?"

"Yup."

"I thought we were taking Lily to the pool."

"We'll bring her along on our second date."

If there *was* a second date.

Evie looked at the rope swing and then the river. Jack could see her working it out, the number of steps it would take to get to the edge, where she might land in the middle.

And then she kicked off her tennies, shucked off her T-shirt and shorts. Even though Evie wore a conservative one-piece swimsuit underneath her clothing, Jack had to look away for a second and pull his unruly thoughts back in line.

"It's higher than I remember." Her gaze traveled upward, pausing for a split second on each knot in the rope until she got to the one lashed to the trunk of the tree.

"You don't have to prove anything to me, Evie. You don't even have to prove anything to yourself. The only reason I want you to try out that rope swing is because you know you'll be laughing when you come back up to the surface."

"*You'll* be laughing."

"Probably."

A smile ignited the gold dust in her eyes. "I love your laugh."

And then she was gone.

Jack's breath cinched in his lungs as Evie ran toward the end of the point. Suddenly he understood why Dan and Max had discouraged her from trying out the rope swing.

What if there was something underneath the surface of the water she couldn't see? A rock? A stump? What if she wasn't a strong swimmer? What if she couldn't swim at all?

Yeah, that would have been a really good question to ask before he'd let her grab hold of the rope.

Jack started after Evie, almost hoping she would lose her nerve and stop when she reached the spot where the bank ended and the river began.

"Evie —"

Too late.

Her feet left the ground and she sailed over the water without a sound. The only thing Jack could hear was the thump of his heart. And the creak of protest from the branch as it bore Evie's weight.

The rope went taut when she was in the middle of the river. For a moment, Jack thought she was going to hang on. End up back in his arms.

But she let go.

Pride swelled up, overriding Jack's initial panic. He lifted his phone and snapped Evie's picture a split second before she disappeared under the surface of the water.

And then he dove in after her.

Evie scooped a handful of wet hair from her cheek and blinked away the water streaming into her eyes. Her nose burned, she'd swallowed a mouthful of river water on the way down, and her palms still stung from gripping the rope . . . and she was laughing.

The current tugged at her, beckoning her to follow.

A strong arm suddenly slipped around her waist, holding her in place. She braced her hands on Jack's bare shoulders. Tiny beads of water glistened on his face and divided his lashes into small spikes.

"I did it! Did you see me?"

"I had my eyes closed the whole time."

"Jack."

"You did good."

"I was terrified."

"And yet here you are."

Yes. Here she was.

Without thinking, Evie closed the distance between them and brushed a kiss against

Jack's forehead.

The flash of heat in his eyes sent a shiver running through her. Raised goose bumps on her arms.

"Time to go back." Jack's voice wasn't quite steady, and then he ducked underneath the water. When he surfaced a few seconds later, he was ten feet away.

And Evie felt closer to him than ever.

She rolled onto her side and swam leisurely back to shore.

Jack was waiting in the shallow water, holding out a beach towel. Neat rows of penguins wearing pink tutus.

He caught her smile as he draped the towel around her shoulders. "Lily let me borrow it."

"She knew about this?"

"Are you kidding? Lily made me tell her everything I had planned for the evening."

"There's more?" Evie couldn't resist teasing him a little.

"I haven't gone on a date for a long time, but I am aware that food is usually part of it." Jack picked up another towel — a more masculine green-and-blue plaid — and rubbed it against his bare torso. "What do you think about dinner at the bistro?"

What did she think about dinner at the bistro?

In her mind's eye Evie saw white linen tablecloths, candles, and fresh flowers. The perfect place for a romantic first date.

If that was your idea of perfect.

"You're not saying anything." Jack looked a little uncertain now. "Is there somewhere else you'd rather go?"

"Actually . . . I'm more in the mood for spaghetti."

CHAPTER 32

Pauline intercepted Evie as she walked into the church foyer the next morning.

"Gertrude is waiting in your office, and Pastor wants to see you. He promised it would only take a minute."

"Thanks, Pauline." Evie stifled a yawn.

The secretary tipped her head. "I was just going down to the kitchen to get Gertrude a cup of coffee. Looks like you could use one too."

"That sounds great. I stayed up a little late last night."

"What were you watching?"

Evie smiled. "A baby."

She'd been at Jack's apartment until almost midnight, wearing a path around the living room with Amber Lynn.

Andy's wife, Serena, had shown up shortly after dinner, crying almost as hard as the baby cradled in her arms. Evie sent her back upstairs with orders to take a long soak in

337

the tub. When two hours went by and Serena hadn't returned, Evie handed Amber Lynn over to Jack for a few minutes while she ran upstairs to check on her. She'd found Serena curled up in a threadbare recliner, sound asleep. Evie left her that way.

She and Jack took turns rocking Amber Lynn, singing and even telling her knock-knock jokes, but the baby hadn't stopped crying until Jack — in a moment of what was either sheer desperation or pure genius — had taken out his saxophone. Amber Lynn had drifted off to sleep as Jack played the last note of "Summertime."

"A baby." Pauline's eyes twinkled. "Practicing for being a grandma? I'll make the coffee high octane."

"That would be great." Evie turned down the hallway and heard muffled voices on the other side of Keith's door. She knocked once and waited.

"Come on in, Evie!"

Evie pushed open the door, her gaze cutting from Pastor Keith to the man standing by the window.

"Harvey."

"Good morning, Evie!" The custodian grinned. "What's going on around here? I walked into my room a few minutes ago, and there's not a Post-it note in sight."

338

"You — you're back." *Early.*

"My sister decided to take a shift." Harvey tucked his hands in the front pockets of his tan Dockers. "She talked to her boss, and he agreed to give her two weeks off. So here I am."

"That's great." Evie injected the necessary amount of enthusiasm into her voice before she looked at Keith. "Does Jack know?"

Keith shook his head. "He hasn't come into work yet, but he knew the job was temporary going in . . . and under the circumstances, I don't think he'll mind."

What circumstances, Evie wanted to ask. Had Keith seen the story in the newspaper about Jack's brother too? Or had Dan or Ryan said something?

She glanced at Harvey. "I'm sure you're going to want a day or two to unpack. Get settled in at home before you dive back into work."

"That's not necessary." Harvey flexed his fingers. "I'm looking forward to putting things back the way they were."

"We won't keep you any longer, Evie." Keith looked a little confused, as if he was wondering why she didn't look happier about the idea. "Pauline said Gertrude is waiting for you in your office."

"And I have to straighten up mine." Harvey's voice dropped a notch. "The building looks good, but the guy you hired turned it into a *lounge.* Radio *and* a coffeepot . . ."

He was still listing Jack's quirks when Evie closed the door behind her. Her feet felt heavy, like her shoes were still weighted down with sand, when she returned to her office.

"Evangeline." Gertrude sat in the chair by the window, wearing a linen pantsuit the same shade of red as her hair. The ensemble reminded Evie of a poppy in full bloom. "I ran into Harvey a few minutes ago. You must be thrilled he's back." Fortunately, she didn't wait for Evie to respond. "I wanted to give you something before I leave."

"Leave?"

"For Texas. The movers will be here on Friday."

"Already?" Evie dropped into the chair across from her. "What about your house?"

"Sold. God took care of that detail before I even got around to asking Him about it." Gertrude took a dainty sip from the cup of coffee that Pauline had delivered and left a half moon of Dazzling in Crimson on the rim. "I called the realtor last week, and she offered to buy it right then and there. It turns out she'd been looking for a house

340

with a lot of room." Gert reached into her purse and withdrew an envelope. "I want to give a gift to women's ministries. It isn't much . . . loaves and fishes, really . . . but God loves to take the smallest things and multiply them."

"Gert —"

The envelope flapped in front of Evie's nose, waving away her protest. "I'm just doing what God told me to do, Evangeline. If you have a problem with that, I suggest you take it up with Him."

"I don't know what to say, Gert. Thank you."

"No, thank you." Gertrude reached across the table and squeezed Evie's hand. "You're the one who gave me the courage to step out in faith."

Evie couldn't tell her the truth. That it was so much easier to encourage others to step out in faith while she stayed put, cheering them on from the sidelines.

"I'm still going to miss you." She wrapped her arms around Gertrude and gathered her close, breathing in the familiar, comforting scents of Final Net hairspray and Chanel N°5.

"I'll miss you too. Now" — Gert patted Evie's back — "I have a mani-pedi scheduled for nine o'clock, and if you get me going, I'm going to need my makeup touched up too."

The statement was classic Gert, and Evie laughed. She slipped the envelope into her desk drawer and followed Gertrude into the hall.

The door to Pastor Keith's office was open a few inches. Keith stood at the window with his back to Evie, talking to someone on his cell phone. Talking to Jack? Letting him know that he didn't have to come into work?

On her way to the kitchen to refill her cup with Pauline's "high octane," Evie peeked into the custodian's room.

Harvey spotted her and waved. "Come on in, Evie!"

There was no sign of Jack, but Harvey was in the process of filling a cardboard box with his things.

"I wonder how this got in here." Harvey picked up Jack's yellow coffee mug. "Looks like it belongs to one of the Sunday school kids."

"Jack's niece made it for him." Evie was suddenly overtaken by an irresistible urge to snatch the box off the table and put everything back where it belonged.

"Not sure what he did to my table." Evie jumped a little when Harvey thumped the wooden top. "Looked fine the way it was."

Fine.

Evie's shoulders twitched. That word? It didn't sit so well anymore. "It's something Jack likes to do."

Harvey folded Jack's denim shirt neatly in half and set it on top of the box. "Keith said he was going to call him. Do you suppose he'll be back to get his stuff sometime today?"

"I can take it to him." Evie crossed the room and rescued Jack's possessions before they ended up next to the box marked Lost and Found.

"So . . . we've got the garden walk coming up on Saturday." Harvey worked free the Mason jar that Jack had used to prop the window open, then closed it, sealing off the breeze. "Ice cream social afterward, same as usual?"

"Same as usual." That didn't sit well either.

"Good. I'll let you get back to work. I'm sure you've got a hundred things to do."

More than a hundred. And none of them as important as talking to Jack.

"I'll see you later." Evie tucked her empty coffee cup into the corner of the box and carried it down the hall to the kitchen.

Jack was walking through the back door,

talking into the cell phone pressed against his ear. He caught her eye and smiled.

"I'll stop by and pick it up about four thirty."

Evie caught the tail end of the conversation before Jack ended the call and slipped the phone into his pocket. He glanced down at the box in Evie's arms. "I don't mind if you borrow my shirt, but I'm not sure it goes with the skirt you're wearing."

He didn't know.

"Harvey's back."

"Okay." Jack blew out a sigh. "I guess I missed that memo."

"So did I." Evie wished Harvey would have called the church and told them he was on his way home. "I encouraged him to take a few more days off, but he's anxious to get back to work. I'm really sorry."

"Not your fault. It's sooner than I expected, but the landlord is anxious for me to finish the first floor." Jack's lips quirked in a half smile. "I'll have time for Andy now too."

"Andy?"

"I ran into him when I was leaving. He asked me to explain a text he got from Serena when he was at work last night."

"What did it say?"

"Take saxophone lessons."

Evie was laughing when Dan walked in. He pulled up short at the sight of them, his eyes narrowing when they locked on Jack.

"Dan." Evie stepped away from Jack, opening up a wider space between them. Jack's hand dropped to his side.

"Keith told Dad there's a section of fence missing, so I offered to drop off the lumber on my way to work." Dan's gaze bounced from Evie to Jack. "Where do you want me to put it?"

"You'll have to ask Harvey." Jack turned back to Evie. "I can take this now."

The weight of the box lifted when Jack eased it from Evie's grip, but the one on her heart felt even heavier when he turned and walked away.

CHAPTER 33

Jack grabbed his toolbox and headed down to the first floor. Lily had skipped off with Bert for her next baking lesson after they'd finished eating supper, giving him a chance to spend a few hours with a crowbar.

Better to punch out a wall instead of banging your head against it.

Oh wait. He'd already done that. After he'd kissed Evie.

Whack.

"It's not all about you, Vale," he muttered. "Evie isn't the kind of person who's going to hold your hand while you're strolling through the halls of Hope Community."

Still, it had hurt when she'd backed away from him. Like she didn't want to give Moretti the wrong impression about their relationship.

"And what exactly" — *whack* — "is our relationship?"

It suddenly occurred to Jack that maybe

Evie didn't want to be seen in public with him. Was that why she'd turned down his invitation to Marie's Bistro the night before?

"Should we be concerned he's talking to himself, Ryan?" Dan Moretti sauntered through the door.

"I thought he was talking to the crowbar."

"Six of one, half dozen of the other, as Grandma Moretti used to say."

Great. Just what Jack needed. A cop *and* a firefighter.

"Did I accidentally dial 911?" Jack patted the phone in his back pocket.

"Nah . . . We're off duty." Ryan's gaze swept over the interior of the room and lit on Jack. "You've made quite a bit of progress."

Dan folded his arms across his chest. "In a short amount of time."

Why did Jack get the feeling they weren't talking about the building?

He gave the wall another whack just because it felt good.

"The wiring isn't up to code." Dan tipped his head toward the gaping hole in the ceiling, where Jack had removed one of the light fixtures the day before.

"It will be." He cast a meaningful look at the door.

Which — big surprise — they totally ignored.

Ryan Tate prowled the perimeter of the room, inspecting the exposed walls as he made his way over to Jack.

"Look, I know what you're going to say —"

The door swung open again and three more guys walked in.

Dan's dad and two of his brothers. Jack recognized them from the engagement party.

The crowbar fell to his side. "Should I be flattered that you rounded up an entire posse to run me out of town?"

"Run you out of town?" Dan picked up a hammer and tested its weight. "We're here to help."

"Help."

Dan grinned. "See, all you had to do was ask."

John Moretti, a man roughly the size and shape of a skid-steer, strode up to Jack and clapped him on the back. "Put us to work, Vale. We're as good at following orders as we are at putting up drywall." His voice dropped to a whisper. "Just keep Trent away from anything with a blade. He's a *lawyer*."

"I heard that, Dad." Dan's brother shrugged off his white dress shirt, revealing a T-shirt with a cartoon shark and the words TRUST ME stamped underneath it.

"What are you listening to, man?" Ryan had traced the music to the corner of the room, where Jack's iPod dangled from a rusty nail.

"Michael Brecker. One of the greatest jazz musicians of all time."

"Can't say I've heard any jazz at all, but it isn't bad."

Ryan strapped on Jack's tool belt.

Was nothing sacred?

"Vale." Something nudged Jack's back. Something like the business end of a cordless drill.

Dan's brother — Will — stood less than a foot away, spinning it on one finger the way a cowboy would spin a pistol in a cheesy Western.

"You better start assigning jobs, or we'll be forced to pick the stuff that looks like it'll be the most fun." Will was eyeing Jack's crowbar when he said it.

Okay, then.

Jack was used to working alone or with Coop, but he put Dan and his father in charge of removing the old drywall and sent Trent and Will down to Lily's "dancing room" to peel the fake wood paneling off the walls.

For the next hour, the only accompaniment to Brecker's sax was the occasional high-pitched squeal of the circular saw and the steady thump of the hammers on percussion.

At this rate, Jack would be finished with the major stuff ahead of schedule.

Dan's father plunged his hand into the cooler Will had lugged in and pulled out two bottles of water. He cracked one open and handed it to Jack. "Here. You look like you could use one of these."

"Thanks." Jack took a swig of water and let it wash away the sawdust lining his throat.

"I've lived in Banister Falls all my life, and I don't think I've ever been in this building before."

"Evie said it was a fabric store."

"What's it going to be?"

At the moment? Jack's only source of income. "I'm not sure. The owner wants to sell it when I'm done."

A frown creased John's forehead. "Aren't there apartments upstairs?"

"Six."

"You've been working on those too?"

"Off the clock." Jack caught the water trickling down his chin with the back of his hand.

"And off your timecard?"

"I'm getting a break in the rent, so it all evens out in the end."

"Uh-huh." John gave him one last, long look before he walked away.

For some reason, Jack felt like he'd just passed a pop quiz of some kind.

"Yoo-hoo, Jack! Is it safe to come in?" Bert reached a hand around the door he'd propped open to coax in the fickle evening breeze and waved a white dish towel. She didn't look the least bit surprised to see the group of men milling around the room.

"Lily and I want to share the fruit of our labor."

"Strawberry pie!" Lily followed Bert inside, a dusting of flour on her nose and a bounce in her step.

"Break time!" Ryan peeled off his safety glasses and tossed them onto the workbench. "I love fruit. Especially when it's inside a crust and topped with ice cream."

"Then you're in luck." Bert swept some of Jack's tools aside and set a wicker picnic basket on the counter. "Because Lily and I just happen to have some of that too."

"What do you say, boss?" Will Moretti was eyeing up the pies. "Do we get a break?"

Boss. Jack rolled his eyes. "Take five. There's a sink in the kitchen."

Lily opened a smaller basket and lifted out a stack of napkins and a bouquet of plastic forks while the crew filed down the hallway to the kitchen to wash their hands.

Jack paused to drop a kiss on the top of his niece's head. "They look delicious, Lil."

"We made one for Evie too."

Just hearing Evie's name sent a rush of longing through Jack. "Evie had a meeting tonight. I don't think she's planning to stop over."

"I'll see her tomorrow, though, right?"

"I'm sure you will." Evie's affection for Lily was the one thing Jack *was* sure about.

"Can you grab that bench over there, Jack?" Bert pulled what looked like a metal garden trowel from the pocket of her housecoat and began to transfer slices of pie from the tin to paper plates. "Maybe someone wants to sit down."

Jack dragged it closer but the men ignored it, bellying up to the counter like the Friday night regulars at Eddie's bar.

Dan, whether by accident or design, ended up standing next to Jack. Providing an opportunity to voice the question that had been plaguing Jack all evening. Hanging drywall together didn't mean that Evie's friends approved of him.

"Something on your mind, Vale?" Dan

352

turned his fork into a blade and scraped the last of the crumbs and filling into the pool of melted ice cream on his plate.

"Wondering why you're here. When you showed up, I thought you'd be grabbing pitchforks, not hammers."

"Number one, you're a brother in Christ." Dan shrugged. "Brothers look out for each other."

Not blood brothers, but a deeper bond. A bond that stretched into eternity.

For the second time in the space of a few hours, Jack felt the warmth of God's presence. He was the one used to taking care of people. His mom. Travis. Lily.

But just when Jack was feeling weak, God showed up.

Reminded Jack that he wasn't alone.

Amazing grace.

He didn't deserve it. Could never earn it.

But God always knew just when Jack needed it.

"And number two . . ." Dan paused, clearing his throat. "This morning . . . at the church. I haven't heard Evie laugh like that for a long time."

CHAPTER 34

"Thank you for agreeing to meet with us tonight." Joanna Mason smiled at Evie. "We heard how successful the fall women's conference at Hope Community was last year, and we're thrilled you agreed to be our keynote speaker."

"You're welcome." Evie tried not to glance at the grandfather clock in the corner of Joanna's living room. Again. Because of an incident involving the woman's twin eleven-year-old boys, the neighbor's birdbath, and a can of spray paint, the meeting with Joanna's ministry team had gone later than planned.

"I know everyone will be inspired by your story," Joanna continued.

Her story. Of course. But for some reason, Evie had to ask anyway.

"Which part?"

Joanna and the woman sitting next to her on the sofa exchanged a quick glance.

"You lost your husband at such a young age," Joanna said carefully. "But you continued to trust God through the grieving process."

Joanna's friend bobbed her head. "And look where you are now."

A loud crash made the ceiling fan above their heads tremble.

"I knew it was too quiet." Joanna sighed. "I think that concludes our meeting for tonight, ladies. I'll e-mail the minutes to everyone tomorrow, and I'll see you next week!"

She dashed toward the stairs.

The women chuckled as they gathered up their things — swapping stories about their own children — but Evie didn't linger.

She checked her phone when she got into the car. A text from Cody, inviting her over for a cookout on Sunday afternoon. No missed calls.

Jack knew she had a meeting, but Evie couldn't shake the feeling his silence meant more than that. Couldn't shake the feeling she'd made a terrible mistake when she'd stepped away from him after Dan walked into the church kitchen.

She couldn't even explain why she'd done it.

The first star winked overhead as she got

out of her car and collected the mail from the box at the end of the driveway. A large envelope was propped against the front door, and she bent down to pick it up.

Too quiet. Too dark.

Evie hung her purse on the wooden coat rack, a part of her still expecting to find Diva asleep on the couch when she walked into the living room.

The clock chimed seven times as she sorted through the mail. When she got to the padded envelope at the bottom of the stack, she flipped it over to look for a return address.

Nothing. No name or address at all.

Evie slid her finger underneath the seal. Tissue paper crackled as she peeled back the flap and pulled out what felt like a picture frame.

Raine had mentioned that the photographer had called, letting her and Cody know the proofs from the wedding were ready. Anticipation made Evie clumsy, and she almost dropped the whole thing on the floor in her haste to unwrap it.

It took a moment to absorb the fact that Cody and Raine weren't in the picture. Another to realize that the person in the photograph was *her*. And she was . . . flying.

Jack had taken it at Sandy Point. Captured the moment when she'd let go of the rope. She was suspended in midair. Arms lifted toward the sky. A blur of light and laughter.

Evie traced the edge of the frame, reliving the feel of the wind in her face as she ran toward the river. The ground giving way underneath her. The laughter that loosened the knot of fear. Loosened her grip on the rope.

And then surfaced to Jack's smile.

Evie pressed the photograph against her chest.

After Jack had found out he was now unemployed, he'd taken the time to print the photograph, wrap it in tissue paper, and deliver it to her front door.

Evie crossed the room to the fireplace. The photograph of Max in his turnout gear, taken his first day at Second Street Station, held a permanent spot on the end of the mantle.

At twenty-five, Max was a slightly older version of Cody. Tall and handsome, white-blond hair and a hint of mischief in his eyes. More boy than man.

She'd been drawn to his confidence. Leaned on his strength.

And when he'd died, it felt like something inside of Evie had died too.

"Look where you are now."

Joanna's friend's words came back to Evie, shining a light in the darkest corner of her heart.

She was in the same place she'd been thirteen years ago when Max had died. A moment that had somehow defined her life. Defined *her*.

She wasn't Evie — she was Max Bennett's widow.

Making Cody's dreams come true had become Evie's focus.

Encouraging women to take a step in faith while she made a safe place for herself inside the walls of Hope Community.

All this time, Evie had thought it was grief that had flash-frozen her heart. Kept her from moving forward. But it was fear.

And when she'd stepped away from Jack . . . that had been fear too.

She was afraid of the feelings Jack stirred inside of her, familiar and new all at the same time. She was afraid to let herself dream again because she and Max had had such big dreams. All those "somedays" cut short . . .

Evie slid the photograph on the mantel between the pictures of Max and Cody on his graduation day.

How had Jack known she'd always wanted

to try that silly rope swing?

Because Jack knew *her*. Maybe — and this was the scary part — better than she knew herself.

See, she was afraid of that too.

God . . . I need Your help. I'm afraid of everything. Loving. Losing. Making mistakes. Not making them. I don't know what to let go of . . . and what to keep.

The words poured out and Evie didn't realize she'd been twisting her wedding ring around and around on her finger until God answered.

Will you trust me, Evie?

Will.

Evie closed her eyes.

Because that's what it always came down to — an act of the will. Evie believed God could heal the past. She believed in heaven. But was she going to trust God with all the moments in between?

Yes.

Not a whisper. A battle cry.

And the fear loosened its grip and Evie knew exactly where her first steps would take her.

She took the stairs two at a time to her bedroom and changed into jeans and a T-shirt. Unhooked the bracelet on her wrist and reached for the porcelain jewelry box she'd found while browsing the aisles of the thrift shop on Bird Street. Max had pointed out the chip in the cover, but Evie had been drawn to the tiny porcelain bluebird perched inside of it, meant to hold a ring. He'd given it to her a few days later, on her sixteenth birthday.

Slowly Evie pulled off her wedding band, knowing she would never forget the day Max slipped the ring on her finger. The love they'd had for each other.

She also knew that Max, the boy who'd always been larger-than-life, so full of courage, wouldn't have wanted Evie to be held captive by fear after his death.

And that he would have liked the man who'd reminded Evie she was still alive.

The door opened and Jack glanced over his shoulder. Blinked, just to make sure he wasn't seeing things.

Seeing Evie in snug-fitting faded jeans, a Post-it note–pink T-shirt, and the tennis shoes she'd worn on the hike to Sandy Point.

Conversation ceased as she wove through the maze of guys and building supplies and stopped in front of him.

"Evie." Jack tried not to stare at the rhinestone — *rhinestone* — heart that almost completely covered the front of her shirt. "I didn't expect to see you tonight."

"I . . . forgot something."

Jack frowned, trying to remember if she'd left something in his apartment. "You did? What?"

"This." Evie went up on her tiptoes, anchored her hands on his shoulders, and kissed him.

Jack's hands instinctively molded to the curve of her waist. To keep himself upright.

As far as kisses went, it was appropriately rated G, especially given the fact they had an audience. But the soft-as-satin touch of Evie's lips ignited a flame inside Jack that would burn for a hundred years. Maybe two.

Lily's giggle brought Jack back to his senses. He felt Evie's smile against his lips right before they stepped apart. But her hand slid down his arm, and she wove her fingers through his, linking them together.

"Your cheeks are all pink, Uncle Jack!"

John Moretti grinned. "It is getting kind of warm in here." He pushed away from the table. "I think it's time to leave, boys."

"Or stay longer," Dan muttered.

Jack couldn't tell if the guy was teasing or not. He joined in the cleanup and followed the men as they filed toward the door. Dan was the last one, and Jack stretched out his hand.

"Thanks again for all your help tonight."

"Brothers, remember?" Dan gave him a smile and a cuff on the shoulder at the same time. "Vale —"

"Don't worry." Jack might be in way over his head when it came to his feelings for Evie, but he wasn't stupid. "Lily makes a great chaperone."

Dan's lips twitched. "Good, because I'd hate to have to break out the pitchfork."

Jack turned, and his eyes met Evie's across the room. Faded jeans, rhinestone shirt, and the memory of the kiss still simmering in her blue, blue eyes, she took his breath away.

And she was here. With him.

Bert cleared her throat. "Lily, what do you say we take the leftover pie to Josh to celebrate the A he got on his geometry exam?"

"Can you braid my hair when I get back?" Lily wrapped her arms around Evie, tight as insulation on a pipe, and hugged her. "Uncle Jack tries but it looks crooked."

"Hey, that's only because I can't use my plumb line."

"I'll send her back down in a few minutes." Bert's eyes twinkled. "My arthritis is acting up today though." She patted her hip.

"We'll have to take the stairs pretty slow."

Uh-huh. Jack couldn't remember Bert mentioning she suffered from arthritis, but he was willing to go with it.

The moment they were alone, Jack drew Evie into his arms.

Touched an emerald-green rhinestone glued to the hem of her T-shirt.

"I cannot believe you did that." Jack's breath feathered against Evie's cheek. "When there were dozens of tools within reach that could have been used against me. Hammers. Wrenches. *Nail guns . . .*" He faked a shudder.

"That's kind of what I thought was happening when I recognized the vehicles parked in front of the building," Evie confessed.

"So you planned to rescue me?"

"I *planned* to kiss you." She peeked up at him through a fringe of gold-tipped lashes, and Jack's heart turned over in his chest. "And no one was going to get in my way."

"You gotta love a woman with a plan."

The smile that curved Evie's lips made Jack want to taste their sweetness all over again.

"Thank you for the photograph."

Jack had forgotten about the photograph. "You're not upset that I took it, are you?"

363

Evie shook her head. "My first thought was *Who is that?* And then I realized it was me. I wish . . ."

"Max could have seen you?"

"That I would have been brave enough to do it a long time ago."

CHAPTER 35

Jack's hands tightened on the curve of Evie's waist.

"Don't be so hard on yourself," he chided gently. "It doesn't mean you aren't brave. And just for the record, I almost had a heart attack when you grabbed that rope and took off."

"But you let me do it anyway." Evie cupped his jaw, every nerve ending in her body responding to the soft scrape of Jack's whiskers against her fingertips. "Thank you."

"You didn't really give me a chance to stop you." He folded his hand over hers and brought it to his lips. Stilled when he realized what was missing. "Your wedding ring . . ."

"It's in my jewelry box at home."

"Evie." Jack groaned. "Please tell me it wasn't because of me. I was being an idiot before. I was afraid people would always compare me to Max — that *you* would compare me to Max — and I'd never measure up —"

"Stop." Evie pressed her finger against Jack's lips. "I didn't take it off because of you — I did it for me. I guess I thought if I took the ring off, put it away, it meant I would be forgetting Max."

"You won't forget him, Evie. I don't *want* you to forget him. Max built a beautiful home for you, provided for you and Cody. Loved you." Regret flashed in Jack's eyes. "When I was that age, I wouldn't have been able to do any of those things. If anything, it makes me want to get down on my knees and thank God for bringing someone like Max Bennett into your life."

Evie could tell he meant every word, and she silently thanked God for bringing Jack into her life too.

A door snapped shut above them, and the patter of footsteps on the outside staircase let them know that Lily was coming back.

Jack's lips grazed her temple. "I told Dan she made a good chaperone," he whispered.

Evie didn't get a chance to ask him why the topic had come up in the first place, because Lily burst through the door, waving a hairbrush and a pink-and-white scrunchie.

"I'm ready!"

Jack released Evie — reluctantly — and she ducked her head to hide a smile. "Hop up on that stool by the counter, and I'll braid your hair while your Uncle Jack finishes cleaning up."

Lily obeyed, chatting about cutting up the strawberries for the pie and how next time, Bert promised, they'd make an apple cobbler.

"There's an orchard a few miles outside Banister Falls where you can pick your own apples in the fall," Evie told her. "There are hayrides and a corn maze and samples of homemade apple cider. Cody enjoyed it when he was your age."

Lily's face lit up and she twisted around. "Can we go, Uncle Jack?"

Jack didn't answer.

Evie glanced up and realized he wasn't paying any attention to them. His gaze was riveted on the man standing in the doorway.

Lily shrieked and launched herself off the stool.

"Daddy!"

Travis was the last person Jack expected to see. At least he could take comfort in the fact that his brother was wearing jeans and a T-shirt instead of an orange jumpsuit.

"Hey, bro." Trav lifted Lily off her feet and swung her around. "How's my favorite girl?"

"Is Mommy with you?"

Travis's smile slipped a notch as he set Lily down again. "Nope . . . just me, Princess. Have you been keeping your Uncle Jack on his toes while I was gone?"

"While I was gone."

Only Travis could make it sound like he'd just returned from two weeks at Disney World instead of a ten-by-ten jail cell.

"Uh-huh."

"That's good." Travis turned his attention to Evie, and the glint of approval in his eyes immediately set Jack's teeth on edge.

"Trav, this is Evie Bennett . . . Evie, my brother, Travis."

"Nice to meet you, Evie." Trav had two ways of charming women — a '57 Gibson Les Paul and his smile — and he played both to his advantage.

"Hello."

Evie returned the smile, but Jack could tell she wasn't charmed.

How had his brother posted a five-thousand-dollar bond?

Why now, God? I thought we decided Trav was better off in jail.

And the honest, gut-twisting truth? It was

368

better for Jack too.

Because when Travis was in jail, Jack knew he wasn't using or snapping at his wife and daughter. A sheriff's deputy wasn't going to wake Jack up in the middle of the night and tell him that Travis had driven his car into a tree.

"I stopped by the house on my way here. Did you know Phil stuck a For Sale sign in the yard?"

"He mentioned it." And Travis would have known too, if he had put Jack's name on his visitors list at the county jail. "Phil decided he'd rather buy and sell than rent, but you're paid up until the end of the month."

Travis's smile hardened. "Looks like you and I have some catching up to do."

Evie took the hint. "I should be going anyway." She reached out and straightened the bow at the bottom of Lily's braid. " 'Night, sweetheart."

Lily detached from her father's side long enough to give Evie a hug. "I'll see you tomorrow, Evie!"

Jack ignored the smirk on Travis's face. "I'll be right back."

He waited until he and Evie were outside before he released the sigh that had been building up. "No, I didn't know."

"Why did they let him out?" Evie shivered

even though the temperature was in the high seventies. "Did he appear before the judge already?"

"He must have convinced someone to pay his bond." Jack had no idea who could come up with that kind of cash, but Travis could have called in a favor from one of his former bandmates.

"What's going to happen now? What about Lily?"

Jack could tell Evie was waiting for him to say that everything would be okay, but he didn't want to make a promise he couldn't keep.

"I don't know."

"It'll be all right."

Evie sounded confident, but Jack saw the question in her eyes, understood her need for reassurance, but he couldn't keep that promise either.

He brushed a kiss against her lips instead.

Trav was waiting on the sidewalk when he crossed the street. "I wasn't gone that long, Jack. Where've you been hiding the beautiful Evie Bennett?"

"Where's Lily?"

"She went upstairs to straighten up her room before she lets me see it — and you didn't answer the question."

"We met at the church where I work."

Worked, Jack silently corrected himself. "She's the director of women's ministries."

"Figures." Travis started up the stairs. "You didn't used to go for the goody-two-shoes type."

"Why don't we talk about you instead?"

"My favorite subject." Travis was all grin and swagger. "What do you want to know?"

"How long it's going to take you to stop pretending that what you're doing is working. You keep doing the same thing and expecting different results."

For a split second Travis faltered. "Victor set me up."

"He forced you to buy those pills."

"His friend was in on it." Travis yanked open the door at the top of the landing. "Who do you think tipped off the cops? I tried to find him so we could have a little chat, but one of his friends said he's 'out of town' for a while. The jerk — "

Jack stopped him with a warning look when Lily poked her head out the door of his apartment.

"Come and see my room, Daddy! Uncle Jack painted it pink."

Trav followed her inside and let out a low whistle. "Uncle Jack has been a busy guy. Looks like someone is settling into small-town life. I wonder why."

Jack ignored the eyebrow wiggle — and the innuendo. "Are you hungry?"

"Do you know how many times you asked me that when we were kids? Right before I got the Travis-you're-in-so-much-trouble lecture, you'd sit me down at the table with a bowl of macaroni and cheese."

"I thought it would go down easier."

"It did — when I was eight." Travis waited until Lily disappeared into her bedroom again. "Now it just makes me want to hit you."

"Please." Jack squeezed his brother's bicep. "The heaviest thing you lift is a guitar pick."

Trav pinned Jack's hand in place. Squeezed back. "It's not your fault, you know." His voice dropped to a whisper. "You did the best you could. I put all the blame on our old man."

"Dad's gone, Trav. You have to forgive him. He made mistakes, but you're not a kid anymore. Now you get to choose."

"Yeah." Something dark flickered in Trav's eyes. "Whether to take the deal or let the jury decide how many years I'll be in prison."

"Trav —"

"My preliminary hearing is on Monday. They'll decide if there's enough evidence to hold me over for a trial. I'm guessing there will be, so I had to get out of there for a few days. Being locked up . . . it was making me crazy."

"Daddy!" Lily's plaintive voice floated from the direction of the bedroom. "You're taking forever."

"She missed you," Jack murmured. "Go on. Spend some time with your daughter. I'll make that mac and cheese."

"Don't worry about it. Lil and I can grab a burger on our way home."

"I thought you'd stay here tonight."

"So you can keep an eye on me?"

"Because there's no food in your refrigerator and all Lily's things are here."

"Fine. You win." Trav's lip curled. "One night."

Jack waited until the door closed behind his brother, and then he slipped onto the balcony and pulled out his cell. Evie answered on the first ring.

"How are things going?"

"Right now, Lily is giving Trav a tour of her room."

"Is Lily . . . is she okay?"

"She's good." Lily didn't hold her father's mistakes against him. When Jesus told His disciples they had to become like little children, maybe part of that was how quick they were to forgive.

"What about you? Hammer in one hand, sword in the other?"

A laugh slipped out. "You remembered."

"I remembered." Evie's voice softened. "I've heard a lot of ways to memorize scripture over the years. But a tattoo? Pretty creative, Jack Vale."

"Right now I'd like to take the hammer and pound some sense into my brother's head. His hearing is on Monday."

Evie was silent for a moment as she processed the news. "Are you still taking Lily to Raine and Cody's tomorrow?"

"I'm planning to call Raine and explain the situation because it sounds like she'll be with Travis. He agreed to spend the night here, but they'll be going back to the house on Brewster Street."

"You're letting him take Lily?"

Jack expelled a quiet breath. "It's not a question of *letting*. Travis is Lily's dad."

"I don't like the idea of her being shuffled from place to place."

"Neither do I, but I have to trust Him."

"But how do you know he's not . . ." Evie couldn't even say the words.

"I was talking about God. If I don't trust Him moment by moment, I get too focused on the bad stuff and miss out on what's good."

"Uncle Jack!" Lily's voice filtered through the window. "Do you want to play a game with us?"

"It sounds like you're being summoned." A hint of wistfulness crept into Evie's voice. "Are you sure you don't want me to come back over for a while?"

"I appreciate the offer —" Jack winced at how formal he sounded. "But it's getting close to Lily's bedtime, and there are a few things I have to discuss with my brother."

"I'll talk to you tomorrow then."

"Tomorrow," Jack echoed.

He hung up the phone, sending up a silent prayer asking God for the strength to get through the rest of the evening and adding a silent *thank you* that Evie would be spending hers on Rosewood Court.

Chapter 36

"Are you getting ready for opening night on Broadway or an ice cream social?"

Evie peered over the vase of yellow daisies she'd been arranging in an old-fashioned flower cart and laughed at the expression on Gin's face.

"Not much goes on in Banister Falls, so women tend to take advantage of opportunities like this. We want it to be special."

The door swung shut behind Gin, and the heels of her cowboy boots clicked against the bricks as she walked across the patio. "How many women are you expecting tomorrow morning?"

"We sold almost a hundred tickets in advance, but there are always a few walk-ins." Evie stepped out from behind the cart. "The garden walk used to end at Marie's Bistro, but when we could no longer fit everyone in the dining room, we moved it to the church."

Gin's eyes swept over the galvanized tubs filled with smaller pots of miniature roses. "Everything looks beautiful, but I thought you had a team of volunteers helping out."

"I do, but there are always a few last things that fall on me. My friend Gertrude is selling her home and doesn't need this flower cart anymore. I thought it would look great with the rest of the decorations."

"Speaking of great . . ." Gin held up a plastic container. "I brought something for you. Just between you and me though, I think Sue is a little nervous about providing the continental breakfast. She said, and I quote, 'What's that Evie Bennett thinking? I don't do dainty, little, frou-frou pastries like Marie. All I know how to make are cinnamon rolls and apple fritters.' "

It was hard for Evie to picture Sue Granger, the diner's gruff owner, getting nervous about anything. "Marie is already providing the ice cream and toppings. I decided that we should give other businesses in the community an opportunity to partner with us too, when we host an event like this." It was the same reasoning Evie had used when she'd approached her team with the idea. "And I happen to love cinnamon rolls."

"I hope you won't be too disappointed then, because that's not what you're getting." Gin peeled back a corner of the lid, releasing the scent of cinnamon and apples into the air.

Homemade turnovers lined the container, the seams of the flaky, golden-brown pastries bursting with fresh fruit and the tops sparkling with a dusting of raw sugar.

"What is Sue talking about? Those look amazing."

"I'm sure she'll be happy to hear that." Gin grinned. "Even though Nicki is the one who made them."

"Nicki?"

"Uh-huh. I could tell she was more interested in making the food than serving it, so last week I convinced Sue to let Nic help her out in the kitchen." The lid came off. "Don't be shy. Go ahead and try one."

Evie reached for a turnover, broke off a corner, and popped it into her mouth, closing her eyes. "I think we just discovered Nicki's spiritual gift."

"She made the pies last week and they sold out in an hour. In fact, a few of the customers ordered dessert first. I think Sue was ready to hang up her apron right then and there." Gin chuckled. "Nicki overheard us talking about the garden walk, and she suggested Sue make apple turnovers instead of fritters."

"And Sue told Nicki to make them herself," Evie guessed.

"Exactly."

"Tell Nicki they're delicious and she should seriously consider becoming a pastry chef."

"You'll see her tomorrow," Gin said. "I invited her to the garden walk."

"That's great —" Evie's cell phone interrupted them. She'd kept it close all day, waiting for Jack to call, but her heart still took a nose dive when his name and number flashed across the screen. "Excuse me a minute?"

"No problem." Gin reached for a turnover. "I'll find something to keep myself occupied."

Evie tapped the screen as she walked to the edge of the patio. "Hi."

"Hey." Jack's husky voice rumbled through the line. "What are you up to?"

"I'm still at church, getting things set up for tomorrow."

"How's that going?"

"Good." Evie didn't want to talk about the garden walk. "I should be heading home in half an hour or so."

As far as hints went, it was pretty blatant. But Evie missed the man. She missed Lily too. She and Jack had talked on the phone several times, but she hadn't seen him since Travis had shown up at Jack's apartment building on Tuesday night.

"I'd love to see you, but Travis's car is acting up again. I told him I'd take a look at it."

"If it's easier, I could always swing by Brewster Street this evening. Bring over something for supper if you're hungry."

The silence lasted so long that Evie wondered if they'd been cut off. "Jack?"

A barely discernable sigh told her he was still there. "I don't think that's going to work," he said slowly. "Nicki is taking Lily and her kids to the pool this evening, and I'll have my head under the hood of Travis's car. It would be hard to hold up my end of the conversation."

Evie didn't care if Jack conversed at all. She'd be content to stand next to the car and watch him work. Hand him tools.

"I understand." She injected what she hoped was the right amount of cheerfulness into the phone. "Cody and Raine invited us over Sunday for a cookout after church, and he said you should bring Travis and Lily along. I already made them promise there will be no karaoke."

Silence.

"I'm not sure what we'll be doing, but I'll

talk to Trav and let you know," Jack finally said. "He's planning to drop Lily off at the church by eight tomorrow morning for the garden walk. You'll call me when it's over and let me know how everything went?"

"Sure." Or even better, she could tell him in person.

In the background, Evie heard a door slam and the sound of a masculine voice.

"Evie . . . I should probably go." Jack sounded distracted.

Evie murmured a good-bye she wasn't sure he even heard. She wasn't sure how long she stood there, riveted to the patio like a garden statue, but suddenly Gin was steering her toward one of the wrought-iron benches.

"Sit." Gin winced. "Oh, oh. Sue must be rubbing off on me. What I meant was, *please* sit."

Evie sat and Gin dropped down next to her. "That was Jack, wasn't it?"

"I'm not quite sure who that was," Evie said honestly.

Gin didn't look the least bit confused — or surprised. "He canceled your plans for the evening?"

"We didn't *have* plans." Evie stared down at her phone, wondering why Jack had cut their phone call short. Wishing he would call back. "That's part of the problem."

"What's the other part?"

"His brother. Things were going really well until Travis got out of jail." Another thing that was difficult for Evie to admit. "I haven't seen Jack for three days, and I can't help but think . . ."

"That he doesn't want to see you?"

Put like that . . .

"How insecure does that sound?"

"You're not the one who's insecure," Gin muttered. "It's not that Jack doesn't want to see you . . . I'm guessing he doesn't want *you* to see *him*."

"What do you mean?"

"My mother was an alcoholic." A myriad of emotions — pain, anger, regret — skimmed through Gin's eyes. "I never invited anyone over to our house when I was growing up because I didn't know if Mom would be sober or sobbing in her bedroom . . . or throwing things around. If there'd be a strange guy sprawled in the recliner or sleeping on the couch.

"When you're a kid, you look around at other families and you can't help but wonder why yours is such a mess. But then you start to realize it's *your* mess. You take care of it. Clean it up. Hide it. Whatever. But the one thing you never want to do is expose other people to it. That's why I left when I found out I was pregnant with Raine. I wanted a better life for her."

Evie's heart ached for Gin. She'd heard bits and pieces of Gin's past from Dan, but she hadn't known how difficult her life had been.

"It took a lot of courage," she said softly. "To leave."

"More like desperation." Gin shrugged. "But I didn't realize I was still running until we ended up in Banister Falls. God and I are working on things but sometimes I still shut Dan out. It's like the messy closet in your house. You don't want anyone to see it . . . and you sure aren't going to invite them in to help you sort through the junk inside."

"What did Dan do . . . when you blocked the closet door?"

A slow smile tipped the corners of Gin's lips. "He ignored me and barged in anyway."

Evie smiled back. "Bold."

"Stubborn."

"I can be bold." Evie *had* kissed Jack in front of half the Moretti family. "And stubborn, when the situation calls for it."

"I believe you." Gin laughed and started to rise, but Evie snagged her hand, giving it a quick, impulsive squeeze. "Thank you."

To her amazement, Gin squeezed back. "How long are you going to be here?"

"Ten or fifteen minutes. Why?"

"The Lullaby Boutique on Main Street is having a sale today, and I thought I'd stop by and check it out. Want to come along?"

Evie hopped to her feet. "I'll make it ten."

CHAPTER 37

The first thing Evie saw when she arrived at church Saturday morning was Jack's ancient, paint-spattered radio sitting outside the door of the custodian's room, the cord wrapped in a tight wand and secured with a rubber band.

"Harvey?" She knocked once and the sound echoed down the hall.

The door opened and Harvey stood on the other side, pointing at his watch. "Seven fifteen. I was getting worried. Thought you had a flat tire or something."

"No flat tire. I didn't get out the door as quickly as I'd planned this morning." Thanks to Ginevieve, who'd talked her into watching a movie after they'd put a serious dent in the Lullaby Boutique's newborn inventory. Evie hadn't gotten home until midnight.

"I've got all the tables set up." Harvey looped his thumbs in the front pockets of his Dockers. "You should be good to go."

Evie fished an envelope from the outside pocket of her purse. "I meant to give this to you a few days ago. It's kind of a welcome-back-we-missed-you gift."

Harvey popped the seal on the envelope and pulled out a piece of paper. "My Place?"

"It's a diner on Radley Street. Sue Granger — she's the owner — has a great breakfast special called The Kitchen Sink. I thought maybe you'd like to try something new."

Evie left Harvey to ponder that and walked back to her office. The red light on the desk phone was blinking, so she pressed the button to retrieve her voicemail messages.

"Evie . . . this is Dawn." The financial secretary's brisk voice came over the line. "Gertrude Fielding mentioned she'd given you a check earmarked for women's ministries, but I see it hasn't been recorded yet. I'll need the total by Monday morning. Thank you."

Gertrude's check.

Where had she put it?

The flare of panic subsided when Evie yanked open the desk drawer and spotted the envelope peeking out from underneath a folder.

Evie couldn't believe she'd forgotten

about it.

Gertrude's loaves and fishes.

Smiling, Evie slipped her thumb under the old-fashioned wax seal.

The check fluttered to the floor, and Evie almost joined it when she caught a glimpse of the amount. She bent down to pick it up, slowly, to counteract the rapid beating of her heart.

"Gertrude." Evie breathed the woman's name as she stared at the numbers, counting the zeroes a second time.

Fifty thousand dollars.

On the memo line, three words written in Gertrude's flowing script: *For the adventure!*

"Good morning, Evie!" Belinda poked her head into Evie's office. Her straw hat, decorated with a cluster of bright-red plastic cherries, spanned the width of the doorframe. "I just wanted to show off my new hat . . . Are you all right?"

Evie glanced down at the check again. No, the numbers hadn't changed. "Look at this."

Belinda crossed the room and gently pried the check from her fingers. Her mouth worked but no sound came out. Evie figured she was counting zeroes too.

"Do you think Gert made a mistake?" Belinda finally ventured.

"No." Gertrude Fielding was as sharp as

the proverbial tack.

Laughter drifted down the hallway as the first group of women arrived. Evie slid the check back into the desk drawer and closed it. "I can't think about this now."

Belinda gave Evie's arm a comforting squeeze. "Gertrude trusted that you would ask God what to do with that money. Trust Him to provide the answer."

Trust.

A word Evie had been hearing a lot lately.

Maybe it was time to start putting it into practice.

The scent of roses mingled with the classical music playing from the speakers hidden in the azaleas that hemmed in Victoria Kellan's patio.

Evie turned the tiny gold spigot on the beverage dispenser, and a trickle of bright-red punch flowed into her glass.

The turnout was larger than they'd predicted, the promise of a beautiful summer day beckoning women to put aside their usual Saturday routine and spend a few hours outside.

Nicki had joined Raine and Gin a few minutes before the tour started, and she'd brought along Ava and Grace. The little girls looked adorable in matching purple sundresses.

There had never been an age restriction on the garden walk, more of an unspoken rule that small children would remain in the childcare the youth group provided, but Nicki must have found out that Evie had invited Lily.

Every time Evie saw the girls, they seemed to be enjoying the outing as much as Nicki.

"If I could have your attention, please." Evie waited until the hum of conversation died down. "On behalf of the women's ministry team, I would like to thank everyone for taking part in the garden walk today. As most of you know, all the proceeds from the ticket sales will benefit a women's shelter in India."

Out of the corner of her eye Evie saw Victoria subtly move into position. "I would also like to thank the people, like Victoria Kellan, who graciously invited us to enjoy their gardens today."

A scattering of applause followed.

"Everyone is invited back to the church for an old-fashioned ice cream social, compliments of Marie's —"

Something bumped against Evie's leg, and she glanced down.

Grace had somehow escaped from her

mother's arms. She held up a dandelion, its shaggy yellow head drooping on the stalk, a white milky substance oozing between her tiny fingers.

"Fower!" Grace grinned up at her.

How many times had Cody toddled up to Evie, a damp bouquet of dandelions clutched in his hand, nose dusted with yellow pollen as he offered her the gift?

A flower, not a weed. A matter of perspective.

"I'm sorry, Evie." Nicki sidled up, her cheeks stained red with embarrassment.

Victoria, Evie noticed, looked a little flushed too, anxiously scanning her manicured lawn for a possible dandelion uprising.

"Don't be." Evie scooped Grace into her arms, dutifully smelling the flower waving under her nose before she addressed the group again. "Victoria's rose garden is officially the last stop on the garden walk, but this year we're adding a mystery garden. That's all I'm going to tell you about it, but if you're up for a little . . . adventure . . . before you cool off with an ice cream sundae, please feel free to follow me."

A low murmur traveled around the patio. Out of the corner of her eye Evie saw some of the women consulting their fliers, searching for any kind of clue that would help them decide what they should do.

Belinda and Sonya materialized at Evie's side.

"When," Belinda whispered, "did we add a mystery garden to the tour?"

"About ten seconds ago," Evie whispered back.

"I thought so."

Jill joined them, her eyebrows practically touching over the bridge of her nose. "Fairview Street?"

"Fairview Street."

"Are you sure about this, Evie?"

"No," Evie said truthfully.

"That's what makes it an adventure." Belinda lifted the hem of her broomstick skirt and revealed a pair of rubber clogs. "I knew there was a reason I wore these today."

Evie looked at Sonya.

"I'm in."

Jill shook her head. "I'll escort the women back to the church. Someone should keep an eye on things until you get back."

It was clear from her tone she thought that someone should be the director of women's ministries.

Evie's hand shook a little when she stuck the key in the ignition of her car. She glanced in the rearview mirror and saw Belinda give her a thumbs-up.

But the closer Evie got to Jack's neighborhood, the more tempted she was to keep driving. Make a wide loop and head back to the church.

God . . . I have no idea what I'm doing, but I'm going to trust that You do.

CHAPTER 38

Evie pulled up behind the apple-red Beetle parked in front of the vacant lot. Maggie, in her patched overalls and a red baseball cap, shaded her eyes against the sun as cars began to line up along the curb.

The women, a small, colorful remnant of the original group, clustered together on the sidewalk, waiting for direction. Evie had expected that Gin and Raine and Nicki would be there, but she was stunned to see Victoria Kellan towering above everyone like an exotic bird-of-paradise in her vivid orange dress and boat-shaped straw hat.

Maggie tucked her gardening gloves into the pocket of her overalls as she strode toward Evie.

"I'd like to introduce you to a friend of mine, Maggie McClain." At least Evie hoped they would still be friends after showing up unannounced. "Maggie's vision is to turn this vacant lot into a community garden next summer, and after you talk to her, I have a feeling you'll be as excited as I am about the project. Maggie?"

"Good afternoon, everyone." Maggie's warm smile expanded to include the entire group. "If you follow me, I'll share a brief overview of the design."

The women followed, the tight knot loosening a bit, and Maggie's laughter filling the spaces.

Thank You, Lord.

The knot in Evie's chest loosened a little bit too.

Maggie might not have fliers or sketches or photographs, but her enthusiasm would bring the garden to life.

"Lily?" Evie caught the girl's hand before she scampered after Ava. "How about we run up to Bert's apartment and let her know we're here?"

Bert had politely declined Evie's invitation to attend the garden walk as her guest, but Fairview was her neighborhood, the environment where she felt the most comfortable, and she liked Maggie. Maybe the younger woman could introduce Bert as her first official volunteer.

Evie and Lily crossed the street together, and Evie noticed that the plywood covering the broken windows was gone and sunlight glinted off the new glass.

Jack had made a lot of progress over the past few days.

Lily broke free and dashed up the stairs to find Bert, but Evie followed the trail of sidewalk chalk hearts to the open door on the first floor, hoping to catch a glimpse of Jack.

Sunlight flooded the space. A clean tarp had been tossed over the countertop. Luke and Ron sat on opposite sides of a spindly legged card table, the checkerboard between them. Andy watched them, swaying back and forth, Amber Lynn in his arms.

Jack emerged from the kitchen, a plate with a crooked Dr. Seuss–like stack of grilled cheese sandwiches in one hand and a pitcher of ice water in the other.

He spotted Evie in the doorway and his slow smile fluttered through her, stirred that sense of wonder that came with the first signs of spring. "What are you doing here?"

Being bold.

Which was why Evie didn't wait for Jack to invite her in.

"We added a mystery garden to the tour." She glanced over her shoulder. Across the street, the women had formed a semicircle behind Maggie as she pointed to the graffiti-stained brick wall. Evie could almost hear her saying *This is going to be a mural* . . . "I sent Lily upstairs to find Bert."

"Evie, look!" Luke pointed to the mound of red checkers beside the board. "I'm winning!"

"Not for long," Ron grumbled.

"Help yourself, Andy." Jack set the plate of sandwiches on the counter. "There's plenty."

Andy cast a longing look at the food. "Are you sure?"

"I'm sure." No one but Evie saw Jack make a neat cut through the center of the stack, dividing the sandwiches in half.

Loaves and fishes.

"I'll hold Amber Lynn." Evie reached for the baby. Andy's daughter was wide awake, mesmerized by the fan chugging in a lazy circle above their heads. "When did you put the fan in?"

"When I got back from Travis's last night." Jack poured a glass of water from the pitcher and set it beside Luke.

"You have to sleep once in a while."

"There's a lot to do."

And a lot on Jack's mind.

"Knock knock!" The women funneled in behind Maggie. They spotted Andy with his multiple piercings and tattoos, and Evie could almost hear the snap as they locked back together in a single unit just inside the door. Gin and Raine, looking a little confused by the unexpected traffic jam, guided Nicki and the children around them.

"We were hoping you could spare a few glasses of water, Jack." Maggie tugged off her baseball cap. "It's pretty warm out there."

"Sure." Jack's smile surfaced, and suddenly he was the focus of a dozen curious looks. A friend of Victoria Kellan's began to fan herself with her straw hat, but Evie suspected it didn't have anything to do with the temperature.

"Can you give me a hand, Evie? I think there are some pitchers under the cupboard in the kitchen."

"Of course."

Now *she* was the focus of a dozen curious looks.

"We also have fresh-squeezed lemonade." Bert, bless her heart, created a welcome distraction when she marched through the door, Hawaiian-print housecoat flapping against her knees and her snow-white Keds stirring up the dust on the floor. Lily was right behind her with a tower of Dixie cups.

"I'll find the pitchers, Evie."

Evie gave Gin a grateful smile. "Thanks."

"And I'll take the baby." Raine reached

for Amber Lynn.

Evie cleared off the bench so some of the women could sit down.

Gin returned a few minutes later with two pitchers of ice water and set them down next to Evie as she ladled lemonade into paper cups.

"This used to be the fabric store. I remember when my mother brought me here to pick out material for my prom dress." One of the women ran her hand along the beveled edge of the counter. "We sewed every one of the sequins on by hand."

"I miss Thomsen's Bakery even more," someone else said. "There'd be a line halfway down the block on Saturday mornings when Mr. Thomsen was deep-frying crullers."

Maggie took a sample of Bert's lemonade, and her eyes drifted closed with the first sip. "Yum."

"My grandmother's recipe. The secret ingredient is lavender." Bert handed Victoria one of the cups and watched while the other woman took a tentative sip.

"This is delicious."

"It's easy to make too. I'll jot the recipe down for you." Bert grabbed a carpenter's pencil and a scrap of paper off the counter.

Ava had found Lily's bucket of sidewalk

chalk behind the counter and lugged it over to Raine. "Can you make a picture with us?"

"I will." Evie nudged her daughter-in-law toward the bench. "I think Raine would like to put her feet up for a few minutes."

"Thanks." Raine wiggled her toes. "In this humidity, my ankles get ankles."

"Me." Grace held up her arms. Clutched in one hand were the remains of Luke's grilled cheese sandwich.

Evie picked her up anyway, propping her on one hip while Luke, Ava, and Lily ran ahead of them and spilled out onto the sidewalk.

The girls immediately flopped down on the concrete and sifted through the chalk, searching for their favorite colors. Luke was more interested in a beetle crawling along the foundation of the building.

Evie set Grace down so she could watch her sister and cousin. Laughter flowed out the door and Evie turned toward the window.

Chrissy Anderson was deep in conversation with Maggie, and judging from the animated expressions on the women's faces, Maggie had found another volunteer.

Bert refilled Victoria's cup and Evie smiled. The two women *did* have something in common. Victoria leaned toward designer labels, but both of them loved bold tropical prints.

Jack sat across from Ron, filling in for Luke at the checkerboard.

Sonya peeked her head out the door. "We better get back to the church pretty soon, Evie. I just got a text message from Pauline, asking if the mystery garden was in another county."

Evie hadn't realized how quickly the time had gone by. She wiggled her chalk-dusted fingers. "I'll wash up and be right over."

"Thank you for letting Maggie share her vision with the group . . . and be sure to thank Jack for letting us interrupt his work." Sonya joined her on the sidewalk. "It was nice to get out of the sun for a few minutes and have something cold to drink."

"I will, but Jack never sees people as interruptions."

"I knew I liked him."

Evie could have left it there, but she drew in a breath and took another step forward. "I like him too."

The women began to file out the door, chatting together as they walked back to their cars.

Lily skipped up to Evie and tugged on her arm. "Can I ride back to the church with Ava and Luke?"

"If it's all right with your Aunt Nicki."

Nicki, in the process of extracting a shard of purple chalk from the pocket of Grace's sundress, looked up when she heard her name. "It's fine with me, Evie."

"Save some ice cream for me, okay?" Evie gave Lily's braid a playful tug. "I'll be there in a few minutes. I left my purse inside."

Ron and Andy were gone — they must have slipped out the back door that opened onto the alley — and Jack was talking to someone on the phone, his cell wedged between his ear and his shoulder as he stacked the empty dishes.

Evie bumped him aside and carried them into the kitchen.

Without the dark paneling closing in on her, the room seemed larger than she remembered . . .

And suddenly Evie had a vision too.

A place where people could gather together. A place where they could be nourished, physically and emotionally.

A place for them to meet with God.

In the heart of the neighborhood. Right across from the community garden.

Evie gripped the edge of the sink, overwhelmed by the possibilities that began to flow through her mind.

"I didn't think Fairview Street was part of

the tour today."

She turned at the sound of Jack's voice. "It wasn't . . . until God put it there."

"I can't wait to hear that story."

"There's more."

A smile teased the corners of Jack's lips. "I'm not surprised."

"I am." Evie pressed a hand against her stomach. She felt the same way she had the day Jack had taken her to Sandy Point. Terrified and excited at the same time. "Why couldn't Hope Community buy this building? It's the perfect location."

Jack went from "not surprised" to stunned. "For . . . ?"

"People to get out of the sun for a little while when they're working on their garden. And there's so much extra space back here. We could have a food pantry . . . or accept donations and have a clothes closet for moms like Nicki who don't have a lot of extra money in their budget . . . *What?*" Evie paused and dragged in a breath. "You think I'm crazy."

"Crazy is the last word I'd use to describe you."

"I know it sounds like a big project." Evie caught her lower lip between her teeth. "But does it sound . . . impossible?"

"Yes," Jack said promptly. "But Jesus fed

the five thousand with a few pieces of bread and some fish. He performed the miracle but He let His disciples get in on the fun. It must have been like handing out presents on Christmas morning."

It's not much . . . loaves and fishes, really.

"Jack." Evie swallowed. Hard. "Do you ever hear God laughing?"

The first time we met, Jack wanted to say, but he didn't think Evie would understand, so he nodded instead.

"All the time."

"Let's look at the rest of the building."

"Maybe I should take back what I said about crazy," Jack teased. "You've already seen it."

"Not like this."

Jack hadn't seen Evie quite like this either. The light in her eyes . . . it reminded him of the day he'd taken her to Sandy Point.

He followed her back to the main room, and Evie pointed to the area in front of the windows. "There's plenty of space for tables. Maybe even a sitting area. And once you refinish the counter, it would be a perfect place to serve water and snacks . . . or a meal once a week."

"A meal?"

"Everyone loves your spaghetti, but we do need to shake things up once in a while."

"Shake things up." Visions of Post-it notes danced in Jack's head, but he tried to keep a straight face.

"I'd have to talk to Pastor Keith, but if the church could come up with the funds to buy the building, the rent from the upstairs tenants would subsidize the cost of the upkeep. As a ministry, it would be practically self-sustaining."

She was right. But . . .

"Are you sure you haven't been planning this for a while?"

Evie didn't seem to hear him. She took a slow turn in the center of the room. "It wouldn't end up being converted into another liquor store either."

"Liquor store?" Jack's gut tightened. "Where did you hear that?"

"From Ryan Tate, when I brought my team here last week."

Jack tipped his head toward the ceiling. "Okay. I'm hearing God laugh right now. I have been praying for this neighborhood since I moved here, but I never . . ." He stopped, shaking his head.

"Never what?"

"Never imagined *you* would be part of the answer. I never thought I'd see you again after we met that night on Brewster Street."

He had Evie's full attention now. "Did you

want to?"

The question made Jack laugh. "Let's just say you make quite a first impression, Blue Eyes."

"So that's a yes?"

"Yes." Jack was about a millisecond away from backing up the words with action when his phone buzzed, signaling an incoming text.

"I have to go," Evie said, "but we're going to finish this conversation later, because I just thought of someone who would be the perfect manager for the building."

The bounce in Evie's step as she walked toward the door reminded Jack of Lily.

And the text message from his brother reminded Jack why *perfect* didn't come close to describing him — or his life — at the moment.

CHAPTER 39

"Raine and I have something for you, Mom."

Cody steered Evie toward the picnic table in his backyard.

"It isn't another celebratory sundae from Quigley's, is it?" Visions of blue ice cream and sprinkles danced in Evie's head. "Because I don't think I can eat another bite."

"It's better." Raine lowered herself onto the bench across from Evie and handed her a gift bag. "Open the one with the yellow ribbon first."

Cody and Raine were practically vibrating with excitement as Evie dug through the tissue paper and lifted out a brightly wrapped present.

"It's our wedding picture!" Raine couldn't stand it anymore.

It was a candid shot, taken after the ceremony. Cody smiling down at Raine — wiping a tear from her cheek.

"I love it. Thank you."

"There's another one." Cody rattled the bag, earning a stern look and a "Careful!" from Raine.

Evie hid a smile. Raine was going to be a good mom. She pulled out — carefully — another photo frame, and this time Cody and Raine didn't say anything.

For a moment Evie couldn't either.

She ran her hand over the black-and-white photograph, tracing every dip and curve of the delicate profile, the impossibly tiny fingers and toes.

"Meet your granddaughter, Mom."

"A *girl*?" Evie breathed the word.

Cody nodded. "Ella Joy Bennett."

"We couldn't keep it a secret anymore." Tears glistened in Raine's eyes. "We had to share."

Evie's throat closed.

"You're not disappointed, are you, Mom?"

"Disappointed?" Evie's head snapped up and she stared at her son. "Why would I be disappointed?"

"I thought maybe you were hoping we would have a boy. You know, so we could name him after Dad."

"I'm not disappointed at all, Cody. I'm thrilled. Ella . . ." The name — the sweet face — took root in Evie's heart. "She's beautiful."

"I know it's not the kind of photo people usually frame." Cody threaded his fingers through Raine's. "But we thought you'd like it."

"I'm going to put both of these on the mantel when I get home."

"It's getting pretty crowded, Mom," Cody teased.

Evie stretched across the table and wrapped her arms around her son and his wife. "I'll make room," she whispered.

The opening notes of a song by Rend Collective Experiment began to play in the background, and Cody wiggled free.

"Sorry. That's me." He dipped a hand into his back pocket and pulled out his cell phone. "Hey. Yeah . . . hold on. She's right here." Cody handed her the phone.

Evie glanced at him before offering a cautious "Hello?"

"You didn't answer your cell phone."

"Jack." Another unexpected gift. "I left it on Cody's kitchen table."

"Just thought I'd check in and find out how your afternoon is going."

Evie slid to her feet and walked a few feet away. Cody nudged Raine and Raine nudged him back, and they both pretended they weren't listening in on the conversation. "I was just about to ask you the same thing."

"Right now . . . good. Travis went over to Brewster Street to mow the lawn and Lily is working on some new dance steps while I finish priming the kitchen."

"Which one?"

"The one that looks like a backdrop on the set of *Leave It to Beaver.*"

"You're painting *my* kitchen? Without me?"

"Your kitchen." A smile flowed into the words.

"I talked to Pastor Keith about Fairview Street after church this morning. He agreed to meet with me tomorrow and I made a few phone calls — gathered some reinforcements. I was hoping you could come too."

Jack groaned. "I can't. I already promised Trav I would go to his preliminary hearing."

"Then you need to be there with him . . . but I miss you."

"I miss you too," Jack murmured.

Good. Evie hoped that meant Jack wouldn't mind when she showed up at his door.

"Well, *hello* there. Aren't you a sight for sore eyes?"

"Where's Jack?" Evie hadn't expected to see Travis saunter into the kitchen while she was trying to locate his brother.

"He went to the hardware store to pick up some paint, but he should be back in a few minutes."

Evie forced a smile. "Every time I come over here, it looks different."

Travis propped his hip against the sink and surveyed the room. His face glowed from being outdoors all afternoon and his jeans were coated with bits of grass, but there was no getting around the fact that the man was extremely attractive. Tousled blond hair and the same lean, sculpted features but with eyes more blue than gray. And they lacked the warmth Evie saw in Jack's.

"I think this building would benefit more from a wrecking ball, but that's my big brother." Trav's lips twisted in a smile. "Trying to make something out of nothing is a personal challenge to him."

There was a double meaning embedded in the words that Evie didn't want to analyze too closely. "Is Lily here?"

"I hope so. I came to pick her up."

As if on cue, Evie heard the patter of footsteps in the hallway and Lily burst into the room. "I made up a new dance! Do you

410

want to see it?"

Evie circumvented the refusal rising in Travis's eyes with a quick smile. "Of course we do."

For a moment Evie thought he was going to decline. But then he swept his arm toward the door. "After you."

He followed them to the mirrored room and pulled his cell phone from his pocket as Lily began to flit around.

Just when Evie was tempted to snatch it away from him, Lily glided up to them. "Twirl me, Daddy!"

Travis looked at Lily like she'd just asked him to launch her to the moon. "There's no music."

"Yes, there is!" Lily reached for his hand. "Uncle Jack says it's inside of you."

Travis glanced at his phone. "Maybe when we get back from Quigley's. You want to go with me, right? I thought we'd get a hamburger for supper."

"Yes!" Lily performed a pirouette and almost landed on Evie's toes. "Oops! I'm sorry, Evie."

"That's all right, sweetheart." Evie wished Jack would get back.

"Can you and Uncle Jack come to Quigley's with us?"

"I'm sure they'd rather be alone, Princess," Travis said before Evie could respond. "It's just going to be you and Dad tonight. I thought we'd get some ice cream and watch a movie."

"Uncle Jack doesn't have a TV."

"That doesn't matter because we have one at home."

Lily's forehead puckered. "Aren't we coming back here?"

Evie hoped that Lily didn't see the flicker of irritation in Travis's eyes as he set his hand against the small of Lily's back and guided her toward the door.

"Let's go, Princess. If I don't get a cheeseburger and fries in the next ten minutes, I'm going to disappear."

Don't get my hopes up.

The thought rolled through Evie's mind before she could stop it and she felt terrible. Summoning a smile, she waved goodbye to Lily, but the moment the two were out of sight, she closed her eyes. *I'm sorry, Lord. I know I shouldn't judge him. I'm worried about Lily. And Jack . . .*

"The color isn't that bad, is it?"

Evie turned at the sound of Jack's voice and some of her tension melted away under the warmth of his smile. "I love the color."

"Good. Because the guy at the hardware store said I can't return them." Jack set two gallons of paint on the floor. "Travis left?"

"He picked up Lily. They're going to Quigley's for supper and then home." The last word stuck in Evie's throat. "I think she'd rather be here though."

Jack simply nodded.

How did he do this? If it was difficult for her, she couldn't imagine how hard it must be on him.

"I wanted to show you something." Evie reached into her bag and took out the photographs. "Cody and Raine gave me these today."

Jack moved closer. "I saw the photographer take this one on their wedding day."

"You did?"

"It was right after the ceremony. Raine told the photographer she wanted all the pictures from here up." Jack tapped his chest. "But Cody said, 'There's a baby in the picture so there's going to be a baby in the picture.' He told Raine he didn't want their child to think they were ashamed when he or she was old enough to do the math. And I remember thinking someone raised that boy right."

"I wasn't so sure of that the night Cody announced he was going to be a father. I was devastated." Evie replayed the conversation in her mind. "I blamed Raine for ruining Cody's future. I was convinced she'd messed up God's plan for my son . . . but I was the one who almost got in the way. I suggested they consider putting the baby up for adoption. I wasn't always kind to Raine or Gin, and there were nights I cried out to God and asked Him to give Cody the courage to make the right decision. And He did.

"I know they're going to face some difficult things . . . but if Cody had listened to me, I wouldn't have this."

Evie handed Jack the other photograph, and he pulled in a quiet, almost reverent, breath as he studied the ultrasound.

"The baby is a she. Her name is Ella. Ella Joy Bennett."

"Your granddaughter."

Evie smiled. "The good stuff."

CHAPTER 40

"Morning, Jack!" Pauline stood behind the welcome center in the church foyer, restocking a small wicker basket with pocket-size devotionals. "How are you doing?"

Jack bypassed the question with one of his own. "Is Evie here?"

"She's still in a meeting with Pastor, but it shouldn't go too much longer." Pauline's voice cut to a whisper. "Evie told me about the building on Fairview Street. I've known her for thirteen years, and I've never seen her so excited about a project. It sounds like Keith is on board, so I have a feeling if it comes to a vote, the congregation will support it too."

"That's great." Jack pushed out a smile. "Do you mind if I wait in her office?"

"Not at all. There's a fresh pot of coffee in the kitchen if you're interested."

The thought of putting anything in his stomach made it tilt sideways. "No thanks."

Jack's smile died the instant he closed the door behind him. He walked over and stared at the watercolor on Evie's wall. A tranquil lake and a blue sky that reminded Jack of her eyes.

God . . .

That was as far as he got. The door opened and Evie came in. Her cheeks were flushed pink, the sparkle in her eyes an indication that her meeting about the building on Fairview Street had gone well. Jack tried to smile, but it must not have been very convincing because Evie's disappeared.

"They found enough evidence to hold Travis for trial, didn't they?" She was at his side in an instant, reaching for his hands.

"Trav didn't show up for court, Evie." Saying the words out loud only made them more real.

"What do you mean he didn't show up? Where is he?"

"He . . ." Jack cleared his throat, trying to clear the lump from his throat, but it continued to expand. Barely allowed a breath to filter through. "I don't know."

"You mean he *left*?"

"He's not answering his phone. I stopped by the house on my way here . . . his car is gone."

Evie stared up at him and Jack could see

416

her trying to fit the pieces together in a way that would make sense.

"He left Lily alone?"

"Evie —" At that moment Jack would have given anything not to have to tell her the truth. "Trav took Lily with him."

No.

Evie's lips shaped the word but no sound came out.

Everything inside of her wanted to reject what Jack had just told her, but the raw pain in his eyes made it impossible.

"I talked to Ryan . . . They issued a warrant for Trav's arrest, but he could be across the state line by now." Jack's voice broke a little on the last word, and something broke inside of Evie.

She didn't even realize she was crying until Jack's arms folded around her. A tremor ran through him, one that Evie felt all the way to her bones.

And all she could do was cling to Jack and thank God, over and over, that He'd brought them together. And that Jack didn't have to go through this alone.

Jack was finally alone.

He'd managed to persuade Evie to go home and get some sleep even though he knew he wouldn't allow himself the same luxury.

Not until he heard from Travis.

After she left, he drove to Brewster Street and let himself in with the spare key Cheryl had hidden underneath the mat on the back porch. The air in the house felt thick, so the first thing he did was open the windows in the living room.

Lily's stuffed toys, lined up along the back of the couch, watched Jack with benign smiles as he filled in some of the holes in the wall and nailed a strip of baseboard back in place.

He was glad Evie wasn't here to see him take out his frustration on an innocent piece of oak.

Evie.

She'd stayed by Jack's side all afternoon while he called Travis's former bandmates and friends. She'd made him eat. Worked out the knots in his shoulders. But somehow everything she did only made Jack feel worse.

Because all he could see was Evie's expression when he'd told her that Trav had taken Lily and left town.

That was something he couldn't fix.

And her tears . . .

The soft scuff of footsteps on the steps

leading up to the porch cut through the silence, and he was at the door in three strides.

"Trav —" Jack yanked the door open and came face-to-face with Ginevieve Lightly.

Her gaze swept over him. "You look terrible."

There was something refreshing about the blunt observation, but it didn't stop Jack from bracing one arm across the doorframe, creating a barrier between the porch and Trav's living room.

"Is that what you came over here to tell me?"

"No, that was just to break the ice." Gin ducked underneath his arm. "The next part requires a cup of coffee."

Jack closed the door behind her. "Don't you work at a diner?"

Ginevieve picked up a stuffed dog, transferred it to the next cushion, and made herself at home on Trav's lumpy couch. "It's been a long day."

Jack couldn't argue with that. He walked around the butcher-block island that separated the living room from the kitchen. He was feeling shaky enough without another dose of caffeine, but reheating a cup for Ginevieve gave him something to do.

"Have you heard anything?"

Gin obviously wasn't one to beat around the bush.

"No."

"You can't blame yourself. Short of locking your brother in a closet — and that involves a few felonies of its own — you couldn't have stopped Travis from leaving."

Maybe Gin was right, but knowing that didn't make it any easier.

"There's a warrant out for Trav's arrest now. I talked to Ryan Tate and they won't issue an Amber Alert for Lily because they don't believe she's in danger."

"I don't either."

For some reason, Gin's matter-of-fact statement sliced through one of the steel bands that had wrapped around Jack's chest that morning. He shot her a grateful look. "I found a dress shirt and tie on Trav's bed. I think he planned to go to court but he must have panicked. Or got angry. It's no excuse, but my brother tends to let emotion cloud his judgment."

"I hope that's not a family trait."

Jack was debating whether to ask Gin what she meant by that when his cell phone rang. He saw the name on the screen and folded the phone into the palm of his hand, letting the call go to voicemail.

When he looked up, Gin was watching him.

"Don't do it, Jack."

"Don't do what?"

"Hurt Evie."

"*Hurt* her?" Jack repeated. "I'm trying to protect her."

Gin set her empty cup in the sink and walked toward the door, but Jack had a feeling she wasn't finished with him yet.

"Are you protecting Evie?" she said softly. "Or yourself?"

Ginevieve's words lingered in Jack's head as he drove back to his apartment building.

For once, no one was around.

He walked through the living room and went onto the balcony. He and Evie had sat out there the night before — it seemed like a year ago now — while the paint was drying, serenaded by the squeal of tires and the jukebox in the bar across the street.

It had seemed romantic at the time.

I've never had this.

Yeah. He'd opened up a whole new world for Evie all right.

Jack's phone rang again, but this time a number he didn't recognize popped up on the screen.

"Vale."

The silence on the other end of the line

421

sent equal amounts of hope and fear rocketing through him. "Hello?"

"Jack."

He sagged against the railing. *Thank You, God.*

"Trav . . . where are you?"

"In trouble." A broken sigh funneled through the speaker. "I messed up, Jack. I messed up big this time. I . . . I panicked, you know? I was going to take Lily out for breakfast before I went to the courthouse and I just kept driving."

"Where is Lily now?"

"She's with a friend of mine. Deidre. Remember her? Used to sing backup for the band once in a while?"

The image of a woman's face uploaded from an old file in Jack's memory. Long black hair, sultry eyes, pouty red lips. Part of the past Jack would rather forget.

Trav's voice dropped to a low rumble. "I need you to drive to Milwaukee and pick up Lily. Deidre still lives above the Lightning Lounge."

Fear grabbed Jack by the throat. "I'll pick you up too, Trav."

"And take me to the police department?"

Jack closed his eyes. "Yes."

"Sorry. I beat you to it, big brother. I turned myself in."

It took a moment for the words to sink in. "You did the right thing."

"For once." A sigh rattled in Jack's ear. "Tell Cheryl I'm sorry. And promise me you'll look out for my family."

"I will."

"I have to go." In the background Jack heard voices. The scrape of a chair against the floor.

"I love you, Trav."

Silence. His brother had already hung up. Jack was about to press the End Call button when Travis whispered his name.

"Jack?"

"I'm still here."

"Don't stop praying for me, okay?"

Hope stirred inside Jack like the whisper of a warm summer breeze.

"Okay."

CHAPTER 41

At five in the morning, before the neighbor's automatic sprinkler system came on and the first chickadee showed up for breakfast at Evie's feeder, she was on her way to Jack's apartment with two large cups of Marie's French roast and a white paper sack filled with Nicki's apple turnovers.

If she hadn't been able to sleep more than a few hours — if you could even call it sleeping — Evie doubted that Jack had been able to sleep at all.

And where had Lily spent the night?

Jack had been on the telephone for hours the day before, calling everyone Travis and Cheryl knew, no matter how fragile the connection, asking if they'd seen or heard from him.

God, bring her home safely. And wrap Your arms around Jack and give him strength. He's been through so much with Travis already.

Evie hadn't wanted to leave Jack, but as

the sun went down and the silences between them had grown longer, he had insisted she go home.

But Rosewood Court didn't feel so much like home anymore.

She turned onto Fairview Street. The rising sun painted the buildings with a rosy glow and glinted off the broken antenna sprouting from the roof of the bar across the street from Jack's apartment.

Evie grabbed the cardboard tray with the coffee and pastries and slid out of the Jeep. As she closed the door, a squad car rolled up beside her and the driver's-side window scrolled down.

Ryan shot an envious glance at the white paper sack on the tray. "Jack's back already?"

"Back from where?"

Surprise flickered in Ryan's eyes. "He didn't tell you?"

"Tell me what?" The tray wobbled in Evie's hands, and she tightened her grip.

"Travis called Jack around midnight. He got as far as Milwaukee and turned himself in."

"He did?" Fear distilled into relief. "What about Lily? Is she all right?"

"According to Jack, Travis left Lily with a friend. He went to pick her up."

"You *talked* to him?"

"I'd asked him to call me if he heard from his brother."

But why hadn't Jack called *her*? Why hadn't he asked her to go with him to Milwaukee?

Ryan must have read Evie's mind because he expelled a slow breath. "Look, Evie, you and Jack had a heck of a day yesterday. He probably didn't want to wake you up. I'm sure you'll hear from him soon."

All Evie could manage was a nod. "What's going to happen to Travis now?"

"He'll be extradited back here. He proved he's a flight risk, so he'll be in jail until his hearing. The judge isn't very understanding when it comes to bail jumping, so the guy probably sentenced himself to a longer prison term." Ryan hesitated, as if he were debating whether to say more. "I recommended to Jack that he file the paperwork to become Lily's legal guardian when he gets back. That little girl needs some stability in her life."

Evie had no doubt Jack would give Lily everything she needed, but the fact that Ryan thought so too meant a lot.

"Here . . . you take these." Evie handed him the tray. "You look like you've been up all night too."

"Overtime." Ryan shook his head. "Chief wants more police presence in this neighborhood now that the community garden got a green light. Are you sure you don't want the coffee though?"

"I can make more."

Ryan left and Evie checked her phone again.

As she scrolled through the call history, Evie went through a whole list of reasons why Jack hadn't contacted her.

Travis had called in the middle of the night and he hadn't wanted to wake her. He'd been in a hurry to pick up Lily. He was driving . . .

I'm going to trust You with this too, God.

Evie walked up the stairs to the second floor of Jack's building, found the door to his apartment unlocked — that made her smile — and let herself inside.

Jack was on his third cup of coffee when Coop set a plate of misshapen pancakes down on the table in front of him.

He winced. "No, thanks."

"You think I spent the last ten minutes trying to make a guinea pig out of pancake batter for you?" Coop chuckled. "These are for Lily."

"She's awake . . ." Jack's chair scraped

against the patio blocks. He started to rise, but Coop pressed a hand on his shoulder.

"Stay put. She and Anne are taking Rascal for a walk around the block. They'll be back in a few minutes."

"Rascal can walk?" Jack had known Coop for years, and the only thing he'd seen the couple's overweight Corgi do was snore on the rug in front of Coop's La-Z-Boy.

"I see you haven't lost your sense of humor." Coop pulled up a chair next to him on the patio. "So what's the plan?"

"I haven't gotten that far." It had been a little after four in the morning when Jack arrived at Deirdre's apartment. She'd met him at the door wearing a red satin camisole that didn't quite meet her low-cut shorts. Fortunately, Lily had roused at the sound of Jack's voice.

Next he drove to Coop's house and tucked Lily into the guest room. She'd clutched his hand as he drew the blanket over her shoulders, her eyes begging him not to leave. Jack had finally fallen asleep in the rocking chair next to the bed until the aroma of freshly brewed coffee lured him downstairs.

"Then how about I start you out?" Coop leaned back, folding his arms across his massive chest. "The house you finished before you left . . . It's yours if you want it."

Jack was blown away by the generosity of the offer. "A house in that neighborhood is worth a fortune, Coop." They could buy and flip two more houses after the closing costs.

Coop gave him a look. "Don't get me wrong," he said dryly. "Anne and I have no problem with you living above our garage, Jack, but it isn't big enough for two people — even if one of them is only four feet tall. You said your sister-in-law isn't getting out of jail until January. Why would you stay in Banister Falls?"

It was a fair question. And one Jack tried to dodge. "Maybe I will have one of those pancakes."

"Is your landlord easier to work for?" Laughter gleamed in Coop's eyes. "Does he give you time off when you need it? Better advice?"

Jack snorted. "None of the above."

"Is it Evie?"

Jack should have seen that coming. He met Coop's eyes and told the truth. Coop had always had that effect on him. "She's the reason I have to leave."

CHAPTER 42

Jack was alone when he pulled into Evie's driveway later that evening.

He'd called to let her know that he and Lily were on their way to Banister Falls, and although Evie hadn't expected Jack to share the details about what had happened over the past twenty-four hours, something in his tone had made her uneasy. And so had the lengthy silence that followed when Evie told him she was waiting for them at the apartment.

"I know you have things to do, Evie," he'd said. "We won't be there for three or four hours, so you should probably go home. I'll call you when we get back."

Evie had tried to attribute the lack of emotion in Jack's voice to fatigue, but the moment she opened her door and saw his face, her heart plummeted to her feet. "Where's Lily?"

"With Bert. She's pretty tired." Jack's

smile didn't quite reach his eyes.

"You look tired too." Tired and wonderful and *here.* Evie wanted to wrap her arms around Jack's waist, but she nudged him into the foyer instead. "I would have come over to your place."

"I wanted to talk to you alone."

Evie's pulse evened out a little for the first time as Jack followed her down the hall to the living room. Of course he wouldn't want Lily nearby when he talked about her father.

"Sit down." Evie motioned toward the sofa. "Are you hungry? Can I get you something to drink?"

"No . . . I can't stay long." Jack remained standing. "This is the first time Lily has let me out of her sight since I got to Milwaukee. Trav did the right thing, but it was pretty traumatic for Lily when he left her at Deirdre's like that. She and Trav go way back, but Lily had never met her. And the neighborhood she lives in makes Fairview Street look like a Rosewood Court."

"No wonder you were in a hurry to get there," Evie murmured.

Something flickered in Jack's eyes. Guilt? Regret? Maybe both.

"To tell you the truth, the last twenty-four hours have been a blur. I was out the door and on the road ten minutes after Travis called. I let Coop know what was going on. I live in the apartment above his garage, but Anne insisted we spend what was left of the night with them."

Evie could admit it. It hurt a little, knowing Jack had found time to call Ryan and his friends but not her.

"I'm just glad you and Lily are back." She reached out and wove her fingers through Jack's, needing to feel connected to him again. "I adjusted my schedule and took a few days off. I'll do whatever I can to help."

Jack didn't move, but Evie felt something shift between them. Right before he let go of her hand.

"Evie . . . I have to go back to Milwaukee."

"For how long?"

She saw the answer in Jack's eyes before he said the words out loud.

"For good. It's where I live . . . and work."

"But Lily's family is here. Nicki and her kids. And what about Bert and Ron? Josh? The apartment building?" The words tumbled out before Evie could stop them. "Keith thought it was a great idea, hiring you as the manager if the church decides to buy —"

"I can't." Jack cut her off. "You know it's not going to work."

"It will. Keith is confident the congrega-

432

tion will love the idea of doing something outside the walls of the church for a change. Gertrude's gift should be enough to cover the cost of the building."

"I'm talking about us," Jack said. "You went through so much when Max died. I'm not going to put you through that kind of pain again."

Evie struggled to make sense out of what Jack was saying.

"It's not the same. Your job is . . . it's safe."

"Don't you get it, Evie? *I'm* not safe. Not for you anyway. Do you know what I used to wish sometimes?" Jack didn't wait for her to answer. "Even after watching our mom go through radiation and chemo, I wished Travis had cancer because that meant he could be cured.

"There's no remission for addiction. It's something Trav will have to live with the rest of his life. Can he have victory over it? Of course, but I don't know if he's going to stay clean. Or if he'll have his head on straight when he gets out of prison. I can't promise he and Cheryl won't make mistakes with Lily . . . I can't even promise they'll stay together."

"I'm not asking you to make promises, Jack. You don't have to go through everything alone. I'll be with you —"

"I don't *want* you with me." The words vibrated in the air between them. "I don't want to have to worry about what this is doing to you. Whether you're getting tired of it all. You don't know what it's like to have someone you love struggle with an addiction. Every time the phone rings, you get this hollow feeling in the pit of your stomach. Every time they take a step forward, in the back of your mind you're waiting for them to take three steps back. The only thing I can do is hold onto Jesus's hand and trust that He won't let go. Your life will be a lot less complicated without me."

Jack's face blurred. Evie tried to blink back the tears, but there were too many. They leaked from the corners of her eyes and zigzagged down her cheeks. But she had to tell him the truth. "You're the one who made me see I wasn't really living at all."

Jack's hands clenched at his sides. "Don't say that."

"Why not? Risk over regret, don't you remember?"

"That's what I'm doing," he said softly.

The door closed behind him.

"We heard you're on a tight deadline."

The hammer almost missed the nail and crushed Jack's thumb when Dan and Ryan

434

appeared behind him. Sheesh. The guys moved with the stealth of Navy SEALS.

"I'll get there." In record time, considering Jack had been working almost round the clock for the past few days. "And you're not going to talk me out of leaving, so don't even try."

Dan and Ryan exchanged a look.

"Don't take this personally, Jack," Ryan drawled. "I mean, you're a decent guy and all, but we think you made the right decision. Moving back to Milwaukee."

How was Jack *not* supposed to take a statement like that personally?

"He's right. It's best to cut things off with Evie now," Dan added. "She's fragile, and I'd hate to —"

"Fragile?" Jack interrupted, almost choking on the word. "Evie is one of the strongest people I know."

Dan's eyebrow shot up. "Well, you haven't known her as long as Ryan and I have."

"Yeah, Evie's great when it comes to planning teas and stuff for the women at church," Ryan added. "But she's pretty naïve when it comes to the real world."

You couldn't get any more real than Fairview Street, and yet Evie had been able to look past the dilapidated buildings and embrace the people living inside of them.

"You're not giving Evie enough credit."

And neither, Jack suddenly realized, had he.

Evie hadn't ventured onto Fairview Street since Jack had told her he was leaving Banister Falls, but it didn't matter. The last three days had been torture. He saw her everywhere. In his kitchen, laughing with Bert. Helping Josh with his homework. Rocking Amber Lynn. Braiding Lily's hair.

Evie had told him how she'd felt about him, and Jack had walked out. Not because he was afraid she'd get tired of his family. No. What Jack had been afraid Evie would eventually get tired of was *him.*

"Are you protecting Evie," Gin had asked. "Or yourself?"

As if God Himself had just aimed a spotlight on Jack's heart, the answer to that was pretty clear.

"Here." Jack tossed the hammer at Dan and strode toward the door. "I have to go."

As he hopped into his truck, through the window he saw Ryan and Dan slap their palms together in a high five.

He'd been totally played.

And the next time Jack saw them, he was going to say thank you.

"Your crown is falling off, Evie!"

Evie reached up and set the plastic tiara back in place, careful not to lose her grip on Grace as she twirled Ava in a circle around the living room of Nicki's apartment.

The children had acted like it was Christmas morning when Evie brought a box of dress-up clothes for the girls and a box of Cody's Matchbox cars to keep Luke occupied for a few hours.

"Someone's here." Lily dashed toward the door, leaving a trail of purple feathers from the boa around her neck.

The only thing Evie heard was the thump of the bass pounding through the speakers and Grace's shriek of delight as Evie dipped the toddler backward over her arm.

Luke, who'd been stretched out on the floor building a bridge out of paperback books for his cars, suddenly rolled to his feet. "Uncle Jack!"

Evie's heart stuttered and then stalled completely when she turned toward the door and saw Jack. He looked . . . good. Too good.

"Evie." Jack's eyes met hers across the room and then traveled over the gaudy beaded shawl draped around her shoulders before pausing to linger a moment on her bare feet.

"We're at a ball, just like Cinderella!" Ava shouted. "Look at my princess shoes!" She stuck out her foot so Jack could admire the sparkly high heels Evie had found at the thrift store on Bird Street.

A smile teased the corners of Jack's lips. "Interesting choice of music for a ball."

So she'd developed a taste for jazz over the past few weeks.

"Nicki isn't here." Evie turned the music down. "She signed up for a culinary class at the Tech, and I offered to babysit."

"I know." Jack's smile disappeared. "I stopped over at Cody and Raine's first."

"You're here to pick up Lily?"

"Actually . . . I came to see you."

Evie swallowed hard. She'd wondered if Jack would make an effort to see her before he left town. She was suddenly glad the children were there to provide a buffer . . .

"I'm tired, Evie." Lily bounded over and reached for Grace. "Can we watch a movie now?"

"Of course." What else could she say? *No, stay. I don't want to be alone with your uncle?*

Luke and Ava scampered after Lily, and they disappeared into the bedroom.

Suddenly self-conscious, Evie reached up to remove her tiara. Maybe it would have been easier if Jack had left without saying good-bye. Then she wouldn't have to watch him walk out of her life twice.

"I don't want you with me."

The words had cut deep, cycling through Evie's mind all day and at night when she tried to sleep. But they didn't stop her from praying for him. From loving him.

"Evie —" Jack extended his hand, and all Evie could do was stare at it.

Was he *trying* to torture her? Were they supposed to shake hands now? Part as friends?

"I . . . I should check on the kids." So maybe Evie wasn't as bold as she'd claimed she was.

"Wait. Please." Jack stepped into her path. "The last time we were together, I told you all the things I don't know. Now I want to tell you the things that I do. I know my family isn't perfect. I know that my God is . . . and I know I'm in love with you. I wish I could give you more, but that's it. That's all I've got —"

He didn't get a chance to finish the sentence because Evie closed the distance between them, framed his face in her hands, and kissed him. And the words she whispered against Jack's lips were a promise she could make to him.

"It's enough."

EPILOGUE

November

Jack opened the velvet jeweler's box and slid it across the table.

"Well? What do you think?"

Cody studied the diamond and sapphire ring, but it was impossible to tell what the kid was thinking. Jack gripped the back of the chair and waited.

It hadn't occurred to him that asking Evie's son for his blessing might be more stressful than the actual proposal. But Jack wanted to do this right.

"Are you going to ask her at Christmas?" Cody didn't answer Jack's question. He didn't give the ring back either.

"No." Because that would mean waiting another month. And Jack was getting tired of having to leave Evie with a kiss good night at the front door. "I was thinking . . . Saturday."

"Saturday the church is hosting the

Thanksgiving dinner on Fairview Street. She's going to be crazy busy that day."

Jack was counting on it. "Then she won't suspect anything. And it seemed like an appropriate time because what I'm the most thankful for is your mom."

A sigh came from the direction of the living room, where Raine was rocking two-month-old Ella Joy to sleep and unashamedly eavesdropping on their conversation.

Jack and Dan had paced the floor of the family lounge together after Raine went into labor, waiting for updates from Gin and Evie, who'd been given front row seats to the event in the delivery room. The VIP tickets had been issued shortly after the birth, and Jack was one of the first people to hold Evie's granddaughter.

Another Blue Eyes.

Lily had proclaimed herself an honorary aunt, demanding an Ella update when Jack picked her up from school every day.

Jack realized Cody still hadn't said anything, encouraging or otherwise, about his timing of the proposal. He waded cautiously into the silence, trying to pinpoint the reason for Cody's hesitation.

"Do you think it's too soon? I realize your mom and I haven't known each other very long, but I love her." It scared Jack, sometimes, just how much. "And whether I hold onto this ring for six days or six months or six years, that isn't going to change."

"Cody and I only knew each other for nine months before he proposed!" Raine called out from the living room.

Jack ducked his head to hide a smile. At least he had someone on his side.

"Mom's been through a lot," Cody finally said. "I don't want her to get hurt again."

"I can't promise that won't happen. This side of heaven, we get hurt. But I can promise that I'll love your mom through everything . . . the good and the bad . . . until I take my last breath. I'm not trying to take your dad's place, Cody, but I hope we can be friends. That's why I wanted to talk to you first. Your blessing means a lot to me."

"You have it."

It took a moment for the words to register. "Really?"

"Under one condition."

"Anything," Jack said. "Name it."

Cody grinned and handed the ring back.

And when he told him what that condition was, Jack couldn't help but grin back.

"How am I supposed to steal a kiss when you're never alone?"

Jack's whispered comment sent a shiver dancing down Evie's spine.

"Behave." She tried to keep a straight face as she dipped the ladle into the Crock-Pot on the counter and smiled at the next person in line. "Would you like some gravy, Ron?"

"Just a little, Blondie. The doc said that stuff ain't good for my cholesterol." Ron held out his plate and watched Evie drizzle it over the mountain of mashed potatoes. "Maybe a little more."

She kept drizzling until Ron smiled. He bypassed the next station — green beans — and shuffled toward Angela, who was doling out still-warm-from-the-oven dinner rolls.

"Aren't you going to ask me what I'd like?" Jack murmured.

"You're so bad."

"Hey, I thought we established I'm one of the good guys." Laughter warmed his silver eyes.

"We're running low on cranberry sauce." Evie resisted the urge to fan herself with a potholder. "Why don't you go see if there's some in the kitchen?"

"Because it's more fun to stay here and make you blush."

She *was* blushing, dang it. Jack had that

effect on her.

"Hey, Mom." Cody stopped in front of her, Ella cradled in his arms. Evie had bought her granddaughter the pink corduroy overalls and matching jacket, Gin the impossibly tiny cowboy boots.

"There's my girl." Evie leaned across the counter to plant a kiss on the baby's downy hair. Ella cooed and waved her arms. "You look as sweet as Lily's apple pie."

Lily, sandwiched in the line between Cody and Raine, beamed from the compliment.

"Raine and Cody invited me to stay over tonight, Uncle Jack." She handed Evie her plate. "Can I? We're going to watch *The Princess Bride.*"

"We'll bring her to church with us tomorrow morning," Raine added.

"I suppose." Jack glanced down at Lily. "And I suppose you already packed your overnight bag?"

"Yup!"

"I sense a conspiracy."

Evie did too, but she loved to see Lily smile.

"Don't forget to show Evie my surprise, Uncle Jack."

"I won't."

"Surprise?" Evie's gaze bounced between Lily and Jack.

"It's upstairs. You'll have to wait until your shift ends."

"And that would be right now." Ginevieve rounded the counter, arms behind her back as she knotted an apron around her waist. "Evie, you and Jack have been here since six o'clock this morning. Time to let someone else feed the multitudes."

The multitudes. Evie smiled. That pretty much described it.

It was the first dinner Evie's newly formed committee had served since the sale of the building had gone through — a process expedited by Gertrude's gift — and no one had known quite what to expect. Evie had been a little shocked when she carried the first tray of sliced turkey into the dining room and saw the line stretching to the door. They'd set up for fifty people, and from what Evie could see, every seat was occupied.

Maggie McClain, who was sitting between Bert and Andy's wife, Serena, caught her eye and waved. Across from them were Josh and his father.

"Did you hear me, Evie?" Gin held out her hand. "The ladle."

"The boss has spoken." Dan squeezed in beside his fiancée. "Give a waitress a kitchen . . ."

"And she — to borrow one of Cody's expressions — totally rocks." Evie relinquished the ladle. "Jack and I will be back to help with cleanup."

"No, you won't. John and Angela have that covered." Gin made a shooing motion with her hand. "We'll see you in church tomorrow."

Evie followed Jack outside and up the stairs to his apartment. After spending the majority of the day in the kitchen, the cool air felt good. But then Jack threaded his fingers through hers, and the temperature spiked a few degrees.

"I better show you Lily's surprise first, or I'll be in big trouble." Jack led Evie through the living room and onto the balcony.

Strings of twinkling white lights were wrapped around the railing, and yellow mums in a terra cotta pot decorated the small bistro table.

Evie laughed. "What's the occasion? Or is Lily getting a head start on Christmas?"

Jack didn't answer. He wasn't even looking at the lights. He was staring down at his feet.

"Is everything okay? You seem a little distracted."

Jack lifted his head, and his slow smile made her toes curl inside her shoes. "It's your fault."

"My fault?"

"Those blue eyes of yours have been a distraction from the first time I met you."

Evie playfully batted her lashes at him. "It was dark," she teased. "I'm surprised you noticed the color at all."

"I noticed everything." Jack reached out, and his fingertips grazed a path down her cheek. "The way you stuck by Ginevieve. The way you marched up to me like I was the one who was trespassing and gave me permission to search the grocery bag you were using as a shield."

"I was scared to death. Did you happen to see that in my eyes too?"

"I saw someone I wanted to get to know better."

"And now that you do?"

Jack didn't respond to her teasing the way he usually did. By kissing the smile from her lips. Instead, he took a step away from her. Took something out of his pocket. "Now I want to spend the rest of my life getting to know you better."

He had a . . . ring. A beautiful marquise-cut diamond framed by two sapphires.

"Will you marry me, Evie?"

Evie's throat closed. Suddenly the twinkling lights and the flowers made sense.

"You *planned* this."

Jack smiled. "With a little help."

"Lily."

"And Raine and Cody."

"They knew about it too?"

"Of course. I had to ask Cody for his blessing."

The sweetness of the gesture brought tears to Evie's eyes. "I'm not surprised he gave it. Cody likes you."

She'd watched the bond between Jack and her son slowly deepen over the past few months. With his friend Coop's backing, Jack had bought Travis and Cheryl's rental house on Brewster Street. In his spare time, Cody had been helping Jack with the renovations so it would be ready when Cheryl and Lily moved back in when she was released from jail in January.

"I thought so too, but Cody had me worried for a few minutes." Jack shook his head. "He even put a condition on it."

"A condition?"

"Yeah, it kind of threw me too, but when I heard what it was, I told Cody that was a given."

"What . . . ?"

"He said he's always wanted a little brother or sister."

Evie stared up at Jack, pressing her knuckles against her lips to hold back a sob.

Now she understood what Bert meant the day Evie had told her about the garden.

This is more than I can hold, Lord.

"Evie?" Jack sounded a little worried now. "I'm still waiting for your answer."

"Yes."

"Yes, you'll marry me?" But Jack was already sliding the ring on her finger — as if he wasn't going to give her an opportunity to change her mind — and Evie laughed as the tears streamed down her face.

"Yes to everything."

DISCUSSION QUESTIONS

1. Discuss the changes Evie is facing when the story opens. What season of life are you in right now? What are the joys and challenges?
2. The majority of Evie's ministry took place inside the familiar (and safe!) walls of Hope Community Church . . . until she met Jack. Has God ever moved you out of your comfort zone? What happened?
3. Do you have a question for heaven? If the answer is yes, what would it be?
4. Jack shares a verse from Nehemiah with Evie. Do you agree that he did the right thing by moving to Banister Falls? Have you ever "fought" for a family member? What were the circumstances?
5. Which character in the book could you relate to the most? Why?
6. Bert told Evie, "You can hold onto the memories so close, so tight, that you don't have room for anything else." How was

this true in Evie's life? What changes did you see in her after she got to know the people in Jack's building?

7. What was the turning point in Jack and Evie's relationship?

8. Loaves and fishes . . . share a time when you saw God take something small and multiply it.

9. Evie realized it wasn't grief but fear that prevented her from moving forward after Max's death. What are some other things that can hinder our growth?

10. What was your favorite scene? Why?

ACKNOWLEDGMENTS

A heartfelt THANK YOU to the amazing group of people who work behind the scenes while I'm busy writing them! Wendy Lawton, agent extraordinaire, whose wisdom and guidance extends way beyond contracts. Editor Becky Monds, who made my day when she said I have a gift for creating "swoon-worthy" heroes. All I can say is that it's easy when you happen to be married to one. ☺ Line editor LB Norton, whose margin notes make me smile and challenge mc to fine tune what I was *sure* was already a brilliant manuscript! Ha!

You wouldn't be holding this book in your hands if it weren't for the talented and tireless Karli Jackson, Elizabeth Hudson, and the entire marketing team at HarperCollins Christian Publishing. Your creativity, attention to detail, and patience make that part of the process a lot easier for social media-challenged writers who, ahem, shall remain nameless.

I confess that one of the reasons I write contemporary fiction is to avoid research . . . unless that research involves an impromptu concert in my friend Thia's living room. A special thanks to Matt, for sharing your musical talent so I could make Jack look good on the saxophone. "Summertime" is now on my permanent playlist ☺ And I owe a debt of gratitude to Steve for answering what were probably weird questions without making me *feel* weird. *"What kind of guitar would a guy play if he wanted to pick up girls?"* comes to mind!

As always, I couldn't do what I do without the support and encouragement of my awesome hubby and my friends and family. Thank you for putting up with the "This-is-your-brain-on-a-deadline" Kathryn. Love you all!

I wish I could reach out and hug every reader who tells me that they want to move to Banister Falls ☺ It was a blessing to be able to tell Evie and Jack's story.

ABOUT THE AUTHOR

Kathryn Springer is a *USA Today* bestselling author. She grew up in northern Wisconsin, where her parents published a weekly newspaper. As a child she spent many hours sitting at her mother's typewriter, plunking out stories, and credits her parents for instilling in her a love of books — which eventually turned into a desire to tell stories of her own. Kathryn has written nineteen books with close to two million copies sold. Kathryn lives and writes in her country home in northern Wisconsin.

Visit her website at www.kathrynspringer.com
Twitter: @springerkathryn
Facebook: Kathrynspringerauthor